'Philip Vega is a man to die for.'

SONS OF THE FATHER

by

JANETTE ANDERSON

BearManor Media

2012

Sons of the Father
© 2012 Janette Anderson
Janette Anderson Entertainment
WGA West 1374532

For information, address:

BearManor Media
P. O. Box 71426
Albany, GA 31708

bearmanormedia.com

Typesetting and layout by John Teehan

Cover photo by Valentin Lieu, courtesy of Jose Rosete

Published in the USA by BearManor Fiction

ISBN—1-59393-383-5
978-1-59393-383-8

Dedicated to
Jose Rosete
And special thanks to
all the men in my life.

Introduction to Vega

Mac Hunter opened the door of the snow-sprinkled limo for his boss. Expensive black leather boots and blue jeans heralded the dark shadow of the man that wore them. His thick, black woolen coat hid the .357 that was tucked neatly into the back of his jeans. As he stepped from the limo into the fresh, crisp snows of the tiny Colorado cemetery, it allowed giant footprints to make deep impressions. His breath streamed ahead of him, and spiraled in the freezing cold air. Here was a man that would worry you; one with a sign of danger hanging round his neck.

Philip Andrea Vega leaned against the shiny black limo. He rested his arm on the hood and fresh crisp snow parted in his wake. The snow, heavier in the last hour, had made the drive hazardous, but it had not deterred Philip from visiting her grave.

Vega removed the shades from his eyes and dark circles lined from tiredness stretched out into the afternoon light. He pulled his thick coat closer around him and pushed his salt and pepper graying hair inside his collar. His deep-brown eyes looked ahead of him and his presence just by being there commanded respect. But still he shivered in the chilling air.

"Sir, would you like to sit back inside the car?" Vega's chauffeur questioned him. No ordinary driver, Mac Hunter also sported a gun, which when tucked away in the inside of his jacket was undetectable. So was the one he carried in his boot.

Philip thought for a moment. "No, Mac, I'm okay. Besides, the air suits me just fine. Good clean air not filled with the pollution of our lives." Philip's tone was as cold as the temperature around him.

"Yeah, and one day you will get your head blown off," replied Hunter with some sarcasm. He pushed the stray blonde hairs from his face and concentrated on his boss.

"No one is going to shoot me, not in a cemetery. You've been watching too many movies." Philip put a wiser hand on Mac's shoulder. This action could often determine one's future. A future without a face.

Mac Hunter was not sure about any gunplay in the cemetery, and he glanced around him. It would be very convenient for someone to be buried, and Philip Vega was a good target: master of all and subservient to no one. Strong and powerful, with success still lingering about him, Vega was a man to be feared. Those large powerful hands that had held small children could also kill, and the mind that could think to love a woman, would never hesitate to kill a man.

Philip Vega had many enemies, both in and out of the business. At the age of forty-eight, time and good bodyguards had been kind to him. But Philip had one more thing left to do in his lifetime, something he should have taken care of a year back. He turned away from the limo and strode out into the snow, his handmade Italian leather boots once more crushing the soft snow beneath them. Slowly he put his hand under his coat and slid his arm round the back of his jeans. Retrieving the gun from its hiding place was an easy task. He kept the weapon by his side and turned to face his bodyguard.

"Not me, Mac. I am not the one who will get their head blown off…" Philip raised the gun high and saw the look in Mac's haunted blue eyes.

Hunter fell to his knees. He did not beg for forgiveness. He knew his boss would kill him at some point and amazed himself that death had not come knocking on his door sooner. Snow seeped water up his black jeans and touched his long grey coat.

"You may just as well of killed her yourself. I told you you would never know where or when, and now is the time… Time to die." Vega's voice rang out in the crisp air, and his eyes were cold and calculating.

Philip aimed the gun at Mac's head, pulled the trigger and with one clean shot ended the life of his longtime bodyguard. Mac slumped down in a pool of crimson-red snow, twitching in death and then he was still, dead eyes staring into cold air.

Philip turned away without showing any remorse. He stood there and looked across to the grave that sported an icing of snow on the flowers of yesterday... her grave, and he waited for the second car to collect him. He could hear the engine and could see the headlights and just for a moment... he saw her, and he thought back four years.

"Philip... please help me," her voice was quiet, but at least she was alive. Tired and dirty, but alive, her jeans filthy and her T shirt ripped open.

He turned sharply, searching for her in the blackness on the cliffs leading down to the ocean shore. The only light came from the headlights of the cars. He could see his young and pregnant mistress held firmly round the shoulders in front of the Don's older brother; a knife firmly stuck so close to her waist that not even a breath of air could pass between them. Damien held her there, his fingers gently caressing her face, pushing her long, blonde hair out of his way as Emma visibly cringed.

"Let her go, you bastard! It's me you want, not her," and Philip took a step forward, dropping his gun to the hard ground, with his spare gun still in the back of his jeans, his hands raised as if to surrender.

"Really? I think it's both of you we want," and another, only angrier voice emerged from the darkness. He, too, carried a gun, but seemed not quite sure how to use it.

"You! What the hell are you doing here with these people? Didn't I pay you enough for you to disappear from our lives?" yelled Philip.

"Money can't buy my wife! All you think of is money! That, and her... She's sleeping with you, so she can die with you!" Steven Sand's voice was shrill and echoed on the evening air, his face contorted in hate for the older man that he was looking at.

Philip was franticly thinking of ways to get her out of there. In the beam of light he could see the glint of steel, but he knew that Mac couldn't see it. If anything happened to him, his men had orders to kill anyone left standing. Anyone!

"Emma… are you hurt, baby?" yelled her lover.

"No… I'm fine," she replied in a desperate tone, her eyes betraying her real feelings.

"And the baby?" Philip continued yelling to her.

Steven glanced at his wife, and just for a second he took his eyes off Philip. It gave Vega time to pull the gun from the back of his jeans. His .357 loomed in the darkness like a canon ready, positioned on the battlements. He was very much in control now and between two hands aimed it straight at Steven.

"Now… tell Damien to let her go. NOW! Yeah, Steven, your wife is pregnant with my child. Shocked? The look on your face says you are. Why would you be? Like you said, we have been sleeping together… Tell him, Steven, or I will put a bullet in you right where you stand…"

"You wouldn't do that in front of Emma… then she would know who and what you are…" Steven laughed nervously, looking from one man to another, the gun wavering in his hand…unsure of what to do.

Philip Vega laughed an almost cruel laugh, and then he stared point blank at Steven. "She already knows, Steven! She's known the whole time!" And Philip pulled the trigger.

Chapter 1

Philip Vega first set eyes on Emma Sands at a wrap party for his own Anglo-US movie, 'Angels and Kings'. Philip was bored, and though surrounded by a bevy of beauties, he was totally disinterested in the evening's events. Only because it was his money that was being totally abused by alcohol, wanna-be actors and women, was he there. He took a long draw on the Cuban cigar he was smoking and inhaled deeply. While blowing smoke rings out above him, he happened to glance up and then across the room full of people. Big burly red-coated bouncers checked ID at the door and made sure that only cast, crew and starlets of Philip's choosing gained entrance to the event. Philip watched very half-heartedly until someone he had seen briefly before emerged through the door. Philip was curious and paid particular attention to this man.

Steven Sands, smalltime exec on the international film, came through the screening with an air of arrogance about him. Tall, almost too slender and with an early receding hairline, he stepped into the room with his wife in tow.

Philip stared through the haze of smoke and lights. It was then he noticed the girl with the long, dark-blonde hair and the slimming black dress. The strobe lighting only emphasized the shape of her body, and someone had forgotten to tell her not to wear white lace lingerie underneath the dress. Philip smiled to himself and his eyes squinted in the fluorescent lighting to get a better look. Maybe he should make it his business to tell her. He clicked his fingers and Mac Hunter stepped forward to do his boss's bidding.

"Sir?" Mac leaned down to Philip so that he might glean his orders above the noise of small talk and of music.

"The girl over there by the door… long hair… I would say about five foot nothing… black dress… get her name and bring her here… nicely!" Philip never even looked at Mac. Just gave him an order.

Nicely meant politely… and not by force. Mac stood up to his six foot height, a tad shorter than his boss. He buttoned the jacket of his dark-grey suit just to hide any threat of a gun, walked away and crossed the crowded room to the girl. Big and powerful-looking he moved with ease across the floor, people parting in his wake. He came upon her right side and scared her half to death.

"Excuse me. My boss would like to buy you a drink… Miss?" He had to lean down a good six inches towards her ear.

"Me?" asked Emma looking quite startled that she had been approached by a somewhat large gentleman that was obvious even to her that he was someone's bodyguard.

"You! Miss…?" He asked her for her name and was not used to being questioned.

"Emma Sands, and it's Mrs." She turned slightly and pointed towards her husband. "That's my husband over there and I would need to ask him if…"

"That will be taken care of," interrupted Mac. "My boss, Philip Vega, the star of the movie, is the gentleman who wants to buy you a drink." He looked down at her. His boss had good taste. Even is this light Hunter could see she had a great shape and her face was very pleasant to the eye. When she turned her head to look for her husband, her long hair bounced on her shoulders, and as she looked back at Mac, her green eyes flashed with some kind of excitement at possibly meeting this man.

"Well, I guess then it will be okay… just for a moment." Emma replied to him in her thick English accent.

"Just follow me through the crowds and I will introduce you to him. This way," and he turned in front of her and lead Emma away.

Emma followed as she was told to do, and they moved across the floor until they reached Philip. She stood still. Hunter leaned in towards his boss and whispered to him.

"Her name is *Mrs.* Emma Sands…". And he turned round to his charge. "Emma, this is Philip Vega, the man who wants to buy you a drink!" Mac said it with such finality and almost but ushered Emma forward, taking her by the shoulders and planting her in front of his boss.

As Philip stood up to greet his guest, he stubbed out his cigar and subtlety pushed the onyx ashtray across the small table next to him. Philip buttoned the jacket of his charcoal-grey jacket, and his dark hair dropped over the top of his collar of the grey silk shirt he wore. As his eyes fixed on the two people in front of him, he deliberately ignored his friends around him. At that moment, he only had eyes for the female in his sights.

"Mrs. Sands…" and he extended his hand to her. "Philip Vega at your service… and *very pleased* to meet you…" he stopped short of saying anything else that he was thinking, especially his comments about her underwear.

Emma looked at the big powerful hand that was ready to greet her. As his jacket sleeve slid back a slim line gold Rolex could clearly be seen. It wasn't there for show, it was just there. Emma put her hand out to greet him and it slipped into his with ease. She raised her eyes to look into his face and saw the deep brown shadows of intense magnetism that had seduced countless women for years. Wealth and success lingered about him, and Emma shuffled in her very high black heels as his hand touched hers. The feeling of his skin on hers was almost electrifying.

As Philip held her hand, his eyes scanned her body. He noted her nervousness and it fascinated him, but also disturbed him. Was he that formidable a man? Usually that would be a good thing. Tonight it wasn't. The girl was scared to death of him and he didn't want that. What he wanted was a shot at Emma, just like he did with any beautiful woman he met…

"What would you like to drink, Emma… Mac will get whatever you want…" and he clicked his fingers to his bodyguard.

Emma tried to pull her hand from his but the grasp was strong. "I don't drink, and I'm fine really," she muttered almost embarrassed at her own accent as stupidity clouded her mind.

He leaned down to her, just very slightly. "I can see you are fine, and your accent is very seductive to any man's ears... I still need to know what you would like to drink!"

"Really, I'm not thirsty and I should be getting back to my husband. He will wonder where I am." Emma was crimson and turned slightly to see if she could find Steven. She couldn't.

Philip also looked across the room towards the doors. "Nowhere in sight!" He chose his words carefully. "Lady, if you were my wife I would know exactly where you were at any given time of the day!" He let go of her hand and spoke gently to her, sultry eyes looking down into her face. "My *assistant* will take you back over to your husband. I have a feeling we will meet again, *Mrs.* Sands. Have a great time tonight." He nodded his head very slightly and Mac Hunter appeared so close to Emma she wondered how he managed it without stepping on her.

Totally flustered at the compliment and his statements, she rocked slightly on the heels. "It was very nice to meet you." Emma didn't wait for him to speak again, and she turned away ashamed of her performance in front of this man.

Philip watched her walk away, her backside in time to the beat of the music. He looked hard through the smoke one more time and then turned towards his friends. Cool and calmly he sat down in his chair, uttering one single line with such deliverance that it made his friends stare at him in shear amazement. "That, my friends, is the woman I intend to marry!"

Chapter 2

The accident was in the local newspapers, but not of International importance. Headline read: '*Local studio man in hit and run*.' 'Steven Sands and his wife, Emma Sands, were involved last night in a hit and run accident. Mr. Sands, formerly of R and R Studios, was released after treatment. His wife remains in critical condition.' There was more. Steven read it again and again, and then dropped the paper, which was now over a week old, onto the dining room table.

Steven didn't know what to do. Emma was in a coma and it didn't look like she would survive the week. He glanced round the room like a lost man. Steven knew that his marriage to Emma was failing miserably. On the night of the accident the couple was out to dinner with friends trying to look happy and not succeeding. Leaving the restaurant arguing, neither was paying attention to the speeding car until there was a screech of brakes and glaring headlights in the thick winter fog. Steven darted across the road to safety... Emma stood frozen to the spot.

Now he held his head in his hands. Emma needed something to pull her out of the coma and Steven didn't know what. None of their friends could help; seemingly no one could brink her back to the real world of light. The one she was living in was confined to the dark depths of nightmares. On this particular night, Steven had noticed an ad for the upcoming movie that he knew by heart... 'Angels and Kings'. An idiotic thought crossed his mind. Philip Vega... maybe if he could get him to do something, send something, anything… Steven knew about Emma's brief, but powerful encounter with him at the movie's wrap party. He also knew that Emma had been totally fascinated by the man and all she had talked about for weeks was her meeting with him. It was worth a try. At least Steven had the right connections to Vega's manager. He sat down next to the telephone stand and with much hesitation dialed the number to the manager's office in London. Steven was polite but firm, explaining about Emma and asking for any help he could get. The receptionist was new and thinking Steven was co- producer on the film gave him Philip's home phone number. Steven copied it down and a little voice inside of him was telling him to call it now… and another one said no. A voice he should have listened to very carefully.

As his fingers dialed the number, Steven gave no thought to the time in the U.S. He really needed to talk to Vega. He finished dialing and waited for either someone to answer or the voice mail to take over. Steven didn't expect it to be the man himself.

"Who the hell is this?" were the only words that escaped from Phillip's mouth as he answered the landline phone that stood on the bedside table. He slouched back in the giant canopy bed. The woman next to him turned in her sleep, pulled black silk sheets over her and moaned slightly. Philip came to his senses and stared at her. He couldn't quite figure out who she was. He shook his head and blinked his eyes, the phone still held to his ear. "I repeat, who is this?" Philip glanced at his watch in the half light. Four a.m. was a stark reality and he was on the verge of hanging up the phone.

"Mr. Vega?" asked a very tentative English voice.

"Yeah. Who the hell is this? It's four in the goddamn morning…" Philip was yelling.

"I'm sorry. I didn't think of that. My name is Steven Sands." There was a pause. "I was hoping you could help me. You met my wife at the wrap party for your film and she is really sick. Her name is Emma. Emma Sands!" His voice was decidedly English and irritating to Vega's ears, unlike Emma's had been.

Philip sat bolt upright, switching the bedside lamp on at the same time. "Go on."

The slumbering female half awoke to the yelling. "What time is it?" she groaned.

Philip stared at her again and she withered under the glare. "Where is she? Is she there in England?" And once again he focused on the caller.

"Yes. Could you help? Send her something to the hospital? She was in a car crash. Maybe ..." Steven didn't know what to say and stopped midsentence. He pushed his hair across his head. He wanted to help Emma but somehow he knew he was changing the course of history.

Philip was looking for something to write with. Gold-trimmed pen in hand and personalized note paper steadied on the bedside table, he continued. "Which hospital and what's the nearest airport to it?" He scribbled down the address of the hospital, not having a clue where it was. "Airport?" Again Philip wrote the name down. Heathrow he did know. "How far are you from Heathrow?"

"Hundred miles or so... you could get a flight from Heathrow to ..." Steven didn't get to finish.

"I will get a car. You'll be at the hospital, if I ask for you?" Philip was blunt.

"Of course, but it's room D, third floor, just in case." Steven paused. He realized that Philip himself was coming, and he didn't quite know what to say. "So, I guess we will see you in a couple of days then?"

Philip stopped listening to Steven, put the phone on speaker, and climbed out of bed, wrapping a black robe around him. "You..." he said half sarcastically to the girl in his bed.

There was a woman's voice coming from somewhere in the room. Steven had a good idea where from.

"I have no idea why I brought you back here, but Mac will show you the way out. Mac..." yelled Philip. "Get in here... now!"

Steven could hear what sounded like the rustling of sheets and the mutterings of a female. He was right. Philip was handing her both shoes and her clothes all at the same time. The next sound Steven heard was the clanking of wine bottles. He wondered if Philip had forgotten he was on the line. Next noise was a door banging; and then a man's voice whom Steven figured to be Mac, who was obviously in hearing range of Philip's dulcet tones.

"Get her out of here and drive her home, or have one of the guys do it." Philip looked at her, and then he remembered last night and the party at the Beverly Hills Hotel where he seemed to have made this lady's acquaintance. She was blonde, pretty enough but still he questioned his bodyguard. "Was I that drunk?" asked Philip.

"Yeah, boss, you were," muttered Mac. "Sir… your phone is still on…" Mac had glanced at the nightstand.

"Shit!" He moved back to the phone. "Steven, you still there? Just something I had to take care of." Philip cursed again, only more profoundly. The last thing he wanted was for this man to hear that he was drunk enough to have a strange girl in his bed. "So, I have the details… anything else I should know?"

"No, I think that's it." Steven didn't know what to say. "Have a good flight," came out anyway and he hung up the phone.

"Damn! Wish you had noticed the phone earlier… never mind! Just make sure the girl gets home and come back up here. I have packing to do. I am going to take a trip to England… alone!" and Philip began throwing clothes on the bed, not in any particular order, just clothes. Walking to one of his many large bedroom closets, he pulled down a small, by Philip's standards, suitcase. He opened the case and picked up jeans and T shirts from the bed. Black clothes seemed to take up the bulk of the suitcase along with a couple of thick black sweaters, thoughtfully packed for the English weather.

Mac escorted the somewhat dazed, half clothed girl from the room and came back in a few moments through the open doors. "Tony is driving her home. Turns out she doesn't live too far from here, but then I guess you knew that…"

Philip's look to Mac was so intense that it stopped him in his tracks. The bodyguard assumed that Philip didn't remember that at all and probably couldn't remember much about last night period.

"You don't mention her again, right?" Philip snapped and carried on with his packing.

"Sir," replied Hunter. "Would you like me to book you a flight?" he asked his boss tentatively.

"Yeah. Any flight that leaves within the next couple of hours for Heathrow. Any class doesn't matter. Just get me on one... and again, on my own. You understand?" Philip could be incredibly mean to his staff when he wanted to be, and right now, with his head pounding from both lack of sleep and alcohol, he wanted to be. "Passport. Where is the damn thing," as Philip rummaged through his oak desk. "It's always supposed to be in here." Philip was flustered. Something he never was and kept on searching through papers.

"It's there, Sir. Top shelf of the desk." Mac could see it and pointed to it.

"Right. Got it." Philip had no idea why his own mood was so foul. He tried to temper it down. It wasn't Mac's fault that the phone had rung and that Emma's name came up. It wasn't Mac's fault that he couldn't forget her from one brief meeting. And it wasn't his fault he had immediately fallen for her that night.

"Mac... I'm sorry..." he put his hand on his bodyguard's shoulder. "It's early and you are right, I drank too much... again..." Apologies did not come easily to Philip Vega. "Maybe you should get yourself a flight also. Maybe *alone* isn't such a good idea. See what the airline can offer. Leave it all to you. Give the household their orders and put Anthony in charge. Communicate straight to him, no one else. Get your passport, some clothes and let's be gone in an hour tops. Okay?" and as fast as his hand was on the shoulder, it was off.

"Tops, boss," and Mac Hunter left the room.

Philip sat down on the side of the bed. He wondered exactly what he was doing. He could hardly wait to see Emma again, yet he couldn't say that out loud. She was a married woman and that's where he drew the line... normally. Philip ran his fingers through his hair and pushed it back out of his eyes. He needed to shower and get himself dressed. Discarding his robe on the bed, he went into the lavish bathroom, stepped into the marble tiled shower and turned the gold-handled faucet to hot. Philip ducked under the water, hot water, which cascaded down his back. Soft soap billowed from a fountain next to the faucet and Philip used it to its full capacity, lathering up his sun-tanned body, a body that was still tight from daily workouts. At least he felt a little more sober when he stepped out of the shower.

Wrapping a thick black towel round his waist, he let his dark hair flop back on his shoulders. He peered into the mirror over the washbasin and wiped away the mist caused from the heated shower. Aside from partially bloodshot eyes, he didn't look too bad for forty-five considering the amount of alcohol he had consumed of late. A knock on the bathroom door disturbed him. Usually only two people were allowed uninvited into his private suite.

"Sir? Dad?" Marc Vega knocked on his father's bathroom door. It wasn't a loud knock, just enough to let his father know he was there.

"Come in, son. It's not locked," and Philip moved towards the door.

Marc was his oldest son, one of four, the other three living with Vega's ex- wife in Florida.

"Almost five, Dad. Hunter said to tell you he booked seats on an American Airlines flight at seven-thirty, so you need to leave here in about twenty minutes. Need any help with your luggage? I saw a case on the bed. You need another one?" Marc was tall like Philip, but blonde like his mother and he looked much more like her than the rest of the sons.

"Nope… just the one. I can buy anything else I need, but I don't think I will be gone too long." He moved past his son and into the bedroom. "Is that all you saw? The suitcase?" Philip didn't particularly want Marc to see another of his indiscretions, even though it was common knowledge that Philip did not have a very high standard when it came to morals and women.

Marc lied. "That's all." He knew his father had been entertaining by the wine bottles and glasses beside the bed, but the less said right now the better. Hunter had told him why they were flying to England.

"Anthony is in charge while I am gone. You need anything just go to him, and I mean anything. Try and stay close to the house, if you can." Philip paused. "One thing you can do, is keep my gun for me, okay?" Philip figured at twenty-five Marc needed to learn some responsibility and now was his chance.

"Your personal one?" asked his son very tentatively, looking at his father like he had gone insane.

"Yeah, why not? It will be yours one day soon..." Maybe that wasn't the right thing to say. Philip knew that Marc didn't want any part of the inheritance, but he also knew that his younger son, Patrick, did. "If it worries you, just put it in the drawer, lock it and leave it there." Philip was a little disappointed in Marc, but he tried very hard not so show it.

None-the-less, Marc knew it. He couldn't stand guns and he didn't really want his father's lifestyle. He already had a live-in girlfriend, one he intended to marry and not end up like his father with a different woman every night. Now he was taking off for England after another one, but somehow Marc had the feeling this one was very different.

Philip finished zipping up his case. He dressed quickly into black jeans and a thick black sweater over a gray T shirt. He thought that would be warm enough along with a black leather jacket that his sons had bought him last years for father's day. Philip sat down on the bed and pulled his very dark- grey, snakeskin boots from beside the nightstand. Pulling them on over grey socks, he grabbed his keys and wallet from the bed. Philip was still confused why he had brought the girl back to his bed, except for the obvious, normally going back to their houses to satisfy his appetite. Perhaps Hunter could fill him in on the way to the airport. Checking his wallet for credit cards, they were all still there as was his ID. "Honest, at least," muttered Philip.

"Sorry, Dad?" stated Marc as he pulled his bathrobe tighter around him. Even for California it was cold at four-thirty in the morning and Philip didn't believe in heating too much. Marc pushed the bedraggled blonde hair from his eyes. This morning he looked more like his mother than ever, even down to the bold suntan and deep-blue eyes.

Philip's thoughts were distracted. "Nothing, son. Just thinking out loud." Philip reached for the suitcase just as Hunter came hurtling back through the doorway and headed for the bed.

"Got it, boss. You ready? Car is outside," asked his bodyguard.

"Your case?" asked Philip.

"Already in the car. Just grabbed some things, tossed them in there. Er, one question, Sir. How do we get guns on the flight?" Loyal... but not always the brightest bauble on the tree.

"We don't. We go without. It's England, not Mexico!" laughed Philip and handed Hunter his case. He turned to his son and hugged Marc to him. "Stay in touch. Cell works anywhere in the world. I'll call you when we land. Or Mac will."

"Right." Marc paused. "Glad Mac is going with you. You should be taking more men with you. Well, you know…" He cut his eyes at his father.

"Yeah, I know. Hazardous job I have," replied Philip. "Back before you know it. Look after that girl of yours, too… and if the kids want to come up from your mother's, that's fine," and with that he let go of his son, turned and walked away. Philip knew this was just another adventure…

Chapter 3

As Mac held the door, Philip hurried into the black stretch limo, pulling his leather jacket around him as he went. Marc was right. It was chilly, especially at five a.m. Hunter jumped in the passenger side next to the driver and the limo sped off at a decent speed down the long tarmac driveway towards the solid steel gate. At the sight of the approaching limo, the tall gates opened to let Mr. Vega's ride through and out onto the suburban road that took them down to the 405 freeway.

Philip lounged back in the luxurious leather seating, and pulled his cigarettes from his jacket pocket. He noticed that the glass partition was down into the front of the limo, so he put his cigarettes back in the leather. Philip really didn't care what the driver heard. He knew the chauffeur, and the man had been on his payroll for many years.

"Mac…" Philip had a way of using one-word sentences.

"Yeah, boss?" and Mac turned straight round to face Philip. "You need something? Your ticket is for first class. I managed to get a seat for me almost on the wing," he said with a wry smile.

"Good," said Philip, without really thinking what his bodyguard had said. He paused. "Last night. How drunk was I? I can't remember a damn thing after being at the hotel till that phone rang at four this morning. What the hell was I drinking? Not the usual, was it?"

"No. You were mixing drinks. Not like you. Seemed like you were bored or preoccupied or something," replied Mac with a tinge of sarcasm.

"Bored! Didn't really want to be there," and Philip slumped further back in the seat, contemplating the window like he had never seen one before. As he did so, small spots of rain hit the glass. First slowly, and then a little heavier. "God damn it!"

"No problem, Sir. Almost at LAX.," announced the uniformed driver and he turned off the freeway onto Century Blvd. "Be there in about ten minutes."

"Flight leaves at seven-thirty, boss. We have plenty of time. It's only barely five-forty-five." Hunter was rummaging in his jacket for his passport, pulled it out and laid it on his lap. "We have to pick the tickets up at check-in. Was no other way at this late stage."

"See if you can get an upgrade to first class. Would rather you were with me, especially as I am not carrying." Not that Philip was afraid, just a lot of unknown people in airports and Philip knew he was a good target.

"Pull over by American Airlines. Right there," and Mac pointed to the stand for AA and porters eagerly waiting to take cases and make some cash that no one would ever know about.

The limo slid out of the darkness and into the fast approaching morning light. Raindrops still hit the windows as the stretch limo's wheels touched the tip of the sidewalk. Mac jumped out of the car and beat the porter to the door. Philip stepped out, an air of confidence surrounding him. The trunk of the car opened and Mac pulled both suitcases out, and set off at great speed after his boss.

The terminal was fairly crowded even for this time of the morning and Philip Vega was still easily recognizable as the movie star he was. Normally, Philip basked in the glory, but today he didn't want to be bothered by idolizing women and signing autographs. He had better things to concentrate on. With Mac beside him, he made his way to the first class ticket counter. This one sported no lines and he went straight to the counter. Philip reached for his passport and let Mac do the rest.

"There should be a ticket here for Mr. Philip Vega flying to Heathrow," stated Mac, severely hoping that the woman behind the desk hurried up a little.

"We have it right here, Sir… Mr. Vega?" the very prim and proper older staff member on duty looked straight at Philip.

Philip looked back at her, now wishing he had worn shades, but they sat in the inside pocket of his leather. "Yeah..." and he sighed like he was irritated, which he was. He handed her his passport and waited for his ticket, something he wasn't used to doing.

She took it from him, knowing full well who he was and she was dying to ask for an autograph. By the look on his face, that was the last thing she would get from him.

"The ticket is one-way only, Sir... is that correct?" Now she felt like she was pushing it, but it was her job.

"Correct, and while you are there, upgrade my assistant, here, to first." No please or thank you.

"I can put him on standby to upgrade, Sir, but at the moment there are no seats open... there is a gentleman already ahead. We're waiting for a passenger to arrive that is a possible opening. There is only a few minutes left, though, to clear customs... so she might not make it."

"How much?" Vega was delving into the back pocket of his jeans for his wallet.

"What?" She looked astonished.

"How much to upgrade him before the *gentleman*?" Now he stared at her.

"I can't do that, sir... it would cost me my job..." and she didn't finish as Philip laid a couple of hundred dollar bills on the counter.

"Really... I think you can..." and Philip switched from mean to flirtatious at the flip of a switch. He turned on the charm like one would turn on the bath tap. He reached for a brochure on the counter. "What's your name?" and he pulled a pen from his jacket.

"Cindy..." and Cindy blushed unashamedly, knowing full well what Philip Vega was doing. "Sir, I still can't bump your assistant ahead..."

"Are you sure?" and then came the deep brown eyes, ones used to get exactly what he wanted.

Cindy glanced at her watch. "Well, I guess the lady isn't going to make it in time and I don't see the gentleman anywhere."

"That's what I thought... so here is your autograph and buy yourself something nice with the money, and thank you, Cindy."

"You have luggage, Mr. Vega," chirped Cindy as she changed the ticket for Mac.

"Just a carryon for both of us. Mac, give the nice lady your passport."

Mac stared at him. Yet again, Philip had wormed his way in with a woman to get what he needed, but this time it benefited them both. All Philip Vega had to do was demand, but he didn't.

Cindy handed them back the passports and tickets. "You can go straight through to customs," and she beckoned a security guard over to her, and whispered to him to take the two men past the lines that were now forming.

Mac carried the bags and followed Philip as he bade Cindy farewell, raised his eyebrows to his assistant, and strode off towards customs. He got the usual looks from the women they passed on the way, but once through customs, they found the first class lounge and large comfy couches.

Philip sat down on the nearest one. He wasn't used to waiting for planes. He was used to either flying in his own, or flying his own plane.

Mac sat on the one opposite and put the luggage by his legs. He glanced around, always watching and waiting… just in case. That's what Philip Vega paid him to do.

"Need a cigarette…" and Philip stood up and pulled his packet from the inside of his jacket and went for his lighter from the back of his jeans.

"Boss, no smoking… remember?"

"Since when?" asked Philip, sporting a frown.

"Since for ever…"

Philip sat down again and leaned back. He was still tired and he had the feeling that this was going to be a very long day. He needed a cigarette and he wanted a drink. He couldn't have either, was agitated, and he wanted to be on his way, which he wasn't.

"What the hell time is it, anyway?" mean and moody man was back in full force.

"Six forty-five. We'll be boarding soon. You need anything, Sir?" Mac called Philip 'Sir' when needed… and right now it was needed.

"Yeah, a cigarette… and a scotch!"

"Aside from that, boss," and Mac dropped his gaze to the tickets. "She got us seats next to each other… except mine is still on the wing…" Mac raised his head, looking at Philip. Vega hadn't heard a thing Mac had said. "You know it's snowing outside?" Mac waited for the reply.

"You say something, Mac?" Philip was miles away in thought.

"Not a thing, Sir… not a thing." Mac now knew that Philip was serious about this trip and this trip was to get the girl. He also remembered what his boss had said that night at the wrap party about 'the woman he was going to marry'. Obviously Philip was serious, and that spelled trouble for anyone who got in his way.

Chapter 4

The dulcet tones of the loud speaker announced the boarding for flight 696 to Heathrow. "Will all first class passengers please check in at gate 45. First class only. Thank you."

"We should go, boss," and Mac stood up, taking both cases with him, tickets sticking out of his jacket pocket.

"At last!" and Philip was gone out of the lounge and towards the gate, not even waiting for his bodyguard. He brushed past everyone else that was standing in line, not caring that they were staring, quite possibly recognizing him.

Philip took the looks for granted. He took his looks for granted. He was still an extremely attractive man and he knew it and, more so, he knew how to be attractive to women. He turned slightly to look for Mac and flashed the famous smile at the women watching him. They blushed. That's what he wanted, as he wanted to be first on the plane.

Mac knew what Vega was doing. He always did that. He wondered if he would stop round the girl. Somehow he thought his boss just might.

Philip acknowledged the attendant at the jet's entrance and carried on down to his seat. Easy enough to find when you were in row 1, window seat. He sat down, inspected the seat, pulled the seat belt round him and leaned back. Mac did the rest, putting the cases up in the overhead bins and generally settling them in. He noted that the seats turned into beds with blankets, pillows, a private television and seclusion. Mac had flown with Philip before, on his own private jet, not a commercial flight. Normally he stayed at the house. He wondered how smoothly the trip to England would go. Hopefully his boss would be tired enough to sleep most of the way. That thought was suddenly dashed.

"You lined up a car the other end of this flight?" Philip's eyes were closed, but not his mouth.

"No, Sir, wasn't time. I did ask Anthony to call ahead and find a service. Hopefully, it will be taken care of before we land."

"I hope so, too. That would make me much happier. He can leave you a message on your cell, right?"

"Yes, Sir. I'm sure he will."

"Good," and Philip turned his head towards the window, staring out towards the runway. The rain had stopped as fast as it started. Another plus. Vega liked to fly, but on his terms.

The plane filled up fast and the captain announced the departure.

"On time for once. Makes a change," mumbled Philip under his breath, and then promptly fell asleep.

For once, Mac was pleased. When the drinks cabinet came round, he grabbed a couple of small bottles of red wine. He thought about waking Philip and decided against it. Might not be the smartest move he ever made. He had been Philip Vega's personal bodyguard for the last ten years and by now he knew his moods well. Mostly Philip was civil, but when he didn't want to be… he wasn't… no matter who was around.

Four hours passed. Then two more and Mac also dozed. When he woke it was to Philip drinking down wine. Mac had noticed that Philip was drinking far more than he used to, and that wasn't good, especially in his line of work.

"Must have dozed off… sorry, boss." Mac sat bolt upright and rubbed his eyes. He hadn't meant to fall asleep.

"You didn't miss anything. Damn, I just want to get there." He turned to Mac. "Does that sound wrong?"

"You are asking me, Sir?" Mac was genuinely shocked.

"Yeah, I guess I am. So?" Philip's stare pierced through his bodyguard.

"I think, Sir, that only you can answer that." He paused. "I do know that she made a big impression on you..." he stopped. "And that's why you are flying to England."

Philip stared at him. Was he that transparent? If Mac had seen it, who else had? Maybe his son? He didn't really want that. They all knew the girl was married. Even Philip had some moral standard, low as it was.

"Yeah, she did... I'm only going to visit her and make sure she survives..."

"Right, boss..." Mac wasn't sure who Philip was trying to convince with that statement.

There was a look in Philip's eyes that disturbed Mac. He knew his boss was on a mission. He also knew Philip had fallen head over heels in one brief meeting and he couldn't say he blamed him either. The girl was stunning in a subtle way. She was young and had been full of life... and now she wasn't. She was struggling to survive. If anything happened to her before they arrived... He pushed the thought from his brain. A slight bolt of turbulence rocked the flight, just for a few seconds, but it brought him back to reality.

Philip knew Mac was analyzing him. Time to change the subject. "I meant to get that piece of business sorted out before we left... with the Bartons. I want that land deal. If he won't play ball and accept the offer, then we need to find another way of dealing with it."

"Anthony said Jack Barton was resisting a little. You want me to call Anthony when we get off this plane and tell him to use other methods?" That's all Mac had to say.

"We'll wait a couple of days. See how long we are going to be in England. Then we'll reconsider. I have a feeling we'll only be there a short time." Philip knew himself that he was lying. If a short time was in order, he would have gone on his own and he hadn't.

What Philip didn't know was that there was one other man on the plane that was also there for his protection. Mac had thought it safer that way and so had Philip's son.

Philip was getting more irritated as the flight went on. They watched the television monitor for a while, ate and slept some more. Philip downed a couple more small bottles of wine as time crept by...

slowly, till at last the stewardess came on and announced that they would be landing shortly.

"Thank god," Philip made one last trip to the bathroom and glanced at his watch. Almost six… no, that wasn't right. It was two in the morning where they were. He hoped to god there was a car waiting for them when they got into Heathrow.

In the bathroom, he splashed water on his face and looked into the mirror. He should have shaved before he left Los Angeles but there hadn't been time. With his dark looks, a moustache was already sprouting and a stubbly beard. Didn't look too bad. Maybe he should let it grow, sport a different look while he was away. He could hear the announcement about returning to the seats and this time did as the speaker asked.

It was a good landing and as they taxied into the gate, Mac listened to the messages on his cell hoping to god there was one about a car. There was. The driver would be at the baggage claim when he and Philip had cleared customs.

At the gate, Philip was the first off the plane, with Mac and the luggage in hot pursuit. He didn't stop till they reached customs. All the passport said was Philip Vega. It was real enough, and so was the name. It just didn't go into any details, nor did his ID.

Customs was cleared without any problem. Philip was recognized as usual, but again he didn't have time for such niceties, and ploughed on through.

Mac was there at every step of the way, eyes always watching his boss. They headed for the baggage claim, not that they had any, but that's where the driver was to meet them. Mac recognized the driver even without the sign. Italian looking, dark shades and long, black leather coat. No doubt whom he was there to meet.

Vega headed straight for him, but Mac spoke first. "Limo?"

"Yes, Sir. Right out front. Ready and waiting for instructions," and the new driver, and member of the family in their life, led the way.

Chapter 5

The chauffeur opened the car door and Vega climbed in. Now he felt more at home. He tried looking through the windows as they pulled away from the airport, but it was pitch dark outside. Once more he looked at his watch. Just after three. How he needed sleep. That wasn't going to happen.

Mac sat next to the driver. "You local?"

"Yes, Sir..." replied the deep Italian voice.

"Mac... Only Mr. Vega is Sir or Mr. Vega," he whispered very low. "Anthony's message said you come highly recommended. Don't let us down, Alex."

"No intention of that happening, Mac. None at all." Alex half turned to view Mac. He had been well informed of his duties for *Mr. Vega*.

"I assume he gave you the address. How long till we get there?" Mac asked, not having a clue where they were going except by address.

"This time of the morning... two, maybe three hours. Should be there by daylight. There are drinks and refreshments to the right side of the car. I stocked the drinks cabinet up." Alex thought Philip was not listening.

"Scotch?"

"Yes, Sir," and Alex could see Philip in the rear view mirror. Vega was everything he had been told and more. "Sir, if you open the cabinet, I think you will find all that you need."

Philip did. Aside from a bottle of scotch there sat a .357. He smiled. Smart man.

Alex reciprocated the gesture and focused back on the driving. They picked up speed as they hit the motorway and Philip leaned back on the luxurious seating. This time Mac stayed awake, talking to Alex in a very low voice, even though the glass partition was raised halfway.

The time went by quite quickly and at six-thirty they hit inner-city traffic.

"You want to wake Mr. Vega?" asked Alex, very quietly to Mac.

"Not asleep, Alex." Philip uttered from the back of the limo. He sat upright in the seat, and ran his hands through his hair. He wasn't asleep; he was just doing some real hard thinking.

Mac turned to look at Philip. "Alex tells me we should be there by seven. You want to stop and eat first or go straight to the hospital? Up to you, boss."

"Straight there. I need to see if she's okay…" He didn't say anymore. His statement reflected out loud what he was thinking.

It was not much longer till they pulled into the side entrance of the hospital. Possibly a limo wasn't the best thing to arrive in at the entrance of a large hospital in the early morning light. Alex pulled over to the entrance, rolled the window down and asked the nearest cop where he could park. Maybe a town car would be better. They should change.

With instructions to the parking lot, Mac jumped out of the limo and opened the car door for Philip. They moved quickly and leaving the luggage with Alex, they strode off into the hospital to the information desk.

The desk had been alerted that Mrs. Sands was expecting an overseas visitor. They didn't know it was a movie star, and Philip was not impressed at the attention he was getting just by standing there, in fact he was quiet annoyed.

"Would you tell us which direction we should take to get to her room?" Mac asked much more politely than his boss would. They got directions and were gone.

The hospital was clinical white and smelled of antiseptic, and even at this hour was busy with morning baths and medications. They climbed the stairs to the third floor and right at the top was room D. Philip stopped at the door. He knew that when he entered that room his life would change. Mac went to open the door for him. Philip stopped him, putting his hand on his arm. This was something he had to do for himself.

Philip pushed the door open, and there next to the bed, sat Emma's husband. Philip was taken off guard for just a moment, and, then, with his usual air of authority, stepped into the room.

Steven Sands stood up as Philip entered the room, with Mac close behind him.

Philip glanced down at the sterile bed, and as he spoke to Steven, he could see Emma once more. She was pale and thin compared to when he last saw her. Her long hair lay flat on the pillow and her eyes were shut tightly, blocking out the world. She wore no makeup and yet she was still remarkably pretty… and his heart missed a beat.

"Mr. Vega," and Steven put his hand out to Philip. "I can't thank you enough for coming, Sir… whatever the reason." Steven looked at Philip Vega. No wonder his wife had been so hung up on the man. Tall, tanned and strikingly handsome… and a walking womanizer. His obvious wealth seemed only to surpass his arrogance as he extended his hand in greeting… not a thing he usually did. Both grips were firm, and behind him was the muscle.

"How is Emma? Any better?" And his concentration was totally focused on the girl.

Mac watched with interest as his boss seemed more than intense. Even if Steven Sands didn't realize it yet, Philip was out to take his wife away from him, and Mac figured Philip Vega wouldn't have to try very hard.

Steven answered, pushing the few strands of hair from the front of his head. His eyes were tired and his faced pinched from lack of sleep. "Just the same… nothing seems to wake her. The car accident caused her to go into some sort of coma. The hospital doesn't know why. She just doesn't want to wake up anymore." He was a lost man and it showed very clearly. Steven was thin, pale and slowly creeping up to thirty… and no match for Vega. Steven looked down at Emma and then glanced at Philip, who was staring intently at her.

"Mind if I try?" and he knelt down next to the bed, resting his large hands on the crisp white sheets.

Philip knew that Steven was watching every move he made, but it was Emma's health that mattered. He looked at her lying there and he wanted to reach down and hold her.

It was then he spoke. "Emma… Emma," his voice was low. He tried again a little louder. "Emma… It's Philip, Philip Vega. You met me at the party in Hollywood," he paused, choosing his words carefully. "You turned me down once, young lady. You will not do it again!" He extended his hand across the sheets until his fingers very gently touched hers. As he did, the sleeve of his jacket slid back and the expensive gold Rolex could be seen quite clearly. "Emma, I know you can hear me, girl. Take hold of my fingers." He leaned closer to her. "Emma…" his breath almost on her face.

Suddenly, without any warning, Emma's fingers moved just slightly and her finger touched his. Her eyelashes flickered just for a second and then she opened her eyes. The first thing she saw was Philip's face. She blinked… hard. She must still be dreaming and closed her eyes tightly. But she could feel the warmth of his breath and she could smell the musky smell of unfamiliar cologne on this man.

"Emma. Open your eyes. Now! You can do it. You don't slip back… not now, not ever!" Philip demanded.

Her hand moved again and she clung to the fingers offered her, like a child lost in the night. "Philip…" Her voice was so low. It was the first word she had spoken since the accident.

Steven stood and watched Philip like he was in some kind of nightmare. This man had walked into the room and Emma had responded to him… however briefly. And she had turned the corner.

Tears streamed down Steven's face. "I don't know how to thank you, Mr. Vega… I really don't. We all thought she would die…" and Steven stopped to compose himself. "I should get the doctor… they need to know she is awake," and he left the room.

Philip nodded, never turning Steven's way. He stood up, but without letting go of her fingers.

"Boss… you okay?" asked Mac. He was genuinely concerned. This was new to him. Normally Philip was extremely dominant.

Philip turned his face towards Mac and in his eyes there was a look Hunter had never seen before. It was the face of someone who had reached a turning point. The look of a man who had finally come home and had found the person he had been searching for all his life. And now he knew what he had to do.

Chapter 6

Philip didn't want to leave the hospital room where Emma was. By now Alex had joined them and the room was starting to get a crowded look to it. Alex was larger than most men and very formidable looking even without shades.

"Mac...wouldn't Mr. Vega like to eat?" asked the good and intelligent new bodyguard. "And maybe step outside in the fresh air."

"Yeah, he should... but he doesn't want to leave her. He has to be hungry and tired by now. You see any decent places to eat on your travels through the grounds of the hospital?" Mac asked Alex, still with his eyes on Vega.

"They have a restaurant on the first floor. A bit cafeteria like, but not too bad. But you know him better. I will leave it to you."

"I'll wait till he's finished talking to the doctor and Steven...."

"Is he always this conversational?" asked Alex. This was not what he had heard about Philip Vega.

"Only when he wants something... or is after..." and Mac stopped, realizing he didn't know Alex that well. And Mr. Vega's affairs were not discussed with the help. "Generally, no."

As if he heard them talking, Philip looked up at Mac and with a very slight nod of the head beckoned him over to where he stood. He spoke very quietly to him and Mac nodded. He did indeed need to eat. Time was passing by and they also had to change cars and find a hotel for tonight.

Mac returned to Alex's side. "He wants to leave and come back later or tomorrow... you go and get the car, and we will meet you by the entrance in ten minutes." He was very much in control.

"On my way," and Alex was gone.

Mac waited by the door for Philip. He watched as his boss shook both the doctor's hand and Steven's, and he could hear him saying he would be back first thing in the morning. He also knew that Philip wanted to be on his own with the girl and that seemed to be the plan that was going down.

Philip said goodbye to Steven and he looked down at Emma. She hadn't woken again, and was sleeping peacefully. Her face was flushed and shades of pink filled her cheeks… and she was almost twenty years younger than Philip. He needed to remember that fact, and that she was the same age as his son.

"Sir, the car will be outside…" Mac looked at his watch.

"Let's go… I'm done here for tonight…" and Philip retrieved his shades from his leather and put them on, mainly to hide very bleary eyes.

Steven noticed. He was also aware of the two men with Vega. Did a movie star need that much protection? He thought not.

They left the room and this time took the antiquated elevator to the ground floor. The limo was there just like Alex said it would be and Philip climbed inside. He leaned back on the leather seat, tiredness literally hitting him in the face.

"Alex says there is a hotel very close to here. Place has suites and good food. Would you like to try it, just for tonight?"

"Why not… he's staying, too, right?" Inclining his head towards Alex… Philip would feel safer with them both there.

"Yes, Sir…" Mac replied.

It was settled. They were on their way. Turned out it was five miles from Emma's house. Alex planned it that way for his new boss, and was able to change cars at the hotel.

On the way there, Philip helped himself to a scotch or two, and he slipped the .357 into the back of his jeans. Now he felt much more comfortable. One more drink wouldn't hurt; after all it was way past six.

They turned into the hotel entrance. It was lavish to say the least and so close to the city… and the hospital. Alex had done well and Philip would note that. The only thing Philip could see was that it was more of a public place. It was busy with cars and people, but high-end kind. Doorman, private cars... the works. But that's what he was paying Mac and now Alex to do... keep him safe.

Now was the time for more caution. Vega was a better target when he was away from the hospital and mingling with the public. Normally, security would be high if he stayed in a hotel. Mac signed them in, while Philip waited in reception. Top floor, best suite... out of the way, and, hopefully, good room service. Mac went in with Philip. Alex was to change the limo for something smaller, making sure to leave the scotch behind with Mr. Vega.

Philip inspected the suite. It wasn't too bad. Not his usual standard but most passable. The best the hotel had to offer. He opened the bedroom door, walked through the room, dropped his leather and shades on the bed, and walked out onto the balcony. The 14th floor gave good views of the city. Dusk was settling in and lights popped on in all shapes and sizes of buildings. Inner-city traffic snaked along the roads, hardly moving. He shivered slightly from the chill of the damp autumn weather thinking things over until Mac disturbed his thoughts.

"Sir, would you like to look at the menu?" Mac asked tentatively. He knew Philip was deep in thought about where he was and the situation.

"No. You know what I like... order something. Chicken, steak, anything that's filling. Drinks. Something for later, too. Whatever you want and food for Alex. See if there is a drinks cabinet in the room." He wasn't facing Mac, and still looking out at the lights.

"Already done and there is. I put the scotch in there. I'll get them to bring ice. Anything else, Sir?"

"Yeah, there is." Philip turned around and leaned on the balcony railing. The cool air was refreshing to him, but he was very tired and it showed. He pulled his cigarettes from his jeans.

Immediately Mac was there, lighter at the ready. Philip cupped his hands round the small flame, let it catch, and then drew on the cigarette, watching the rings floating upwards into the air.

From the back of his jeans, he pulled out the .357. "Maybe you should keep this," and he went to hand it to Mac.

"I have one, too, boss. Alex is pretty good!" and Mac smiled.

"Yes, he is. A keeper. Wonder if he wants to immigrate to the USA?" Philip walked back into the bedroom, pushing the gun back into his jeans. "This place isn't too bad. Maybe make it like a base, at least for now. I need to call Marc. Let him know we have arrived and give him the number here at the hotel."

That was Mac's cue to leave and do what he was asked to do. He turned almost reaching the bedroom door.

"Your room okay? The suit has three bedrooms, right, couple of bathrooms?" asked Philip, causing Mac to stay longer.

"Two of each. Alex and I can share when he is here. Everything alright, Mr. Vega?" Mac knew it was not. "I mean if the hotel isn't to your liking, we can get another one. It's not too late tonight to change…" He knew full well that's not what was bothering Philip.

"Mac… I did the right thing by coming here… didn't I?" His look was very pensive.

"Yeah, boss, why…" Mac stopped.

"You know damn well why! Steven Sands knew why this afternoon! I plan to take his wife away from him." Philip's eyes sported unfathomable depths of despair and his voice meaning every word.

"You're that sure…" Mac inquired, already knowing the answer.

"Yeah… I'm that sure!"

Chapter 7

They ate dinner on the balcony leading from Philip's room, instead of the dining area. Philip had left a message at the house for Marc to call him. Although a little chilly sitting there, it seemed to suit the whole of the events so far. Chicken and steak, potatoes, rice, a veritable collection of food graced the very nice glass table that sat on the more than ample patio. A couple of bottles of wine and a bottle of scotch sat there, mostly consumed by Philip, who also smoked half a packet of cigarettes. At least the hunger factor didn't figure into the equation any more. The night was illuminated by the stars and office buildings housing late night workers. Very preoccupied, Philip didn't seem to notice the noise from the traffic. Tired as he was, he wanted to wait and talk to his son. He stood up from the table and moved to the balcony looking over at the lines of people waiting at the neighboring movie theatre.

"Must be a good film showing there… anyone know what?" Vega asked, very nonchalantly.

"Yeah, boss… late showing of 'The Godfather'," Mac blurted out, without even thinking what he had said.

Philip turned to look at Mac staring at him, and then he started to laugh. "Yeah… good one, Mac," and lines creased on his face.

Just then the phone rang on the line by Philip's king-size bed. Mac jumped up and took off into the bedroom and answered it. "Your son, Sir," and put the call on hold to allow Philip time to get there.

Philip stubbed the cigarette out under his boot and disappeared into the room. Mac left him there and closed the balcony doors behind him.

"How many children does Mr. Vega have?" asked Alex keeping his beverage to water. He still had on his long leather, but had removed the shades, revealing eyes much like Philip had.

"Four sons at present… I think he wants more. He often talks about having a little girl or two." Mac looked out into the evening air. He had a feeling deep down inside him that Emma was to be part of those plans for the one or two little girls.

"How long have you worked for the family?" Alex leaned back comfortably in the large chair.

"Ten years as his personal bodyguard, twenty years total," he replied as he sat back down and picked up a glass of red wine.

Alex raised his eyebrows. "You rose up fast through the ranks! Personal connection?" Alex was very direct.

"Yeah… my father worked for his grandfather, then his father. Right place right time. Mr. Vega is a good boss, fair till you get on his wrong side… which some people have found out… the hard way, so to speak. What did Anthony tell you?"

"Probably as much as I needed to know. To take very good care of Mr. Vega, back you up and keep him safe at all times. And he emphasized the 'all times'. He mentioned there is someone else over here with your party…"

Mac stopped him. "There is, but the boss doesn't know that. Better he doesn't know at this point. Thanks for the guns by the way… how did you know he likes to carry a .357?"

"Anthony told me. So instead of one, I put two in the limo. This might be England, Mac, but in this line of work, most of us carry a gun. No one knows it, that's all."

Mac couldn't help but think how perfect Alex was for Philip. If they had flown over and handpicked him, he could not have been better. Mr. Vega was right. They should take him back with them.

"Ever thought of moving to the US?" asked Mac very casually.

"Yes, why? Some of my family lives in Chicago." Alex answered him.

"You might just get your wish! Mr. Vega likes you! And I think we may have a travelling companion on the flight back, if you know what I mean." Chicago didn't surprise Mac at all. It really seemed very likely he belonged to a family there.

Alex smiled. He knew. He saw the way Mr. Vega looked at the girl and he also knew she was married. "Any enemies over here that I should know about?"

"There are always enemies in his line of work. But to answer your question… yes. But he needs to tell you, and I think today he made one more!" Mac took another sip of his wine.

"Yes, he did. Mr. Sands all but telegraphed his dislike of your boss. But Sands is no threat, is he? He is just a person in the film business, right?"

"More than likely he is, but I would like you to check him out tomorrow after you drop the boss and me off at the hospital. Mr. Vega will want to be there early. I think he wants to spend some time with her, maybe not with the husband around. But we shall see," Mac shuddered. "Always this cold in the fall… I mean autumn?"

"Generally… but not this damp. I will check Mr. Sands out first thing." Alex looked towards the doorway. "You think everything is going okay in there? It's been a while…"

"Yeah it has… I'll go check…" Mac stood up and opened the door, and stepped into the room. He was back out in about ten seconds, and quietly closed the door behind him. "He must have finished the call and fallen asleep. He's out to the world, sleeping like a baby." Mac looked round the balcony to the other side. "We can go in the other way. I'll wait a few hours then go back and make sure he is okay. That's his second night without sleep. Don't know how he does it… got to admit I am tired though after one without sleep. You wanna take the couch in the room for a spell. I just need a couple of hours sleep…" and Mac led the way round to the lounge via the extended outdoor balcony.

"Sure… I'll stay in here. You go. I'll wake you in a while. No sense in us both not sleeping," and Alex took off his coat and threw it on the back of the hard backed chair next to the soft, cream colored leather couch. Magazines adorned the pine coffee table and he picked up a couple to read. He set them on the couch beside him and then pulled his gun from the back of his jeans and laid it right next to him.

Mac was impressed and set off for the spare room.

Alex read two magazines. Vogue wasn't quite his style, but Racing Weekly was, so was Gun World. Several hours passed before the door from Philip's room opened and a very bleary-eyed man stepped out.

"What the hell time is it?" asked Philip, still fully clothed and still sporting the .357.

"Two a.m., Sir. Mac didn't want to wake you. He is also catching a nap. You need anything, Sir? Food, liquid…" Alex stood up, almost to attention. "Your case is in the room…"

"Yeah, I found it. Think I'll go get a shower and go back to bed." Philip, starting to go back into the room, turned slightly towards Alex. "You showed good judgment today. I could use a man like you on the way back to the States… maybe in Los Angeles, too. I'm not expecting any trouble, on the trip nor back at home, and I won't tolerate any, either. Do I make myself clear?"

Alex nodded. "Perfectly, Mr. Vega."

"Anthony must have checked you out and you turned up okay. He has been with me since I took over the family business some twenty years ago. Much has gone on since then and much is still to go." He paused. "The girl you met today… she will be going back with us. First, I have to get to know her and her me. Secondly, she has a husband. I don't want her by force. Oh, that would be the easy way," he shrugged, "but in this case, not the right way. Usually, it would be the way I would handle anything I wanted." Vega pushed the hair from his eyes and touched the stubble on his chin. "Maybe shower when I get up. Oh, and Alex, when you check Sands out… find something, okay? That's what I will be paying you for!"

Now Alex saw the real Philip Vega, and he was all he was told on the phone and a hell of a lot more! Not surprising that he was one on the most respected family heads in Los Angeles.

Chapter 8

They left the hotel at eight this time taking the town car which stayed with them most of the trip. All of them were carrying and Alex had made sure there was a place set aside in the car for the scotch.

Philip's phone call home had been just that... fine. He had learned though that the rest of his children had decided to come and stay with Marc while their father was away. Philip had sent his own private jet and two bodyguards to Florida to collect them. This information was only shared with Mac... his confidant.

It was raining slightly when they arrived at the hospital, looking like there was a lot more to come behind this shower. Dark thunder clouds hung over the hospital entrance and Philip hoped that this was not an omen for the rest of the day. Once inside, the two men made their way to Emma's room. Alex left on Mac's errand as he was ordered to. When they entered the room, Steven was already there, watching Emma like a hawk.

"Mr. Vega. I thought you might be early. I need to go to the studios today. Mind if I have a word with you... in private?" His approach was timid giving Vega the immediate upper hand.

Philip didn't hesitate. "Anything you want to say, you can say in front of Mac." Philip stood there, quietly confident.

"Very well." He glanced down at his wife who was still asleep. "I wanted to thank you again for coming. I am sure you have a very busy schedule and want to visit with Emma a little longer, so today is your day here while I am at the studio."

"Thank you, Steven. I appreciate the gesture, but I have no immediate plans to return to the States just yet. In fact, I thought I might stay a couple of weeks or more. Take in some of the sights in your little country; spend some time with *your* wife. You live near here don't you?"

"Yes, very near…"Steven was completely taken off guard. He looked at Philip, who was once more dressed in black and looked more menacing than ever, with his bodyguard standing right behind him. "Well, I am sure we don't mean to keep you from your own life…"

"*You're* not…" interrupted Philip.

It was Philip's American accent that woke Emma. She could hear both voices, but on hearing Philip she was trying to convince herself he was really there.

"Philip?" Her voice was quiet, expectant, but her eyes were open wide.

Philip immediately stopped speaking to Steven and looked down at the girl in the crisp white nightgown, one that blended into the sheets. She was so thin… She moved her head very slightly, looking up into his face, and as Philip glanced at the monitor, her heart rate increased. He reached down to her fingers, just touched them and once more the heart rate went up on the monitor. If Steven had any doubts… now he didn't…

"I would be glad to stay with Emma today and any days that you have to work," and he sat down on the hard-back hospital chair next to her bed, never letting go of her fingers. He felt hers tighten on his and he reciprocated the gesture, wrapping his fingers further round her hand. Mac saw it and wondered if Steven had. Obviously Philip had made the same impression on her as she had on him. Philip didn't look up. "How are you feeling? You were kind of out of it when we arrived yesterday?"

"We?" Was he married? Her heart missed a beat and she looked into his brown eyes.

"Mac, my… assistant… and myself. You just rest. We can talk later…" Philip knew that Steven was watching every move he made.

She glanced at his fingers. There was no ring, and on hers there was.

"Then I will come back later, Mr. Vega. Emma...I'll be here before lights out," and Steven was gone. Obviously he had seen what had happened... and he was not happy.

"I think I've been resting long enough... I need to sit up a little," and she tried to move on her own, with all the trappings moving with her.

"Here. Let me help you," and Philip slid his arm under her back, holding her, while Mac plumped up another pillow for her.

"Thank you... er..." Emma had no clue what to call him.

"Mac, Ms. Emma," and he stepped away from the bed.

And so with the ice broken, Philip sat down beside her and asked about the accident, explaining to her how Steven called him.

Mac sat at the back of the room by the window. He could hear them talking, but not what was said. And it wasn't his business to know, just to protect Philip. Mac could not help but notice how pretty Emma was. She looked at Philip like she still didn't believe he was there, but, right from that first moment, Mac knew there was a bond between them.

"Philip, it was so good of you to come here. I hope Steven thanked you. Are you staying long?" There was so much she wanted to ask him, and she knew she was acting like a woman that was infatuated with a man. That had to stop right now. Philip was just as she remembered him from the party, and Emma could only imagine what she looked like to him.

"He did. I'm staying till you are well and out of here." He glanced around the room. It was so stark and hostile, not like the hospitals back home. No television, not even flowers... nothing. "Then I am going to steal you away, Emma Sands, take you home with me to the States and marry you!"

She stared at him, her green eyes wide. She blinked her long dark lashes at him, and she blushed unashamedly. "That's a joke, right?" and she laughed a very precocious laugh.

"No. That's the truth. Right, Mac?" laughed Philip, his hand still tight on hers and his other hand resting on the pillow.

"Right, boss," chimed in Mac, having no idea what he was saying 'right' to.

Just then Philip's phone vibrated in his pocket. Letting go of her hand, he pulled the offending object out and looked at the number. "Need to take the call," and he was gone out of the door to the landing.

She cornered Mac as he went by her. "He was joking, wasn't he?" she asked him.

"About what?" Mac asked as he tried to get to the door to follow his boss.

"Marrying me…"

"I don't think he was, Ms. Emma. I really don't think he was!" and Mac went after his boss.

Emma lay back on her pillows. Had to be a joke. No one knew they wanted to marry someone that fast, not in her world anyway. She lay there thinking. If it was a joke then it was a cruel one. But the point was he had come all this way to see her. And then there was Steven… she just couldn't up and leave Steven, whether the marriage was a sham or not. He depended on her. He needed her. That's what she had told herself. What Steven really wanted was Emma's money, of which there was a lot. An inheritance and quite a large one and the house they lived in was hers, too. Tears rolled down her face. Emma knew her marriage was over. She had known the night of the accident and then it all came flooding back to her. The arguing in the street, the car, and her standing there wanting to die and that was her chance! Her cries became louder, much more hysterical.

The door opened and Philip rushed to her, his eyes full of concern. Without even thinking what he was doing he put his arms round her, and she cried into his jacket, clinging to him as her sobs escalated. He held her to him; his face nestled into her hair. He could smell her, touch her and feel the closeness of her.

"It's okay, Emma. You cry it out. I know what's going on in your life. No one is ever going to make you cry again." He cradled her as he thought about the message from Alex about Steven. Mr. Sands wasn't at work, or anywhere near work, nor had been since he quit his job at the studios some weeks ago, sometime around the time Emma came into money. Alex had followed Steven from the hospital to a woman's house, and watched from outside… He'd also found out about the money and the house they lived in. Steven was totally living off his wife. Mr. Sands wasn't so clean after all and Mr. Sands, at some point, was going to let Emma go, one way or another.

Chapter 9

A week passed and Emma was much more like her old self. Philip visited by day and sometimes night. Steven pleaded he had a lot of work to catch up on. It gave Philip time to get to know Emma, and Emma him, and she really didn't care that Steven stayed away more and more. Gave Mac time to read books! Lots of books and magazines. Philip didn't mention the marriage joke again and Emma never asked him about it.

They were doing very well together. Philip showed Emma pictures of his sons on his phone, and just a few chosen ones of his home. He took it slowly not wanting to scare her, and both of them knew they were building some kind of relationship. Only one of them knew where it was heading.

On the following weekend, Philip went to the hospital as usual only to find that Emma was dressed and sitting on the edge of the bed. She wore jeans and a T shirt, older clothes that hung off her. One of the first things Philip intended to fix. In his world, the man bought the clothes.

"Well, look at you! Going somewhere?" asked Philip, half joking, as he looked her up an down.

"Yes… home…" Her face was blank and unreadable.

"What? Since when?" He didn't look pleased that he had not been made aware of the fact.

"I only found out late last night… I can go home… I didn't like to call you." Emma did not look as happy about it as she ought to.

"You should have called me, honey. I gave you my cell number for emergencies or anytime you needed me… does anyone else know you are leaving?" and Philip half turned to Mac, who shrugged his shoulder that he didn't know either.

"Steven… he arranged it… He will be here very soon to collect me." Emma looked up at Philip almost pleading with him to rescue her.

"Really…" Now Philip was not at all pleased. "Is that where you want to go? Home?" He didn't banter words.

"Of course…" She dropped her eyes as she spoke.

"The truth, Emma. Do you want to go home…" and he lifted her face with his fingers, and looked into her eyes.

"Where else would I go?" She paused. "All my things are there and Steven…" and her voice trailed off.

"Just what worries me. I have a better idea. You should come and stay at the hotel where you can be waited on hand and foot," and he let his fingers drift to her shoulders.

"I can't do that, Philip! I have to go home. It's my home and my house…"

"Yes, I know it's yours…" He stopped; aware he was giving too much away.

"What Mr. Vega means is that you could relax at the hotel. They have an indoor pool and a gym, all kinds of good things to help you recover. There's a movie theatre next door, stores…" Mac jumped in also trying to convince her. "Maybe you could show us all some of the countryside." He stopped speaking as Philip turned and stared at him like he was nuts. Mac moved close to Philip. "You can't let her go home, boss. You will never see her again! He will send her somewhere to *recover*."

Philip knew Mac was right. Steven would make her a virtual prisoner in her own home. By now Steven would have figured that Philip had plans for Emma and he wasn't about to lose his way of life.

Just then the door opened and Steven stepped into the room. "Oh, good morning. Didn't you get my message? Left one at the hotel for you. Emma is going home today, all thanks to you." Steven turned away from Philip. "You ready, Emma? The car is out front." Steven smiled a very false smile at his wife.

It was then Philip took charge. "I thought maybe she would like to come back to the hotel for a few days. It's a really nice place. I'm sure you know it. The Hilton. She could relax there, be waited on…"

"She would be much better at home… wouldn't you, Emma? Plenty of time to relax and get over all this. All your things are there, besides you don't have anything with you…" He put his hand on Emma's arm and she pulled away very slightly from her husband.

That was all the prompting that Philip needed. Without hesitation he put his hand on Steven's arm. "I think the lady would be better off in the hotel… with us. I will pay for her to be there, won't cost you a cent and you can visit when you are free. Doesn't that sound better, and then when you are working she will have company? Much better idea."

Steven didn't have a comeback for that statement. Philip was right.

"But I really think it's up to Emma…" Philip turned to her, his face very unreadable. "Let's leave it up to her. Whatever she wants to do. Emma, you chose."

Emma stared from one to another. Her husband and her marriage were at stake. On the other hand Philip was there with her and she looked at him like he would fade away from her.

"That's a great invitation, Philip, but I think maybe I need to go back to the house and get some things, you know clothes and some personal items. Everything I have is there…"

Philip had lost… something he wasn't used to doing. He frowned at her and shook his head just slightly. But she had made her choice, and he had to abide by it.

"And then I can stay at the hotel for a few days…" Emma was aware that she had made the call and she could never go back… whatever happened.

Philip hadn't lost and he recovered quickly addressing both Mac and Emma. "Mac, call Alex and get him to bring the car. Emma, if you ride with us, you can show us the way… or we can just follow you, Steven. After that we can take you back to the hotel and get you a suite."

Philip watched Steven's face. He was furious, with his cheeks turning red and his eyes pin points of anger. Philip had a distinct feeling that pay back would be a bitch, but still he had what he wanted.

"As my car is already parked in the ten minute zone, Emma and I should go down. I am sure your man can follow us." Steven put his hand back on Emma's shoulder. This time Philip let it go.

"I am sure he can. If you would wait for us, please." Philip had a quiet confidence surrounding him. No one was going to push him around and survive, much as Steven wasn't.

"Of course. We will wait out front," and Steven almost ushered her out of the room and down the stairs, not even giving her time to say goodbye to the nurses that had looked after her for so long.

Philip and Mac followed closely behind not letting her out of their sight, hurrying down the stairway two steps at a time.

"Mr. Vega… she doesn't want to be on her own with him…" Mac was concerned for her.

"I can see that, Mac. I'm not god damn blind… let's hope Alex is there with the car. We are not leaving that house without her, whether she has everything she wants with her or not."

"You can't kidnap her, Sir… this is England…"

"I can't? Watch me!" and Philip walked to his waiting car with Mac very close to him.

Alex opened the door and Philip sat inside. Mac gave Alex instructions and they pulled out of the ten minute zone after Steven's smaller car. The pair seemed to be arguing; certainly it wasn't the happy home coming that it should have been.

It took only fifteen minutes to get to their house, all climbing out of the cars at the same time. Emma turned her face away from Philip so he would not see it was tear- stained. Philip could see plainly enough and he was seething, but right now was not the place to lose control. Emma was Steven's wife and Mac was right, he couldn't just kidnap her, much as he wanted to.

Philip looked up at her home. It wasn't bad. Must have cost some money… Emma's money! The faster they were in and out of it the better he would like it. Maybe he should just send Mac in.

Philip leaned on the side of the car, pulling his leather round him. Today, it seemed especially chilly and the rain hung in the air like a shroud. "Mac… you go in with her. Make sure she gets everything she wants to take, and I mean everything, because she damn well isn't coming back here, not if I have anything to do with it!"

"Yes, Sir, Mr. Vega..." and he was gone. Mac knew why Philip would not go in the house. He knew his boss would do something to Steven, and Philip could not afford to be arrested on British soil. The whole situation was getting just a little too close to something blowing up in their faces. On American soil it would have been taken care of. Philip would have given an order, and Mac would have just taken his gun out... and blown Steven away.

Chapter 10

Mac walked out with Emma and behind her followed Steven. Between them they had two large suitcases and a box of toiletries she needed. On the top of the box sat a rather odd colored bear that looked older than Emma. Philip stepped forward and he took the box from her, handed it to Alex to be put in the trunk of the car, along with the cases.

"That's all you have? Don't you have more luggage than that?" He was looking at the bags thinking if it was him leaving home there would be a ton of stuff, but then Emma didn't know she was doing that.

"This is all I need." Suddenly she was distant from him, hardly looking him in the face.

"You have ID with you?" he asked her, bending down and almost whispering to her.

"I have my passport in my purse as ID... always carry it with me, if that's what you mean?" She had donned a jacket, again way too big for her and her hair sat tousled on top of the collar. Still she wore no makeup and to Philip she was stunning, with her big green eyes, and long dark lashes.

"Yeah, that's what I mean. Come on let's get you into the car and to the hotel. At least you have a jacket now. Anything else you might need... I will get for you."

Emma didn't understand the last statement and she just nodded to him, and at the same time climbed in the car. Philip held the door for her. Not a thing he did for anyone. He turned to face Steven.

"She will have her own suite at the hotel. She will also have protection there so no one will bother her. Of course, you are welcome anytime. You are her husband," Philip toned the dominant attitude down a little. "I am sure she will be glad to see you, and any of her friends. A couple of weeks with some luxury and being waited on, while you work, will do her a world of good. Pity it's not summer and she could use the pool, but I think there is an indoor one," Philip continued. "Anyway, we should get going, get her checked in. Say, why don't you come tomorrow and we can all have lunch together. I am sure she would like that…" now he was pushing it with Steven. "That is unless you have other plans?" Philip smiled.

"I'll be there. What time?" Steven was forcing the words out through gritted teeth.

"Noon." Philip turned to make sure Emma was comfortably in the car and then walked to the other side of the vehicle. Mac was there, ready with the door, and Philip climbed in.

Steven watched as the car, containing his wife, drove off. She didn't even really know this man she had left with and yet, Steven had a feeling she did. He waited till they turned the corner and then rushed in the house to make calls.

Emma leaned back in the car and looked out of the window. It was now raining hard and as she looked at the large drops on the glass, tears rolled down her face and onto her old grey coat. She clutched her purse tightly to her and Philip could see her hands tighten round the straps of the bag. Philip very carefully slid his arm round the back of her and rested his arm on the leather upholstery. He felt her back tense as he touched her shoulder.

"You okay? I know you are crying…"

She turned to face him, tears streaming down her face and then without warning she leaned forward into his arms and sobbed. And he was the one who had told her no one would make her cry again!

It was like she had suddenly put the pieces of the puzzle together and she had the whole picture. "I'm not going back home, am I?"

"No, honey, you're not. Not unless you don't want to come with me." He held his breath. He had to say it sometime.

"To the hotel, you mean?" she blurted through her cries.

"You know that's not what I mean. Why do you think I asked about ID?" He raised his voice so they would hear him in the front of the car. "Alex, pull over a moment. You and Mac take five. Something Emma and I have to sort out right now."

Immediately the car stopped at the side of the road and both Alex and Mac climbed out, darting undercover of a nearby shop canopy for protection from the rain.

Philip waited till her cries subsided, then lifted her face with his fingers. His voice was gentle, his eyes concerned. "There is something you should know, baby. I came here to take you back with me to the States. It's what I do. Go after people. I told you back at the hospital that I was going to marry you. I am, when the time is right. First, we have to get to know each other, and there is more to know about me than there is to know about you. You think that's what you would want? A life with me in the States?" he stared into her eyes.

Emma knew he was dead serious. She also knew that he was far more than *just a movie star*. Even she knew that, and they didn't carry guns! She had felt the gun in his jeans waistband while he hugged her the day at the hospital. She had wanted to ask him about it, but it wasn't her business then. Now it was.

"Philip, why do you carry a gun?" Only one way to find out was to ask.

He looked shocked. "How did you know I do..." and he drew back very slightly from her.

"The other day in the hospital, when you held me... I could feel it in the back of your jeans. I'm young, Philip, not stupid. My father used to hunt, so I know a little about guns... and just now, you didn't deny it."

Philip was really taken off guard. "You surprise me more each day that I am around you. To answer you, all three of us carry guns. They carry them to protect me. I am not quite what I seem, Emma. I cannot tell you ..."

She reached up and put her finger on his lips. "I don't want to know what else you are just yet, Philip. I want to know you, the person. Philip Vega. I know you are kind, thoughtful, obviously very generous, and I know you care about me, something I had forgotten how to accept from a man. I know you love your children, even though they are not with you. You have a lovely home… and Philip, I made my choice ten minutes ago. I don't want to go back there to a broken marriage and a man that has affairs. Oh, I know he does. I just can't prove it. What ever happens now happens. I have money in the bank that Steven can't get to. I have two suitcases and I have Toby bear… that's all I need… that… and someone who cares about me."

She never blinked, just kept looking into his eyes. Suddenly she had grown up. Very gently, he pushed her hair behind her ear and leaned forward just enough to be able to kiss her lips. It wasn't long and lingering, just gentle and warm on her mouth. Soft and sweet, fleeting… like it should be. Philip knew she was hooked, right then and there. Now he had to take it slowly, step by step. And Emma knew she wanted that kiss to last forever, and how she was terrified it wouldn't. She was trying to be so grown up and underneath the bold exterior she was still crying. She had been hurt too much for it just to go away. She was twenty years younger than this man, and he was all in life that she wasn't.

Philip banged on the window and Mac and Alex returned to the car.

"Let's get you a room. We have plenty of time to talk. First a meal… I don't even know if you drink alcohol…" He laughed. "I hope to god you do…"

"I do… a little wine… and I don't smoke and I don't do drugs… which reminds me…" Emma opened her purse and pulled out a pill bottle with her name on it. She popped the top and took one out. "You have any water?" she asked him.

"In this car…" laughed Mac, from the front seat. "This car only carries scotch…"

"I guess that will have to do…" and she looked expectantly at Philip.

"Are they pain killers? You can't take them with scotch…" commented Philip.

"Yes… and I need one," she replied.

"Is it still that bad?" Philip really wanted to know, and took the pill container from her, looking at the label as he did.

"Some of the time. Just my back, tops of my legs. It's where the car hit me..." and Emma stopped. It was the first time she had told Philip anything about the pain. "Hopefully it will subside in time. They said it would."

Philip thought he'd never seen such a brave woman in his life. His ex-wife certainly wasn't like Emma, nor were any of his past dalliances. He fished out the scotch for her.

"Just take one gulp of it," and he handed it to her.

She drank it down taking the pill with it... and dually grimaced. "Oh, my god... that's awful. How can you drink that?"

"Yeah, boss... how you can drink that..." Mac thought it rather funny. Perhaps this girl would be good for him.

"Very god damn funny, Mac... Are we there yet?" asked Philip, changing the subject.

"Almost," replied Alex and as he spoke he turned into the driveway of the Hilton.

Philip watched Emma's expression and smiled to himself. This was a life she was obviously not used to and one he would have to introduce her too very quickly.

The car stopped and the doorman approached her side. She stepped out of the car as Mac opened the door for Philip. He moved round the car to her and slid his arm onto her shoulders, resting it very lightly there.

"Welcome to my world, Mrs. Sands," and Philip smiled.

Chapter 11

A lex checked her into the suite next to Philip's, adjoining doors between the bedrooms. Philip ushered her into the suite. The rooms were huge by Emma's standards, a king-sized bed and giant closets with a bathroom that could have hosted a whole family. Mac set her things in the bedroom and then left her and Philip alone. She slipped her jacket off and dropped it onto the chair showing Philip once again her too slim body.

"You need some help putting your things away?" Philip asked her.

That was the last thing she wanted, him to see her clothes. She was embarrassed that she virtually possessed nothing. "No… I can do it later." She turned to face him and smiled. "Thank you, Philip."

"For what, honey?" He looked confused.

"For saving my life…" she didn't cry, much as she wanted to… but mostly she wanted him to hold her tight and never let her go.

As if sensing her feelings, he stepped forward, towered over her and took her very gently in his arms. "Emma," he sighed, "I have to admit to you that I had ulterior motives. I wanted to see you again and you gave me that opportunity. I also meant what I said in the car. When the time is right, I will marry you! So either Steven gives you a divorce or we find another way…" Philip stopped speaking. He just wanted to hold her.

"Philip, how can you really be sure you want to… I mean, look at you and look at me. You must have a different woman every night…" Had she said that out loud? She had, so she continued. "I am not them, Philip. I am me." Again, as she slipped her arms round his waist, there was the gun. She knew if she pulled away from him now, she would lose him. She could not show any fear.

"Emma, I don't care what you are. It doesn't matter to me. What does matter is what you will think of my lifestyle. I can give you everything you want. A big house, money, my love and anything you want…"He avoided saying children and the family…

"Philip, I don't need money. I don't care about material things. I'm twenty-five and in a failed marriage. Are you sure you want to take that on? Look at me Philip… please take a good look… I can't go through more heartbreak!" Now she tried to pull away, but he was much stronger than her and he held onto her.

"Listen to me. First… you don't need those pills for pain. Your pain isn't in your back; it's in your heart. I give you my word, Emma, I will never cheat on you. Yeah, I cheated on my ex wife… I don't deny it. I played the field, and yes, I've slept with women since I saw you at the party." He had started so he may as well finish. "They were for sex, and if that makes me sound like some kind of male whore, then fine. But from this day on, there will never be another woman in my life except you. I know this is all happening so fast for you, but your husband was taking you away Emma. You do know that don't you?" he questioned her.

"Yes, I knew that's why you brought me here. He has friends, Philip, that are not so nice. They can make life a little uncomfortable." She had to tell him, had to make him aware.

"Really," and Philip almost laughed. Now he didn't feel so bad at all. Emma knew he had them. "Good!"

"What?" She looked dismayed.

"I said good! Now I don't feel as guilty for taking you away from him," he laughed and in his eyes there was smugness. "Little Emma, don't you worry about a thing. You just worry about getting well and the trip we are going on next week." He didn't even give her time to answer or ask where. "Now, you hungry? I know I am." He also knew he had to get away from her. The closeness of her body was getting too much for him. "If you brought that black dress with you, you know the one from the party, change into it and let's go have some dinner. After that, you should get some sleep. Tomorrow, when Steven joins us for lunch, let me do the talking." Philip took total control the only way he knew how… as head of the family.

She looked into his face and she knew he was right. She also knew she was in love with him. Philip watched as she pulled the black dress from her luggage.

"This one?" she asked him, knowing full well it was the one.

"Yeah, that's the one… think you could wear the underwear under it like the last time…" His voice was low.

She blushed. "You could see that? And you didn't tell me?" She was genuinely embarrassed, her eyes looking away from him.

"Why tell you… it just gave me a chance to see more of you… and what I saw, I liked," and he turned and left her standing there.

Philip knew Mac was waiting for him in his suite. "Tell Alex to sleep in the other room in Emma's suite. Also make it clear to him to stay out of her way and make it very clear, if he touches her… he's dead!"

"Yes, Sir…"Mac knew that Philip was more than serious. He also knew that Philip knew more than he was letting on. No doubt he would share it later.

"Go and get changed. Tell Alex, also, when he returns, we are all going to dinner. Call down to the restaurant and make a reservation for four at six. I'm going to shower and make some calls. You listen out for Emma. We will talk when Emma is asleep, and Mac, you were right about Sands… he wasn't going to let Emma go." Philip left Mac standing there a little confused.

Mac stood for just a moment and realized there was a knocking on the adjoining suite door.

"Philip," Emma whispered.

Mac opened the door. "He's in the shower, Ms. Emma. Can I help you with something?"

"I just wanted some help putting the suitcases away, and to find out what time dinner is. Did Philip tell you?"

"Six… and I can help with you with the cases. Mr. Vega has to make some calls to the States and the family." Mac said it with a great finality that almost frightened Emma.

There was that word 'family' again. She had heard it a few times from all of them. Emma was starting to put two and two together…

"Thank you, Mac. I would appreciate the help," and as they walked back into her room, Mac looked at Emma. Philip was a lucky man, and if Philip couldn't see it he was blind, something his boss was not.

"The room is way too big for me and the shelves… well…" and Emma laughed,

"And the bathroom is big enough for a family." She was obviously very nervous around Philip's bodyguard and what having one meant.

He felt he should say something. "Ms. Emma. Mr. Vega has asked both Alex and me to look out for you while we are here. If you need anything, you let one of us know. You don't have to do things like lifting cases or carrying things anymore. Alex will be sleeping in the spare room in your suite. Mr. Vega doesn't think there will be any trouble and he won't tolerate it. But just in case, someone will be with you at all times. I hope that doesn't frighten you, but he is looking out for your safety much as we look out for his."

"Mac… can I ask you a question?" She looked at him. Mac was huge compared to her, being almost as tall as Philip and obviously well fed.

"Sure you can," and his tone softened to a much nicer level.

"You are Philip's bodyguard and you all carry guns. That much I know. Does a movie star really need protection like that in England? Or is there another reason?"

"I think Mr. Vega is the one to ask about that…" That was not the statement he expected her to come out with.

Neither of them had noticed Philip in the doorway. He had been about to take the shower, when he realized the adjoining door was open, allowing voices to be heard. Curious, he decided to check it out.

"What should she ask Mr. Vega, Mac?" Philip stood there bare-chested, unshaven and unkempt, and in the front of his jeans he holstered the .357.

Chapter 12

Emma's eyes locked onto him. Firstly the gun… and then his body. She could not stop looking at him. He knew what he was doing… Philip always knew. Still she could not take her eyes off his body.

Mac looked from one to the other and he felt like he was intruding. "She should ask you what time dinner is." Mac didn't falter in his answer.

"Is that all she should ask me?" Philip pushed the gun further into his jeans, leaving his hands on the handle.

This time Mac didn't answer his boss feeling he might be in for the sharp end of Vega's tongue.

Words made it from Emma's brain to her lips. "I asked him a question, that's all… no problem." She realized her mistake. Quite innocently she had gone to his bodyguard behind Philip's back. "So what time is dinner?"

"Six… Alex, and the three of us," and he turned back in his suite leaving them standing there.

"Mac… I am so sorry. I didn't mean to get you into trouble. I can tell him I asked you questions…" She didn't know what else to say and was extremely embarrassed.

"He's not going to say anything else about it. He would have said it right there and then. Perhaps now, though, you get more of the picture," and Mac left her alone to change clothes.

Perhaps now she did. Philip Vega was a boss, more than a boss… she didn't know quite how much more. No wonder he was not afraid of Steven's friends. But maybe now she better do as he asked her to do and get herself ready. She showered very quickly, pulled her hair on top of her head, donned the white underwear and on top the black dress. She rummaged through her things till she found black high heels and some pretty earrings. She also realized she had left things behind. Sitting at the vanity mirror, she looked hard at her face. She knew Philip was coming onto her, and what did she think she was doing?

As she put makeup on, she knew exactly what she was doing. Her eyes were round and much larger with the mascara and just a hint of shadow. She found her lip-gloss and lastly her perfume. She looked at the label and laughed. Obsession. How appropriate. Emma stood up and looked at herself in the mirror. The heels were not the best idea with her back hurting, but tonight she needed them. She had to look good for him as he was risking so much for her. She felt she was ready and glanced at her watch. Five minutes to spare.

There was a gentle tap on the connecting door. She looked round to see Philip watching her.

"How long have you been standing there?" she stammered, a little embarrassed.

"Long enough, lady... long enough." His face gave nothing away.

"Maybe I should start locking this door," she joked.

"Maybe you should, just in case I forget my manners!" Philip wasn't joking.

Emma blushed profusely, and then took a closer look at Philip. He was wearing tight black jeans and a black silk shirt, with the first two buttons undone. He hadn't shaved and his hair was still damp. God knows where the gun was in those pants.

"You should blush more often. It really becomes you. Now," and he took her hand, "dinner. Alex," yelled Philip, "let's go."

"Coming, boss," he yelled back from the other room. "You look shocked, Emma. He was there the whole time. You just didn't see him, and he certainly did not see you getting ready! Mac... come on. If none of you are hungry... I am." He marched her to the front of her suite. "They can follow us." Philip knew they would go crazy trying to get there at the same time as him. He played on the fact that he could protect himself and often enjoyed their worrying, after all Philip was a crack shot.

As he pushed the button for the elevator the two men came tumbling out of the door behind him.

"About time. Who is protecting who here?" asked Philip.

"Sorry, Sir..." and Mac was still pulling his jacket on as he raced to the elevator.

"No harm done... this time..." and Philip turned serious. "Don't let it happen again!"

"No, Sir..."replied Alex.

Philip didn't let go of Emma's hand as they walked into the dinning room. One woman and three men... two of them very Italian looking, was a pretty obvious situation. This procured them the very best table and the utmost attention from the waiters, who were vying for a hefty tip. The restaurant wasn't the best on earth, but it wasn't too bad either.

"You want me to order for you?" Philip asked Emma. Not so much ask, but more like a statement that she would get used to saying yes to.

"Thank you, Philip," and she smiled at him.

Then he leaned into her chair and right near her face. "You do eat steak or chicken, right?"

"Actually, I don't," she said sort of screwing her face at him.

"You do now! You need some meat on those bones, young lady! You don't weigh ninety pounds soaking wet!" and he raised the menu up to see what he could order for her.

No one said a word. Emma was crimson, so he had been watching longer than she knew. Tonight she would take his advice and lock her bedroom door. She had a feeling that Philip was not a man you would say no to twice in one lifetime.

Both red and white wine arrived at the table. Emma drank quite a lot of white wine, and the men red. She suddenly felt very alone sitting there taking baby steps in his world, and one that she had no clue about. Quite obviously everyone else knew what he was, and she was still there figuring it out, and tomorrow her husband was visiting them for lunch. This morning she was still in hospital. It was like her world was spinning out of control and she couldn't slow it down.

The steak came... a very large steak. She pushed it round the plate, and when he looked at her, she ate a couple of mouthfuls. There was also a crisp green salad, much more to her liking and she devoured that. Philip insisted she had desert. Anything to keep him happy, but she was tiring rapidly, and Philip knew it.

"Would you excuse me? I need to go upstairs and lie down for just a little while… It's been a very different kind of day for me," Emma stated, a confused look on her face.

Philip clicked his fingers and Alex was on his feet. "Go with her. I'll be up in a little while."

Emma went to open her mouth to say she could find her way and happened to look in Mac's direction. He was shaking his head just very slightly from side to side; as if to tell her not to say a word.

Mac and Philip stood also, and Philip pulled her chair out for her, and then watched her walk away with Alex, turning back to his bodyguard.

"Playing big brother, Mac? I saw what you did. She's afraid of me, isn't she?"

"Yes, Sir, I think she is. Maybe not so much of you, but what you stand for. I think… she is figuring it out what you are for herself…" Mac stopped. Maybe he had overstepped his bounds.

Philip sat back down and Mac followed suit. He leaned back in the chair. "I'm totally in love with her, Mac, and I guess I am trying not to show it, but apparently not doing such a great job. I know it's unusual for me, but it's true." Philip sat quietly, obviously considering what he had said.

"I think, Sir, she knows that. I also think she is overwhelmed. This morning she was in hospital, now she has stepped into a world she doesn't understand." He paused. Philip might fire him or he might not. "That's what she was about to ask me in the bedroom when you came in. She did ask about dinner too, that was true… why don't you sit her down and tell her? She is an intelligent woman. Wouldn't it be better to come from you rather than someone else?" Mac waited for the explosion.

Philip looked Mac square in the eyes. "Anyone else would be gone for that comment… but you are right, and she needs to know before she gets on the plane. Tomorrow, when Steven has been, I will sit her down and tell her that she is going to be living with the finest 'family' in Los Angeles."

Chapter 13

Alex escorted her into the suite, and she excused herself to the bedroom. She slipped her shoes and dress off and lay on the bed, pulled Toby to her and held him as close as she could. She didn't cry... she just lay there staring at the ceiling. She was very tired and turned on her side in the half light of the bedside lamp, drifting into an uneasy sleep.

Alex sat in the lounge and waited for Philip and Mac. He made a couple of calls on his cell and leaned back on the couch. He didn't have to wait very long for his new boss.

They knocked quietly on her door and Alex opened it and let them both in. Philip immediately made for her drinks cabinet and poured himself a large scotch. He nursed it in his hand, moving to the tan, leather couch in her suite.

"You want me to leave, boss?" asked Alex.

"No. You should both stay." He sat down, still nursing the drink, then it reached his mouth and went down in one go. "Is she okay?" and Philip looked towards the bedroom door.

"She's fine, boss. She wasn't crying, if that's what you are wondering. I think your lady is getting just a little stronger."

"Good, that's good. Tomorrow we face Steven and then I am going to tell her what's waiting for her in Los Angeles. Speaking of which, we need to book a flight for the end of the week, maybe sooner. No good putting off going home. Mac, book four seats... first class... use my card. She has her passport and I assume you do, Alex?"

He nodded.

"Good… Mac, when we leave here, you will also be Emma's body-guard as well as mine." He looked at his watch. "Almost nine. Think I will hit the sack also. Been a very long day. We'll meet about ten in the morning. Steven arrives at noon. After that we will decide which day we leave for the States. Emma has to be fit enough to travel. It's not like it's our own jet we are travelling on where she would be more comfortable." He stood up, set the glass on the table and left the suite by the main door, not the connecting one.

Inside his suite, he threw the room key down on the table, and walked into his bedroom. It was his way of saying he did not want to be disturbed. In his room, he pulled the gun from his jeans, slipped the shirt off and he, too, lay on the bed. So much was going through his mind. How he wanted to hold Emma right now and tell her everything would be fine and how he knew he could not. He wondered if she had locked the door… rising up from the bed, he moved to the door that connected his room to hers. He tried the handle just once. It wasn't locked. He moved away from the door back to his own bed, lay down and slowly fell asleep still clad in his jeans.

Philip was awakened about three by someone's disturbed dreams. He heard her yell and he shot off the bed and into her room at the same time as Alex. Both of them had their guns in their hands ready for trouble. Philip rushed to her side, with Alex staying by the door.

"Emma… honey. It's okay. You're safe. Emma," and he shook her very gently, putting his arms round her trying to comfort her. He had a feeling there had been many nights like this and there were many more to come.

She had dropped Toby on the bed and now she clung to Philip. All she wore was the thin, white lace underwear and all he had on was his jeans. This time it was almost too much for him and he pushed the hair from her face and kissed her. Much to his amazement, she kissed him back, clinging to his back as she did.

Alex slipped out of the bedroom door and left them alone. She had Philip with her now. Philip kept on kissing her and she snuggled into his body. She wanted him as much as he wanted her.

He pulled back just slightly a little afraid of his own feelings… "Nice underwear…"

"I didn't think you had noticed…" she replied flustered.

"I noticed, baby. I noticed…" He paused. "Emma, I want you so badly… but not with two bodyguards outside the damn door…" and he let go of her, standing up as he did. He took hold of her hand and led her into his bedroom and whispered. "I'm not going to make love to you Emma, not tonight, much as I damn well want to. I just want to hold you in my arms, okay? I think it would be too much for you in your condition. But when we do, I want you fully awake and knowing what you are doing. I think, well, me for one, have had too much to drink and maybe you, too… And, Emma, whenever I take you, I don't give you back. You do understand that, don't you?" He stopped speaking and pulled her down onto the bed with him.

"I understand, Philip," she replied.

He lay back on the duvet pulling her with him. Setting the gun on the nightstand, he wrapped his arms round Emma and she leaned on his chest. "Sleep, honey… just close your eyes. You're safe. I'm here with you. No more nightmares."

Philip didn't sleep again that night. He watched over her like a lion over his pride. A song kept running through his mind, one he had heard recently… 'Run to me, whenever you're lonely'… Right now that seemed very appropriate. He could almost hear her heart beat as her breasts pressed to his chest. He kissed her hair and nestled his face into it. How long they lay there like that he did not know. All he knew was that he was totally in love with her, and he had meant it when he said there would never ever be another woman in his life, more than she would ever know. The room had a chill to it and, very carefully, he pulled the duvet round her.

The next thing he knew was Mac knocking very lightly on the bedroom door. Maybe he had dozed for a moment. He hadn't meant to.

"Yeah…"

"Mr. Vega… it's almost ten. Mr. Sands is due here at noon. Should Alex wake Emma?" Mac was trying to be as subtle as he could

"Mac… very quietly come in and close the door behind you." Philip slid from under Emma and sat on the side of the bed. He looked up at Mac. "As you can see she is here with me… untouched, just sleeping off bad dreams… let Alex think she is in the other room, and mostly certainly don't let Steven Sands know anything about this. He would have grounds to accuse me of adultery, or at least think he had." Philip stood up, but not before making sure that Emma's body was completely covered.

"Yes, Sir…"

"And Mac, this is our secret! I'll wake her…" out of time.

"Philip… I thought I heard voices…" and Emma peered out from under the duvet… "Oh, I did…"

"Honey, it's okay… Mac being around us is something you will get used to. Has to be that way… especially back in the States… Emma, while Mac is here, do you think you would be up to flying say about Wednesday or Thursday? Or would next weekend be better to go home?"

Home! They were going home! His home… his life… his family.

"You decide Philip. What ever you want is fine with me. I am sure your family is looking forward to having you back…" She caught the look Mac gave Philip and she saw Philip move his head side to side.

She thought she had it and she didn't. Then there was only one other answer. Family meant gangster, or mob… as in fiction novels! He was in the mob! What had she got herself into… and yet, somehow, she wasn't afraid because he cared about her, maybe even loved her, and, most of all, he respected her. She still had her clothes on and so did he, which, if she had known Philip better, was a first when sharing a bed with a woman.

"Philip…" and she half sat up, making sure that only he saw her, but at the same time scanning the bed for some kind of robe.

"Yeah, baby…" and he looked down at her lying there thinking maybe he had put her in an awkward position in front of Mac.

"Philip, are you some kind of… well… are you some kind of person in the mob?" At last the question made it out of her mouth. She was half joking and half not. She had to know right now, before her husband arrived.

Mac looked shocked that she had asked his boss outright. But she had, and now Philip had to answer, either to lie or tell her the truth.

"Yeah, honey. I am some sort of person like that. You want to know exactly what?" He peered at her and leaned down slightly, his voice raised. He wasn't too thrilled she had called him out in front of his bodyguard.

She was red in the face. "I think I know… you said you go after people… do you kill people? Are you some kind of hit-man? Are you?" Her voice got louder and she threw the duvet off her, jumping out of his bed in full view of Mac, who could see pretty much every-thing.

Philip was furious. "Mac, get out of here! Now!"

Emma was shaking as Philip took hold of her arm and led her into her room. He grabbed a robe and pulled it round her, forcing her arms into the sleeves.

"Don't you ever do that again!" Philip was yelling at her, loudly. "They are staff, Emma, and you are nearly naked! Do I make myself clear? No man will see your body again… except me!"

So that's why he was so angry. She tied the robe up with the belt, pulling it tight.

"You didn't answer my question, Philip. Who are you, Philip Vega?" Now she was screaming at him.

"You obviously think you know so much, what do you think?" He was giving her back as much as she was giving him. Blow by blow. "Maybe you should not be here. Maybe you should go back with Ste-ven! That can be arranged, much as anything that I want can be ar-ranged!"

"Maybe I should! At least he's not a killer!" And she started pull-ing clothes from the closet.

He grabbed her by the arms to make her drop the clothes. "Stop it right now! You're not going anywhere. You made your choice yes-terday by getting in the car with me, and last night by sleeping in my bed!"

"You said we didn't make love… you said… Who are you, Philip, to have such power over people? Tell me, or I will leave! I don't un-derstand, Philip…" and once more tears streamed down her face, but tears of anger.

He let go of her, ashamed he was treating her like this. He reached in the back of his jeans for his true ID, and handed it to her. At the same time, Alex knocked loudly on her bedroom door.

"Is everything alright, Sir? Don Andrea, are you alright in there?" and Alex burst into the room with his gun in hand worried at what he might find.

Emma stared at him. Dear god, what had she unleashed?

Chapter 14

Emma clutched his ID in her hand. His whole name was on there. He was head of a Los Angeles family. She had been in bed with a family head! She ran into the bathroom and threw up in the sink, washed her mouth out and stared in the mirror. He went after her, leaning on the door frame.

"So now you know! I had planned on telling you tonight. Nothing else to know, except, I don't normally kill anyone. That's their job!" and he inclined his head back to Alex, and Mac, who had joined him in the room. "You wanted to know, Emma. Does that change how you feel? If it does then you should leave. But answer a question for me… are you in love with me?"

She looked hard into the mirror above the extremely expensive basin she had thrown up in. She could see Philip standing there watching her. He already knew what her answer would be.

"No." She didn't turn around.

"The truth, Emma… I will ask you for the last time. Are you in love with me? Before you answer me, let me tell you just in case you have any doubts. I have never slept in a room with a woman before without having sex with her. So that has to tell you something. Either I am not attracted to you, which you certainly know is not the case, or I have enough respect for you to wait till you are ready and last night I don't think you were. Now for the last time, are you in love with me?"

"Yes…" she whispered. "God help me, but I love you, Philip Andrea Vega, right from the first time you shook hands with me at the party." She could still see his face through the mirror, his expression softening.

He left the doorway then, closed the door after him and moved behind her, encircling her with his arms. She leaned back on his chest and he whispered in her ear. "Then… God help us both because, I'm in love with you, too, Emma Sands and right now I'm not sure how we are going to handle it. Your husband is in the way, Emma, and we have to see how lunch goes today before we say or do anything."

Philip turned her round to face him. He was so much taller than her, even both barefoot. "Emma, I knew my feelings the instant I set eyes on you, but it took a long time to get back to you. Things got in the way, business things, some things I will never be able to share with you, Em. Best if you don't know. What you do need to know is what you are stepping into. The family is one of the biggest in L.A. My father left it to me some twenty years ago. Rightfully it should have gone to my older brother, Damien… actually half-brother, but Damien never played straight. He was skimming money… well; let's just say he was not what my father wanted as an heir. So the job fell to me. I can't say I didn't want it, because I did. I craved for the life my father had." He stopped. He had not planned this especially with Steven due so soon. "But it's a very different world, Emma. Certainly not on the right side of the law, although they don't bother us and we don't bother them. Tonight, I will tell you more and tonight, maybe we won't drink as much and see where the night takes you and me. What we do have to do now, is get showered and ready to greet Steven." He felt her shudder in his arms. "You, okay? Was it what I just told you, or because Steven is coming?"

"Because Steven is coming. I would rather just run away with you…" and she laughed a kind of uneasy laugh. "Is that crazy?"

"No, baby… it's not crazy. After Steven is gone we'll go into the city… some things I want to get you… okay?" and he moved stray strands of hair from her face with his fingers.

"Philip, you don't have to buy me things… that's not necessary… I have money, quite a lot actually." Her face nestled into his fingers.

"I know I don't have to… I want to. There are some things a man likes to see his woman in and some things that he buys for her, so no arguing… just get used to it, baby…" and he let go of her and as she turned away, just smacked her very lightly on her backside.

Emma blushed. She was not used to this from a man. Certainly Steven had never shown her any affection like this. She could only imagine what sleeping with Philip would be like.

"Pity there isn't time to shower... together, I mean..." added Philip, and opened the door, walked out of her suite and into his own, leaving her standing there.

In the shower, she thought more about Philip, wondering what it was like to be made love to by him. Her mind raced and she came back to the present, thinking that it had to be getting close to noon and that she needed to get ready. She found some tighter fitting jeans and a pretty top that she had been saving, a very tight, long-sleeved baby-blue T shirt, low cut, warm but also very sexy. She left her hair down and donned a pair of black boots, not too high but a pair she had bought recently. She wore a coating of makeup, not too much, just enough. Then she saw Philip's ID on the bed and stuck it into the back pocket of her jeans, meaning to give it straight back the moment she saw him.

There was a knock on her bedroom door.

"Ms. Emma. Mr. Vega would like you to join him by the bar in the lounge. I will be right here ready to escort you to him," Alex added. "Are you almost ready?"

Emma opened the door for him. "I am, Alex. Let's go meet your boss and my husband," and she grabbed her purse as she left the room.

Alex gave her a very admiring glance. "If I may so, Ms. Emma, you look very nice. I'm sure Mr. Vega will be very pleased," and they took the elevator down to the first floor and to the bar.

Alex and Emma walked across the floor to where Philip and Steven stood talking. Next to Philip stood Mac nursing a soda. She looked at Philip and Steven. There was no comparison in the two men. None at all. She knew at that second she would not have stayed with Steven even without Philip, but she also knew what ever happened now she was head over heels in love with Philip... and whatever he wanted, she wanted.

Mac saw her first and whispered into his boss's ear. Philip turned to see her and a smile spread across his face, winking at her at the same time. Steven could not miss the look of admiration on Philip's face. He turned to see his wife accompanied by a bodyguard and he knew that any chance of keeping Emma had gone. He couldn't tell if Philip and Emma had spent the night together or not. Coming down to meet him separately was a smart move on Philip's part.

When Philip smiled at her, Emma reciprocated the gesture twice over. She beamed at him, blushing at the same time, dipping her eyes just a little, enhancing the fact she was overwhelmed with Philip's attentions. Alex was right, quite obviously Philip was pleased. As she neared them, Philip extended his hand towards her arm and very lightly just rested it there just as a friend would do.

"Good morning, Emma. How are we today…" Philip played it to the end.

"I'm fine. Thank you for asking."

"Steven," and Emma looked at her husband. He was immaculately dressed, and she wondered whose money paid for the expensive dark grey jacket and jeans he wore. More than likely she had without knowing it.

"Emma. You look much better even after one day away. Expensive hotels must suit you." Steven looked at his wife, knowing full well it wasn't the first time Philip had seen her today.

"This one must. Did you look around? It's very nice," and she hoped he didn't ask her about it as she had only the restaurant and the suites. "The food is very good here…"

Philip watched with interest. Emma had gained a lot of confidence very quickly, and he thought the confidence sprang from not being around Steven.

"Would you like a glass of wine, Emma?" Philip asked curious as to her reply.

"White, please. Just one." She never looked Philip's way, knowing well there would be a smile on his face.

Mac handed her the drink and there was a look between them that Steven could not miss. He was protecting her, just like a personal bodyguard would do. Steven looked at Philip, who gave nothing away, and behind them all stood Alex. Steven was surprised that he wasn't carrying a violin case under his arm.

"Shall we all go into lunch? Emma is right; the food is pretty good here. We ate here last night... all four of us. The wine is okay, as well. You might like to try a glass, Steven. It's better than the beer," Philip pointedly said as he looked at the beer in Steven's hand.

Noon saw them entering the restaurant. Philip had had Mac reserve them the best table and one that seated five. The seating was well planned at the circular table. Philip, Emma, Mac, Steven and Alex. He wasn't about to allow Steven to sit next to his wife and blow her new found confidence. Steven also noticed it and he realized that Philip and Emma were flanked by his bodyguards... and more to point so was he.

Chapter 15

Lunch went by smoothly enough. Philip downed three glasses of wine, but looked contented. Emma stuck to her one glass as she had stated. Steven noted these facts and also that Philip rested his arm on the back of her chair. Emma didn't even seem to notice. They discussed the weather, Emma's health, the food, the hotel, and then came the bombshell. Philip waited till they had completely finished the meal. He sat back in his chair, a very serious look on his face, and his jet black sweater and jeans he wore gave him a very ominous look. He pulled his cigarettes out and before he even had put the packet back Mac was there with a light.

"Steven. I have something to ask you. I would like to take Emma back to the States with me for a vacation. I think it would do her the world of good. Of course, we need to check with the hospital first and see if they agree, but I was thinking maybe next weekend… or maybe sooner. I have some business to attend to and I can't do it from here." Business was right. He wanted land that belonged to someone else. Philip paused, more for effect than anything else "It would just be for a week or two. She wouldn't have anything to worry about, just to get well. I have a very nice house in Los Angeles, couple of maids and as you see, bodyguards. My four children are there and my brother, so you know she would be well looked after. It's still quite pleasant weather there so she could use the pool…" Was he listening to himself? Nice house was a mansion with high security, gated, and surrounded by ten foot walls; men with guns; maids and bodyguards was the understatement; his brother was about to be booted from the household and his kids were sometimes beyond reproach. Other than that, it was the truth! He watched the smoke rings float into the air and he heard Emma gasp. Even she didn't know he was going to say it like that.

Steven looked at Philip. He should have known that he would pull something like this. His look turned to his wife who had composed herself enough to look back at him.

"Isn't that going to be a lot of money for you, Emma?" He was thinking she was paying and it was coming out of their funds.

Philip stepped right in. "Won't cost her a penny. The flight is on me. Mac is going to get four first class tickets for Thursday evening from Heathrow, providing the hospital says it's okay. Now, of course, if she eats a lot, then I may have to charge her… or find something else for her to do," Philip laughed and leaned forward, stubbing the cigarette out like he was snuffing out a life. He only half glanced at his empty glass and Mac leaned forward and filled it up for him.

Alex was paying great attention to Mac. He needed to watch and learn how to treat Mr. Vega, and right now Mr. Vega was in total control.

Steven was still looking at Emma. "Is that what you want, Emma? To go on holiday to Los Angeles?"

"It would be nice. I liked it the last time… met some nice people…"

"A little too much and too many, apparently…" muttered Steven under his breath.

"What?" Now Emma felt uncomfortable. "Would you excuse me while I find the ladies room?" and she stood up, clutching her purse to her.

Immediately Philip and his two bodyguards stood with her while she left the table, and Philip murmured, "Alex…"

Steven stared and raised his eyebrows. "Impressive, Mr. Vega. But that's not going to carry weight with my wife. She will tire of it as she will of all the niceties you bestow on her. Emma is very independent."

"Really? Good to know. I like that in a woman!" Philip sat down and leaned across the table in Steve's direction. "You obviously don't approve of her taking a vacation, especially not with me. So… while Emma is gone, let me phrase it this way. Emma *is* going on vacation with me. I will take very good care of her, on that you have my word…"

"I am *sure* you will…" he looked Philip in the face as he said it.

"Does that bother you, Steven? You were the one that called me to help her. So, I am helping her, and she will be fine. She is free to do what she wants, right? She is a grown woman… and she is still your wife…"

"Yeah, she is, and you might want to keep that in mind…" added Steven.

"What the hell is that supposed to mean…" Now Philip was getting irritated with the conversation, and his voice was raised. "She's over twenty-one… and she is my friend."

Mac could see it and he could see trouble looming fast… and this was not the place for it. He leaned towards his boss, whispered something and Philip nodded his head.

Philip turned the anger down a notch. "When Emma gets back to the table, you tell her it's fine to go… she is really looking forward to seeing the States again. You don't spoil it for her, okay?" There was more than a threat in his voice, but at least he was quieter about it now. "From now on, you don't spoil anything for her!"

"Is that a threat, Mr. Vega?"

"No… just telling you how it's going to be… probably more like a promise," and he looked Steven in the eyes never flinching, and then just slightly adjusted his sights to also include Emma and Alex.

"Can you back it?" asked Steven, eyes glaring at Philip, and knowing full well he could.

"Any which way you want to play…" Philip leaned back in the chair, a smug smile on his face, firing on all cylinders.

"Who are you, Philip Vega?" Steven's eyes narrowed at the older man.

"I don't think you really want to know, Steven…" Philip was surrounded in confidence and a lot of arrogance.

Now Steven knew Philip was serious. He glanced at Mac, who seemed to have his hand on his belt. Steven had a good idea why, but this was not a good place to ask. He thought Mac was carrying a gun.

"I could stop her going with you. She is not really fit enough to travel, you know…" He was trying everything he knew.

"You could try… but it's not really up to you. I am sure Emma will make her own decisions." Then Philip lowered his voice. "I do know, though, that you are not working at the studio anymore and that you are living off her money. Wonder how she would feel if she knew that? Of course if she is on vacation, she won't know will she? Why not think of it that way? A friend giving her a nice vacation." 'A vacation she won't be coming back from!' Philip thought, as he leaned forward in the chair.

"You son-of-a-bitch!" and Steven almost rose up from the chair.

"Really? Me? Never thought of it that way… Oh, and Emma says she left some things behind at *her* house. I have a list of them here. Maybe you would be so good as to pack them for her and Mac here will pick them up tonight," and Philip fished in his pocket for the list of stuff that Emma had given him last night.

"Be glad to, boss," and Mac's hand moved just slightly, inferring he did, indeed, have a gun.

"Good. Then it's all settled. We fly out Thursday. And you are more than welcome to come see her. One of us will know where she is." His authority was final. As he said it, Philip stood.

Emma and Alex approached the table. Philip didn't offer her a seat, instead very casually slid his arm round her back just touching her very lightly.

"Okay. We are done here. I thought we would take Emma shopping for a few things. So, Steven, Mac will be round tonight for the extras that she wants. Emma, you need a jacket? Here you can borrow my leather," and he slipped his jacket off and put it round her shoulders. Ready or do you need to go back to your suite?"

"No. I'm fine. Have my purse. Do you have my list?" She asked Philip.

"Already taken care of, honey. Steven," and Philip put his hand out to her husband.

The only thing Steven could do was to reciprocate the gesture or look like a fool.

"Going shopping to get new things for the trip! Do you mind?" asked Emma to Steven.

Steven looked at her and also looked at Philip's face as he shook his head side to side. Steven knew there and then that he would never be alone with Emma again.

Chapter 16

"That's all you want to get? Just a leather jacket and some jeans? What about some pretty underwear and nightwear," Philip was teasing her and she knew it.

She blushed, again. "I really don't need any. I don't wear them that much…" and she stopped. "I mean…"

Philip laughed at her, aware he was going obviously where no man had gone before. "Come on then. Let's get them and get going. I know you are tired…"

"A little, yes…" and Emma took out her debit-card to pay for them and Philip let her.

"I'm sorry, madam, but the account is declined," and the over made-up counter- assistant, who was eyeing up Philip, handed her back the card.

"That can't be. There are several thousand dollars in that account." Emma looked horrified at this news.

"I'm sorry, but it's declined." The girl actually looked pleased at the news.

Philip stepped straight in and handed the assistant his credit card, the one with no limit on it. It went straight through and the items were paid for. "Come one, honey. Has to be a bank error. We'll get it checked out back at the hotel." He knew full well where the money had gone, but now was not the place to tell her. He nodded to Alex who collected the packages for her and they left to find the car. On the way there Philip excused himself for a second and stopped Mac. They were only talking a minute or two, but Philip conveyed his sentiments to Mac. He wanted something said to Steven when he went to get the rest of Emma's things.

Emma looked shattered, her misery hard to hide. She knew deep down where the money had gone. She had another account that Steven could not touch, but would need to go into the bank to get the money, and tomorrow that's what she would do, with or without Philip. She was humiliated, and Philip knew it.

In the car, she didn't speak, just sat looking out as darkness fell on the city. It started to rain and a slight mist hit the headlights. What had started as a fairly good marriage had ended up a nightmare, and she was trapped in it. She didn't cry, she didn't do anything except stare through the window at the darkness.

Philip rested his arm on the black upholstery. There was so much he wanted to say and how much he knew he couldn't. It wasn't far to the hotel and once there, they went in silence to his suite, just Philip, Emma and Alex. Mac disappeared per instructions.

"Anyone like a drink?" and Philip went to the cabinet, got three glasses, and a fresh bottle of white wine. He didn't wait for Alex, just opened it himself. He set the bottle down on the large coffee table and set one glass for each of them.

"You want me to stay, Sir, or I can go…" Alex didn't finish.

"Stay. Have a drink with us. Maybe we should order some food. Alex, get room service. Emma what would you like to eat?" Philip was pouring drinks… glasses full to the top.

"Nothing, thanks. Just some wine, then maybe I will go to sleep…"

"No, you won't! You will stay right here and you will eat… or I will make you eat." He knew she just wanted to leave the room.

"You are not my keeper, Philip! If I don't want to eat, then I won't. I am really not hungry."

"Actually, I am your keeper… now…" he replied, half joking. Half not.

Emma stood up, dropped his jacket on the couch and grabbed her purse. "You sound more like my father!" She yelled at him and turned to leave.

"Maybe, I'll act like one then. Sit down! Alex, order some food… from the other suite," and he handed him a glass of wine to go.

Philip waited till he left the room. "That's something else I should keep in mind, too. Almost twenty years difference in our ages. Now, lady… or should I say… young lady. This wasn't quite what we had planned tonight, was it? So we may as well get a drink instead." Now Philip sounded pissed off. He hadn't got what he wanted. He picked up his glass and took it to the window with him, displaying his apparent displeasure at the whole situation.

Emma picked up her wine and drank half of it straight down without stopping. It burned in her throat but she wasn't about to let Philip know that. She looked at him standing there. How she wanted to run to him and him tell her it would all be okay. She knew that he had heard her drink the wine down, yet he never moved. Slowly she walked across the room to him and slid her arms round his waist till she was so close to him that she was leaning on his back, her face turned sideward to him. She clung to him frightened he would let her go at any moment. She reached into her back pocket and pulled his ID out and pushed it into Philip's jeans, letting her fingers linger there.

Philip set the empty glass down on the window ledge and turned around in her arms. He bent his head and kissed her till she couldn't breathe. He held her so tightly that she felt like she would black out. His kisses were electrifying, passionate and intense, and then he reached down her back as far as his arms would go. One hand slipped just inside her jeans, and as it did, she could feel his loins pressing against her, wanting her, and he could feel her breasts on his sweater. If he asked her now to go to bed with him, she would say yes, half a glass of wine in her or not.

"You could never be my father," she whispered. "Philip, please don't ever let me go…"

"I have no intentions of doing that. You are coming back to the States with me and that's where you will stay." He paused. "We should continue this is my bedroom…"

As if on cue, Alex opened the suite door, albeit slowly… and the moment was lost.

"Sir, I am so sorry…" and he went to close the door, embarrassed.

"Alex, come back… you didn't know." Philip looked down at Emma and whispered to her. "I don't think we are meant to sleep together tonight, honey, and maybe we should just wait till we get home, where we will have a lot more privacy!" Then Philip laughed. He was going to let go of her and realized he couldn't. "Don't move, baby. Bad timing for me…"

"I hope I always have that effect on you…" and Emma laughed.

Alex smiled. "Ordered food for four. I assume Mac will be back soon."

"Mac is back now," and he, too, bounced into the room, turning a shade of red as he did. He tried to hide his face behind the rather large box he was carrying, so that he didn't look at the obvious. "Sorry, boss…"

"Nothing to be sorry for. You guys better get used to Emma and I …" Finally he could let go of her, but bent his head just a little first and whispered in her ear.

She blushed unashamedly and hit him on arm, trying hard to concentrate on the box that Mac had brought her.

Mac set it on the table and Emma sat down on the over-large couch.

"Did you have any problems getting my things, Mac?" asked Emma, almost afraid of the answer.

"No problem, Ms. Emma," and he glanced at Philip.

She pulled the flaps of the box and there inside were all the things she asked for. Some photo albums, couple of things from when she was a child, a few more clothes that she had left there and her bank account books, both checking and savings. She leaned back on the couch and opened the checking. It was totally empty. She let out a gasp. It was all gone. She dreaded opening the savings account. It was still there. It was the only account in just her name, and tomorrow she would empty that account, too.

"You okay, baby…" and Philip moved towards the couch.

"I'm fine, Philip…" Her voice didn't betray her real feelings

He noted she didn't look at him. "Of course you are," and he reached his hand over her shoulder and laid it there. "But Emma, one word of advice… from now on don't feel any guilt. You don't owe Steven one damn thing!"

Philip moved away from her and towards his bodyguards, leaving Emma still looking in the box. "Mac, change the tickets, we are leaving first thing Tuesday morning, early as possible. I need to get her out of here before there is no young woman to take with me. Tomorrow, we go into the city, so she can cash in her account and also get her some luggage. Then we get the hell out of here and we don't come back. None of us! And Alex... before we leave here, you will take care of Steven Sands! Tell him not to come near her again and also tell him to file for divorce... or I will end him!"

Chapter 17

"**B**oss, Alex or I can…" Mac looked shocked that Philip would even suggest it.

"This is personal," interrupted Philip. "Would not be the first time and will not be the last time that I take someone out myself. Look at her… he has stripped her of everything. How would you like to have your things in a box and a couple of suitcases? I know I wouldn't. Speaking of which… Alex you need to go and pack also. I never asked you if you have a place here or what…"

"Live with my sister and her husband. As I told Mac, my family is in Chicago. I came here for a change. It was better for my health… at the time. No problems now. All I need is an hour or two to get my stuff together. I could go tonight after we eat, leaves me free for tomorrow."

"Sounds fine. Mac will be here with us and the gentleman down the lobby!"

"You knew?" Mac looked very surprised.

"Of course. I wasn't just handed my position in life. My father made me earn the right. Came up the hard way, just like you. And, Mac, I appreciate the concern. I assume he will be travelling back with us also… on my card?"

"Yeah, sorry, boss…" and his gaze extended to Emma. "Would you like us to leave the two of you alone?"

"No… better if you guys stay… mainly because I don't trust myself with her…" Philip stopped and cleared his throat. That was an admission. "Well, you get the gist… or I could just go out and end Steven tonight!"

They were interrupted as room service arrived heralded by loud knocking on the door.

Alex made for the doorway and Philip joined Emma on the couch. A whole trolley load of food appeared into the suite. Philip turned to look.

"Jesus! How much did you order? Why don't you invite the guy from down the lobby to join us…"

"I am already here, Sir," and the 'waiter' laughed.

"The whole time?" asked Philip.

"Yes, Sir, Mr. Vega."

"Impressive."

"Thank you, Sir," and the waiter left.

Emma looked from Philip to Mac… she had no clue what was going on. She did know, as she looked at the food, Emma was hungry. She pushed the box to one side and leaned back on Philip, who was sipping his wine.

"Maybe, I am hungry…" and then she whispered in Philip's ear, so only he would hear. "If I eat, can I sleep with you tonight?"

Philip almost choked on the drink and made strange gurgling noises. "Did I hear you right?"

"Yes. That's what alcohol does to me…"

"Really? Have some more…" and Philip knew even though she was coming on to him, she would eat then fall asleep. But still, she fascinated him and he really appreciated the gesture. He intended to sleep with her, *sleep* being the word.

"Too much food here. It will keep for breakfast, too." Philip stated as he leaned back on the couch with Emma curled up beside him, her head resting on a cushion on his lap. "What time is it, anyway? Seems like we have been eating and drinking for hours…"

"We have boss. It's nearly eleven."

"God almighty. I gotta get this lady to bed…" and she moved slightly as he slid from under her, lifting her at the same time.

"Need any help there, Sir," asked Alex.

"Alex… I have never known our boss to need help getting a

woman into bed in his entire life…" Mac wondered if he had really said that out loud. By the look on Philip's face, he had.

In the bedroom, Philip slid her out of her jeans and top, put her in one of his T shirts, and tried not to think of the obvious. He climbed out of his jeans and shirt and into sweat pants, lay down beside her, turned out the bedside lamp and he, also, was asleep in two seconds.

Alex slipped out of the suite to get his clothes and was gone only an hour or so. Mac cleaned up and took the room in Philip's suite, so he could monitor both his charges.

Philip woke first and took himself into the shower. Emma was still asleep when he came out. He figured not so much asleep but hung-over. Opening the door quietly, he slipped into the main room. The food tray was there, mostly covered, and the pastries sat there, still looking really good.

At the sound of doors, Mac came into the room.

"Morning, boss… you… er… sleep well?"

"I think we all did! I need to go wake Emma. We should be gone by ten, into the city and get this bank account sorted for her. Any luck with the tickets?"

"First flight out at seven a.m. tomorrow, non-stop to Los Angeles. Cost you a bit, boss… sorry…" and Mac made a face.

"No, that's fine. Don't care how much. Did you call home to make arrangements for us to be met?"

"Yes, boss. Anthony is sending the limo with strict instructions that everyone is home to meet you and your lady. Flight gets in mid morning. No excuses."

"Sounds good… anything else… Damien still there? And all the kids?" he asked, devouring a pastry in two bites.

"Yes, Sir."

"So let's get this day over, get an early night, and board the damn plane and go home. There is only one thing I want from this country and I already have it. She's in the bedroom." Philip's whole demeanor had changed from last night. Quite obviously he wanted out and what Philip wanted he got. "Speaking of getting out, aren't we too far from the airport, like a hundred miles too far away?"

"Yes. I was going to ask you did you want to go down there this afternoon after we get her luggage packed. We actually have to be at the airport at five a.m. We can either leave here about one a.m. and get there early, or travel down this afternoon. We can make use of the first class lounges and facilities or we can book into another hotel…"

"No more hotels! We will stay here till midnight or so and then head down, take advantage of first class. I'll let Emma sleep a little longer. We can pick her up a couple of suitcases on the way back from the bank. Book the restaurant for dinner at six for all of us. Emma can take a nap before we go and we'll head out tonight."

"Got it… boss… everything okay?" Mac broached the subject carefully.

"I'll just be glad to be back in the States. I can't say I am looking forward to the flight and I am a little worried about Emma. She thinks she is handling this well. She's not. She drank too much, and she was talking in her sleep about Steven and him coming after her. I don't think she realizes yet what will happen if he does. I would rather he just give her a divorce. When Alex visits him today make sure Steven understands I am serious, that he gets out of her life. And then we have to introduce her to the family…" Philip drank some juice.

"Second thoughts, boss…" Mac asked hoping to god he was wrong. He really liked Emma and had realized she would be perfect for Philip, even calm him down a little, and stabilize him.

"About Emma, never… I would die for her! I am worried she's not going to handle this entire situation too well."

"Mr. Vega. I think you underestimate her. She has a lot of guts. She hardly knows you, yet she left her husband and is getting on a plane to god knows where with you. She hasn't met your children, hasn't seen where you live… not many women would love someone that much to trust them with their future. She is giving up everything for you."

Philip had not thought of it like that. "Good point, Mac." Pausing, Philip moved to the drinks cabinet. He knew Mac was watching him. He picked up the bottle of scotch and he put it back down again. He didn't need it today. Today he needed to have a clear head for Emma. It was a start. "Okay, I will go wake her. Plenty of food still here, if she wants to eat. You want to put her suitcases on her bed for her and she can pack as much as she can in them. Help her, would you? Then we will go. Want to make a couple of calls."

"Yes, Sir."

"Let's get this show on the road... both you and I can pack in fifteen. We already had practice. Mac, make sure that Alex does what I ask and also that Steven does not know we are leaving early. Nice little present for him to come to the hotel and find us gone, much like Emma's money did. Pay back is a bitch!"

Emma had climbed out of bed and finding Philip gone, made her way to the door still clad in Philip's T shirt... and she had heard every word. She moved back into the room towards the night stand and the phone. She dialed Steven's number. He was still her husband and she felt she owed him.

Philip glanced down at the phone as he heard the main line click and saw the extension line turn red. He knew it was her and that she had more than likely overheard the conversation. He watched the phone... and as fast as it was connected it was disconnected. She hadn't made the call and he smiled. She was learning his ways very fast!

Chapter 18

At one a.m. they checked out of the hotel. Philip didn't ask her about the call to Steven. She had hung up and that's what counted. They had eaten dinner, downed a couple of glasses of wine, and had 'bags to go' containing bagels and fruit.

It rained most of the way to Heathrow, cold, damp rain and in the warmth of the car Emma slept. With his arm round her and she resting on his chest, Philip stared out of the window into a dark place. His thoughts very mixed. Damien loomed into his mind, a half-brother that had to go. His four sons waiting for his return... three of them were visiting their father again after weeks apart. And in his arms, Emma, soon to be his mistress and then his second wife, something he never thought would happen. He wondered how she was really feeling about all this. Whisked off to the USA with a man she hardly knew and a life she certainly didn't know. He noted she had packed Toby in her carry on luggage along with the mementos from home. He pulled her tighter to him, protecting her like he always would be. She was dressed in her new leather that he had bought her and the new jeans, which fit her like a glove. Philip certainly noticed those.

"Mr. Vega, we are almost there. About another ten minutes and we should be at the terminal. Someone will collect the car from us. It's all arranged. If you and Ms. Emma care to get out of the car, Alex and I can get the luggage."

"Fine." He leaned over Emma, and whispered to her. "Baby, time to wake up. We're there. Couple of hours and we will be on the plane, hon. Emma, baby... you awake..."

"Yes. What time is it…" she moved in his arms and rubbed her eyes.

"Almost five a.m. Be light soon. Collect your purse. The rest will be taken care of." Philip said it with such finality. They all had noticed a change in him like he was dreading going back to his old life.

Emma clutched the purse and carryon that stood on the sidewalk while Mac and Alex checked in the luggage.

After the tickets were presented at first class, the bodyguards ushered the pair through to customs. There, both Alex and Emma went through together, and Philip and Mac through US. They met the other side and quickly descended to the first class flight lounge where they were safer, and Mac and Alex could breathe easy again.

Emma whispered in Philip's ear. "Over there, end of the lobby. Alex…" and they took off for the ladies room.

Philip couldn't smoke and he was agitated. Even for him, it was too early to drink. He sat down on the couch. "Mac. When we get home, as I said, you are both mine and Emma's bodyguard. Let me tell you now. Even though you are part of 'the family', if anything happens to her… you are a dead man! Tell Alex that he is working directly for you and to report only to you… or me, but mainly to you. He does not report to Anthony and neither do you. He backs you… clear?"

"Yes, Sir…" Mac was taken by surprise and it showed. "Very clear!" He had been promoted and declared 'dead man walking' all in one go. Now he knew his boss was uptight about something and this would not be a time to cross him.

"Where the hell is she?" asked Philip looking at his watch like it was lying to him.

"It's only been five minutes, Sir…" and Mac stopped talking as Philip glared at him. He knew his boss hated not being in control and right now he wasn't.

It was almost six and he was extremely relieved when both Alex and Emma returned. They had brought coffee with them, and she sat down on the couch next to Philip, handing him a cup. He took it from her, had one sip and put it down on the table. At the same time he felt his phone vibrate in his jeans pocket. He pulled it out and answered it.

"Yeah… this better be good news! She's there now? Then for god's sake get rid of her! Of course she is with me and I don't want Sally there when I get back. What the fuck is she doing there anyway? Damien asked her to be there? Since when has Damien had any authority in my home?" Now Philip was really angry and he stood up, moving away from his party and to the lounge window.

Alex started to stand and Mac motioned to him to stay put. "We can see him from here. Best not to follow him right now."

Emma didn't know what the hell was going on. "Mac… why is Philip so angry? And who is Sally?" She looked from Mac to Philip and back.

Now it made sense why his boss was in such a bad mood. He remembered Philip saying he had calls to make. "Sally is Philip's first wife. He doesn't want her there when you arrive. He wants you to meet his children…"

Emma started to stand as if to go to him.

"No, Ms. Emma. Do not go there. He won't tolerate that, even from you!" He paused. "There are things you will never know about him. Things he cannot tell you, but I have no doubt that he will always love you and always come back to you. This you must accept, this and his way of life… if you love him, and Ms. Emma, always be there, ready and waiting… you understand what I mean?"

Emma looked into Mac's eyes. Her big brother, literally. She knew what he meant.

"I understand you. You mean always be there when he wants anything… including sex…" She stopped speaking, embarrassed in front of these two older men.

"That's exactly what I mean. You are young and he wants more children. You can give them to him. You have to be his wife, lover, mother of his children, confidant, his everything… can you do that?"

It was a big question with a one word answer. "Yes…" and Emma realized she could.

They all heard him hang up the call, still very unhappy. He retuned to the couch and sat on the arm of it looking at Emma like he could burn holes in her with his eyes. It was obvious to them what he wanted and Philip Vega was not a man to be kept waiting. "Let's go to the terminal and get this boarding crap over with and the twelve hour flight. Mac, when we get off the plane you don't leave her side, right to my bedroom if needs be!" inclining his head at Emma. "Alex, you have your instructions from Mac?"

"Yes, Sir…" and he almost stood to attention.

"I won't tolerate mistakes in or near my home. I pay very well, Alex, as Mac can confirm, but money doesn't always buy loyalty, especially from one's brother and an ex-wife!"

Now Emma saw the real Philip Vega for what he was… boss of a mob family.

Chapter 19

The flight was a long twelve hours. Luxurious to Emma... commonplace to Philip. Emma slept as much as she could. Philip changed seats twice with Alex, so he could talk to Mac. They ate first class meals and the 'go bag' meals, watched the movie, drank wine, read magazines and waited for the time to pass. Emma discovered Philip was a bad passenger. She was a nervous flyer, but she wasn't going to let him see that. Very obviously, he had enough on his mind without worrying about her.

It was stuffy on the flight and Emma had removed her jacket. Underneath she wore a very tight white T shirt with tiny buttons down the front. Philip happened to turn in her direction and his look even amazed her. If he could have, he would have made love to her right there. He reached over and undid one of the buttons on the top of the T, and then another, letting his fingers just rest there.

"Ladies and gentlemen, please be seated and prepare for landing." She was saved at the last second by the monotone voice heralding landing.

"Tonight, Emma... I can't wait for you any longer... tonight, baby!" and he kissed the side of her face.

Now Emma knew what Mac had meant about Philip. He obviously knew his moods better than she did. She did up her seatbelt and prepared for the landing, the worst part of flying for her. She clung to the arms on the seat and Philip realized she was terrified.

"Hey, honey. We are nearly down," and he prized her hand from the armrest and held it tightly to his chest. "You're fine, baby, just fine. The limo will be outside and we will be at the house in an hour or so.

Just want you to meet the children and then if you wish, go to our suite. You will like it, Emmy. It's large, airy and overlooks the swimming pool. I have a Jacuzzi in there, a small gym, TV and, of course, a bar…" There it was said. She wasn't getting a say in the matter.

They landed, did the customs thing again and Mac and Alex collected the luggage. In front of the baggage claim stood two men, very Italian looking, all in black with shades, and obviously waiting for Philip. Philip took her hand and Mac and Alex fell in behind them. The two men bent their heads so slightly to Philip it could have been missed, but it was there.

"Anthony… good to see you and Rossi… ..this is Emma, the future Mrs. Vega!" And then he spoke to them in Italian.

Emma tried not to gasp. Of course Philip could speak the language. He was Italian. She just hadn't heard him speak it till now.

"Let's go home," and with his arm round her shoulders he ushered them out of the airport.

The two men had acknowledged her with the same nod of the head as to Philip. No handshake, no anything. As she would later come to learn they were his lieutenants… Anthony, head of the household and Rossi, his second, a very menacing older man who at first sight would scare one to death.

At the curbside sat a stretch limo with tinted windows, and a cop sat on a motorcycle beside it, just watching and waiting.

"Mr. Vega," and the cop all but opened the door for Philip. Rossi beat him to it.

"Louis. Good to see you. How's the kids?"

"Fine, Sir. I'll be on my way. Have a good day," and with that he pulled out into the traffic, lights flashing.

"Ms. Emma," Mac held the door for her and she climbed into the car. She looked around the stretch. It was enormous. She dropped her jacket on the seat next to Philip, but she still clutched her purse.

As Mac climbed in opposite her, he put her carryon bag in front of him and sat facing her. Next to him sat Alex right across from Philip, and next to Philip were the drinks. Anthony climbed into the driving seat and Rossi next to him. Emma was wide eyed. She knew what he was and she knew he was wealthy, but he had certainly downplayed exactly how much security he needed and how wealthy he was.

"Won't take us long to get to the house. You want some water? Plenty of refreshments in the car. You need anything, baby, ever, you let me know and if I'm not around you let Mac know. You understand?"

"Yes, Philip..." and she felt him squeeze her shoulder and his hand slide just onto her skin.

They drove along the sun-filled streets, the houses getting larger as they went. Emma marveled at the splendor of the driveways... and the cars parked there in.

As Philip watched he was almost amused by her. He saw her hands tighten on her purse, and the look on her face.

"Baby, when we get to the house, just stay close to me. Just follow my lead... it's just a different way of life, hon, that's all. Mac will be right by you at every turn, okay?"

She nodded, and as she did the limo slowed down and turned into the driveway. The huge, spiked iron gates opened and the limo came to a stop. At the gate were two men, who looked into the car. Both quite clearly had guns and both looked like gangsters, dressed all in black even down to their boots. Shoulder holsters were a dead giveaway. They touched their foreheads to Philip and at the girl with him.

Emma looked ahead of her and there down a long driveway stood the biggest house she had ever seen. It wasn't a house... it was a mansion. Why in god's name hadn't Philip told her it would be like this... why? And another question she had for Philip: what had happened to her husband? All she had was a brief call from him saying he was busy working and he hoped she had a great vacation. That was it... nothing. He must have known the account was empty by now, and she knew Philip had had a hand in it somewhere. In fact, she had a lot of questions for Philip, but she had already learned not to question him in front of his men.

The house loomed closer. The gardens on each side of the driveway were immaculately manicured. Small trees and shrubs dotted themselves in various patterns right to the front door, and then, posted by the door, were men... a lot of men.

Emma shuddered. It was a fortress from the outside. Philip felt it, and whispered in her ear. "You'll get used to the security, honey, and the inside is very different. Look…" and he pointed through the window to the door.

Mingled with the security were two young men, one girl and two young boys, who were clamoring to look for their father and the woman with him.

As the limo stopped the two youngest Vega sons ran to Philip's side. Rossi jumped out and opened his boss's door.

"Daddyyyyyyyy…" and Daniel and Orry, two carbon copy eight-year-old Vega kids, hurled themselves at their father. One was blonde and one dark haired, otherwise they were identical.

Philip threw his arms round them and hoisted them both into the air, showing a lot of strength. While he held them there, his oldest son, Marc stepped forward and whispered something to his father concerning his mother and Philip's brother, Damien. Philip nodded his head, a serious look on his face.

Rossi opened the door for Emma and she walked around the limo. Philip put the twins down, and slid his arms round Emma's shoulders. He waited for his middle son, Patrick, to join the group. He didn't wait for Marc's girlfriend.

"This is Emma Sands. Hopefully, soon to be Mrs. Philip Vega. So she doesn't have to answer all your questions… she is twenty-five, English, still married, as you can see very attractive, and before you ask, yes, I love her!" That about covered it. No, it didn't. "And she is scared to death, and shaking here. So I want everyone to be nice to her… permanently! You can all meet her tonight after she has rested. Now, I am taking Emma inside so she can see her new home. Dinner will be at six. Tonight is casual as I think we are all too tired to care what we look like." He smiled and hugged her even tighter. "Mac…"

Patrick and Marc smiled back at him, but they stared at Emma. She was the same age as Marc and a year older than Patrick. Even by Philip's standards, she was very young, and she did indeed look terrified.

Patrick thought maybe his father had not told her too much about the house and his lifestyle. He watched Emma and actually felt sorry for her. Even encased in his father's arms, with her long hair pulled into a long ponytail, she looked about sixteen, and could have been his younger sister. He knew Marc, without even asking him, could see it, too. The twins probably thought it was exciting. They had never actually met one of his father's 'friends' before. He and Marc had, a couple of times, but never in such a public way and never had he said 'future' anything. His father was obviously serious about her and was now holding her hand in full view of staff and family, allowing everyone to know her rightful place in the household. Philip had announced her, and his intentions, all in one swoop whether anyone liked it or not. What the Don wanted… he got one way or another!

Chapter 20

Emma looked up at the house. Ivy clung to the walls hiding its true identity of the person it belonged to. Philip and Mac escorted Emma through some of the house, enough for her to take in for one day. It was resplendent with antique furniture in some rooms and only slightly more modern redwood in others. Ruby red velvet couches graced the lounge and the dinning room matched, with a huge dining table in the middle and a half -dozen chairs each side. Above it hung a chandelier, with smaller lights round the room and from there the dining room doors led to the patio that came with a very favorably sized pool.

"This is all yours, Philip… you own this?" Emma stared round the room.

"This… and another two homes… a winter place in Denver, and my ex-wife's house in Florida that houses my three sons. Secretly, I think Patrick would like to live here, so maybe we can change that and he can stay this time. He's a man and needs to make his own choices now, in more ways than one."

"Why didn't you tell me this in England… the houses and the wealth and the… ."

She didn't know what to call it, a kind of expectant look on her face.

"Protection? Would you have come back with me, if you had known? Somehow I think not." Philip bent his head slightly and whispered to her. "And now for my suite…" and he laughed. "Mac, talk to Marc and find out more about Damien and Sally, then get Alex, and you and he stay around the first floor by my suite."

Philip led her up the stairs. Family portraits hung there, large mirrors and more. She had never seen anything like it, and then it was at the end of the corridor, the door to Philip's suite. There was a man outside it, waiting… Pauli, the enforcer. As Philip approached, the man came forward and leaning down, kissed Philip's hand.

"Pauli," and Philip spoke again to him in Italian and he opened the suite door for him.   They stepped inside and Emma stood in the doorway staggered at what she saw, but more shocked as Pauli bowed his head to her.

"Ms. Emma. It is my pleasure to meet you. I have heard only good things about you from the Don." He didn't wait for her reply. "Sir, I will be in the next room should you need me…" and he was gone, as the door closed behind him.

Philip turned the key in the lock and looked straight at Emma. He had waited long enough to make her his woman. He leaned his head closer to her and brought his mouth down on hers. She dropped the purse on the floor and returned his kisses with a fierceness she didn't know she possessed. He reached into her jeans and slid his hand down clutching at her firm young body, pushing her underwear out of the way. Still he kissed her, her face and neck, and down onto her shoulders. Right now she needed him as much as he wanted her. He stopped.

"This isn't the right time, Emma… I wanted it to be in my bed, with the lights dimmed and you in white lingerie that I have bought for you…"

"Philip. I don't care where it is… I just want to be in your arms with you making love to me. Philip, I love you so much…" and she undid the buttons on her white T, slowly one by one until the white lace bra was clearly visible, all the time looking him in the eyes.

With one movement, he picked her up off the floor and carried her through the suite and towards his bedroom. He kicked the bedroom door open with his foot and there, in front of her, was a beautiful array of fresh cut flowers. On a small table at the foot of the bed was an ice-bucket with champagne and two glasses. Next to it was a tray of assorted fruit and chocolate strawberries, and on the bed lay a white, lace nightgown.

Philip looked at her face, one of sheer adoration for the man holding her. He let her slide through his arms to a standing position.

"Oh, my god, Philip… oh, my god… you did this for me?"

He nodded. "Go change, baby… I'll wait… couple of minutes anyway…" and he reluctantly let her go. "Bathroom is right through that door."

She picked up the nightdress and took it to the bathroom, opening the door into a world only seen in magazines. There was a giant bathtub and a Jacuzzi… a shower, two gold-tapped hand basins, giant fluffy white towels everywhere, soaps, lotions… Vogue magazine would have been proud of Philip's bathroom. There was a large window that overlooked the almost Olympic-sized pool. It was wonderful. She could see the two boys playing in there. Two kids, having fun…

She slipped her clothes off and donned the nightdress… it was a perfect fit. Philip had obviously paid great attention to her body. It was then the door opened and Philip stood there just clad in jeans. Gone was his shirt and boots. Mac's words went round in her head… be ready… and now she was.

Philip moved closer to her across the bathroom, the look in his eyes said it all. Once more he picked her up in his arms and carried her back into the bedroom. The covers were back and silk, black sheets greeted her encasing king-size pillows. He lowered her gently onto them, his eyes never leaving hers, until he was almost on top of her. Gently he moved the straps of the lace gown down from her shoulders and kissed her neck, then down her breasts. She could hardly breathe as her nightdress slipped away from her and he carried on down. Her hands dug into his back and her hair draped across his shoulders. Undoing his jeans, he slid out of them. There was nothing underneath except his body, ready and eager to please Emma.

He looked into her face. "Remember, Emma, what I take, I don't give back…"

She nodded. "Just never leave me, Philip…"

"Never!" and Philip lowered his body onto hers and entered her with such force of lust and power that she cried out. He subdued her cries with his mouth over hers and Emma felt like she had never been made love to before. No wonder he had had so many conquests. He rose up slightly; sweat pouring down his chest and Emma kissed it away. Nothing could stop them now. He entered her again and again; each time he held her tightly to him hoping that it wasn't too much for her. They came together, not once, but twice. Two lovers becoming one, her hair dripping water, the sheets wet and sullied. Neither knew how long they were there, neither cared, for both of them it was like they found their soul mate.

Philip turned on his back and pulled her with him. "You okay, baby?'" he whispered huskily.

"Yes, Phil… I'm fine… a little tired, but fine…" and she giggled and blushed.

He liked that. "Cold?" he said as he looked at her raised nipples.

"Maybe you should keep me warm…" and she smiled a rich warm smile.

"Your wish is my command, my lady…" and he rose up from the much disheveled bed, pulling her with him, and handed her a robe, while he wrapped a sheet round himself. He removed the champagne from the bucket and popped the cork, pouring two glasses of bubbly and handing her one. "Drink it slowly, baby… if you are not used to it, you will get a buzz very quickly…"

Emma drank it straight down, and handed her glass to him for more. She picked up a chocolate strawberry, bit half of it, kept the rest in her lips and offered that half to Philip.

He kissed her and ate the chocolate strawberry from her lips. "Ever made love in the shower, Emma?" and he handed her back a half-filled glass of champagne, and watched her down that one in one go "Baby, slow down… Emmy… hey, I know you are uptight about being here… and perhaps me…"

"You… no. You, I want… do you always make love like that? Can we do that ten times a day… please… I have never been made love to like that… the shower you said…"

And she took his hand leading him into the bathroom, shedding her robe as she went.

Philip was amused by her. The champagne had changed her into a different woman, a very fiery woman that he had not seen till now.

"Baby," and he leaned forward kissing her passionately as they stepped into the shower. He turned the water to warm and stood her under it.

She leaned back on the wall and Philip moved towards her lifting her up to waist level. Instinctively she wrapped her legs round his waist, the towel dropping into the water. Her head fell forward and she kissed him over and over again. He wrapped his arms round her, held her to him and entered her again. Her hands clasped his hair and she moaned loudly and he rocked her to let her down gently. He had wondered what it would be like with her and now he knew. It was better than even he imagined. And Emma, she had never had a man like Philip before. They were both in love and lust with each other at the same time.

He stopped the water from running, and they slid down to the seat in the shower.

"Emma, are you okay…" He knew he should have stopped after the bedroom, but he wanted her from the moment he saw her and now she was his. And he would want her day and night, and by the way she had reacted, she felt the same. "Emma, baby… come on, let's get you dried…" He climbed out first, Emma leaning against him and he wrapped one of the giant towels around her. He grabbed one for himself and propelled her back into the bedroom, lifted her up and onto the bed. He lay down beside her and she snuggled into him, contented, half awake and half in a champagne and sex high like she never thought possible, one she never wanted to end.

Philip awoke to the bedside phone ringing and darkness coming through the window. He could see the hands on the clock on the wall… six-fifteen…

"Shit!" and then he looked at Emma and he didn't care. They could wait. He hit the speaker phone button. "Yeah, a problem?"

"No problem, Sir. Just to remind you dinner is at six…" Mac's voice was low.

"We'll be down in about fifteen minutes. Have them wait," and he hung up the line. "Emma, honey… lets go eat… it's way past six… honey…"

"How long was I asleep… I must have dozed off after…" and she smiled remembering the shower.

"How's your head? You drank a lot of champagne. Remind me to keep a bottle up here, if that's what it does to you…" and Philip smiled, touched her on the end of her nose, went to kiss her and thought better of it, knowing if he did they would never go downstairs.

He slid back into his jeans and grabbed a T shirt from the chair. Emma climbed off the bed also and was looking for her clothes.

"Here… wear my shirt over your jeans… no one will know you don't have on underwear… except me… baby, anyone ever told you you have great legs.." and he watched her dress, shirt first, his eyes still glowing. "Ready… not quite how I hoped we would be dressed to talk with the family, but good enough for me and that's what counts! Just stay close to me, baby. I will teach you what you need to know," and he unlocked the door. Outside sat her carryon bag, which Philip lifted into the room for her, and then the Don and his lady descended the stairs, with Mac right behind them.

Chapter 21

Going down the stairs was much different to going up them. Emma was a transformed woman, and even Mac could see it. He also could see she had been drinking. Her legs were slightly wobbly and even though Philip held her hand vey tightly she was still in a sleepy state, with her hair damp. Mac moved to the right side of her with Philip on the left mainly for support.

Philip saw the look Mac gave him. "What?!"

"Nothing, boss…" and Mac looked at her outfit.

"So, we couldn't find her clothes, and yes, she drank champagne. I didn't know it would have that affect on her…" Philip was almost apologetic… but it was funny.

"I'm here you know. I can hear you. And it was my fault I drank two glasses… but it was fun though… wasn't it, Philip, especially in the shower…?" and her eyes sparkled at him, and she hit him playfully on his arm, stopping before she said anymore.

Philip smiled at her, a warm and full smile that told Mac all he needed to know. Philip was really in love with her. This was truly a first, especially for him.

"Look… I forgot my shoes…" Emma looked down at her bare feet, and wiggled her pretty pink toes at the two men.

Philip's expression was amazing. If she was changed, so was he. Mac wondered exactly how much sex they had had in five hours. Obviously she had rocked his world and vice versa. He thought that Alex, for one, would see it and possibly the rest of the family, too.

As the group approached the dining room, Philip could hear them all talking round the table, and then as the family heard them coming, all talking stopped very abruptly. Philip entered the door-way first, his T shirt hanging over his jeans and sporting flip-flops. They all turned to look at him, his new look of a slight beard and moustache creeping in.

And then followed Emma, still grasping Philip's hand, just dressed in their father's shirt, extra tight jeans and no shoes. Her hair hung round her shoulders and a gleam in her eye put there by a man… their father.

Patrick was the first to stand at the table and then Marc, both walking forward to Philip.

"Marc, Patrick, please say hello to Emma. Patrick, tomorrow, I would like you to show her the rest of the house. All she has seen is this room and my bedroom… Show her the pool and if she wants to go swimming, you stay right with her, okay?"

"Absolutely, Sir…" and the twenty four-year-old turned to his step-mother-to-be. "You swim, er… Ms. Emma…"

"Emma… just Emma, Patrick. I do, but only a little… but it would be lovely to swim… and it's very nice to meet you, and," and she turned to Marc, "Marc, it's really great to meet you, also. I have heard a lot about you from Philip," and she let go of Philip's hand and moved to where the twins sat. "Can I guess? Orry, you are the blonde, and Daniel, you have to be the other twin."

They giggled, dropping their big round eyes at her, then looking up and laughing with her. Then Orry showed her the band-aid on his finger and the bruise on his knee and really warmed up to her like he had known her for years.

Emma glanced up from the boys towards Philip, who sported a huge smile on his face and also one on Patrick's.

"She gonna fit right in, Dad…"he whispered to Philip. "She's beau-tiful, Sir… pity I am not a few years older! You are a very lucky man."

Philip smacked him on the back… "Good job you are not, son…" and he walked to where Emma stood. "You have to be hungry. Come on, you sit there next to me," and Philip took his seat at the head of the table, and as he went to the chair, Mac stepped up behind him and pulled his chair back. As he did, Anthony stepped behind Emma and did the same.

'This is casual?' she thought, as she sat down.

The table seemed full of food, wines, water and a host of cutlery that she wasn't quite used to using. Spaghetti ruled the day, with giant meatballs, home made crusty bread, washed down with sparkling water and more wine. There were crisp fresh salads for anyone that wanted them, and fresh fruit on the side. Strawberries, pineapple, grapes and melon all graced the table.

An hour went by. Everyone seemed to be talking, and Emma thought it resembled being in a restaurant. She was tiring very quickly and Philip could see it. For her and Philip it was now very early morning UK time. Philip was just about to rise up from the table when there was a commotion in the hallway.

Immediately, Anthony and Rossi left the room and rushed into the hallway. Rossi had his hand on the gun that was tucked in the side of his jeans, as a woman's voice echoed into the dining room.

"Sally! What the fuck is she doing in my house?" and Philip jumped up from his seat with Mac right on his heels.

Sally made it to the dining room door before she was stopped and quite forcibly so. Philip met her face to face.

"What the hell are you doing here? I was informed you had left this morning, rather they asked you to leave before I returned..." and he glanced back at Emma. "You came to spy..."

"I did not! I came to see the twins before I go to the airport!" replied a blonde, very made-up, over-dressed ex-wife. She peered round the door as far as she could, taking Emma into her sights. Sally was visibly shocked. "My god, Philip. She's our children's age!"

"That's it Sally, enough! *Please* leave... now. Next time there wont be a please!" and he nodded his head to Rossi, who had his hand on her arm. He was only being this nice because of Emma.

Emma pushed her chair back herself and stood up. She was tired and she was angry. "Hello, Sally. I am Emma. I might be young, but I happen to love Philip very much and..." she looked Sally up and down, all five feet of her, clad in Philip's shirt, "unlike you, I plan on keeping him happy!" Emma returned to her chair, unaided, and sipped her wine.

"I think, Sally, you get the gist there of what she said! Emma might be young, but she is not a pushover... say goodbye to your sons and do not, and I emphasize this, do not come back here, ever…" His face was contorted with displeasure. "Goodbye, Sally…" This time it was for good from her ex-husband.

She was forcibly escorted to the door, and the security from outside took over. Philip waited till Anthony and Rossi came back into the room and then, standing next to the table, he let fly.

"How the hell did this happen?" and he smacked his hands down on the table with such force that the crockery jumped. "If this ever happens again, you will all be looking for new jobs… with another family. Do I make myself perfectly clear?! Do I?" He was more than furious, and the veins in his neck stood out, making him look very menacing even to Emma. He wanted today to be perfect and now it wasn't.

"Yes, Sir…" came the reply in unison, and some raised eyebrows. They weren't used to a tongue lashing like this in front of the younger children. They realized just how angry the Don was.

Mac could not ever remember seeing Philip this annoyed without pulling a gun on someone.

But Philip hadn't finished yet. "This was supposed to be a homecoming for me and the start of a new life for Emma… and meeting her new family. She met them all right! Too many of them!" He wasn't calming down anytime soon. "Never, ever let there be a next time… ever. Anthony, this is on your shoulders! This was your job to make sure it ran smoothly and it didn't. Get out of my sight!" and Philip turned to his enforcer. "Pauli… make sure she gets on the flight…" He looked at his children and dared them to speak back to him.

"Emma… let's go…" and he reached down, grabbed her by the hand and helped her up.

She had the distinct feeling he was mad with her, too, and had no doubt that he was going to impart that fact to her upstairs. He went up the stairs two at a time with Emma racing behind him. Little did Emma know when he was angry, his sex-drive went sky high.

Chapter 22

Philip slammed the bedroom door behind him and turned to face his mistress. "How much did you drink?"

"What? Philip, I'm sorry if I was out of line..." she wasn't able to say anymore as his mouth covered hers.

"What the hell are you apologizing for, baby... you were great! You were the only one that was..." and he led her to the bed, pushing her down on the pillows that sank under her. If she thought this afternoon was out of this world, now was even better. Philip tried hard not to let half the house hear them, but he failed. She laughed and she cried. They drank more champagne and ate more fruit, made love, stood on the balcony and watched the moon, Emma in just his shirt and Philip in jeans, with her leaning back on him, while he pointed out the star constellations to her. Not till around one a.m. did they finally fall asleep wrapped in each others arms. Emma was happy and in love for the first time in her life, and Philip satisfied both in bed and out. He pulled her closer and her legs automatically wrapped around him. He smiled and kissed her hair. She smelled so good to him, her hair of strawberries and she of him, and he made love to her again with her barely awake.

No one slept till the Don did. Now the whole house was quiet, and the two oldest brothers were extremely grateful that Emma had come into their father's life. She seemed to be the only one that would be able to handle him, and his tempers, in the future, making this a very big responsibility for her, and tomorrow Patrick would talk to her about just that.

Emma woke first, and found she couldn't move. Philip was wrapped completely around her. She smiled and cuddled into him. She could wait. There was still a tinge of musky cologne on him and a just a slight smell of alcohol on his lips. She lay there wondering what life would bring with this man, wondering if they would have children. That made her smile. It was quite obvious that Philip had no problem in that line. She turned her head slightly and glanced at the bedside clock. Nine a.m. already.

He woke and smiled as he looked into her face. "Morning, sunshine…"

"Morning, you… before you move… how did you know I like white lace?"

"I saw it under your dress, baby… so I called ahead and had Marc's girlfriend go pick it out. You like it, right?" his eyes and mouth questioning her.

"I love it…" and she was going to ask about Marc's girlfriend.

"Good, because there is more where that came from… over there in the top drawer of the large dresser, and tomorrow we are going shopping to get you new clothes."

"Really… can I go and look?" She was an excitable teenager.

"Of course… they are for you…" and he didn't have time to finish the sentence.

She rushed to the drawer and opened it. Philip lay on his back watching, reminding him of his kids at Christmas. She pulled out lace underwear both black and white… her eyes wide.

"Try them on, baby…" he said in a low voice, "so I can see they fit…"

And she couldn't refuse him… nor did she want to.

At ten Philip's private line rang. It was Mac. Damien had returned home an hour ago.

"We will be down!" Instantly, Philip's mood had changed. "Go get showered, Emma. Be quick, if you would, baby. I'll follow you in. Just want to make sure that things are taken care of."

In other words he wanted her not to be in the room for a moment. In the bathroom, she showered quickly, used the facilities and then wrapped a towel round her and went back into the bedroom.

Philip had disappeared into his lounge, but the door was open and she could hear him giving orders. She found her carryon bag and pulled out some clean clothes… cut off jeans, that were very tight, and a nice T shirt that she had never worn. She pulled her hair into its famous ponytail and added just a touch of makeup. She pulled Toby from the carryon and sat him on her pillow. By now, Philip was done and came back into the bedroom.

"Wait for me, baby. I'll be five minutes in the shower."

True to his word, he was, and he came back into the bedroom and donned jet black jeans and a grey shirt, open to the waist, showing the dark hair on his chest. His hair was still wet, and he sat down on the bed to pull his boots on.

"Okay, baby… lets go do this… let me look at you…" and he looked, and liked what he saw. Emma had worn the new black lace bra and panties under her clothes, and Philip was more than pleased. As he spoke, he put a gun down the back of his jeans and he saw Emma's face. "It will always be with me, baby, you know that."

"I know. Just, I haven't seen you with one since we got here."

"Emma, we all carry one… even Patrick. Marc, well, he is not so keen … and you, I'm going to have Mac teach you. We'll find you a small gun to use…"

"Me? Why would I need one…" she was horrified.

"To project our children." and he opened the door for her and ushered her out of the suite and down the stairs. On the way down they picked up Mac and Pauli. "You want someone to come after our children like Sally came here today?" he didn't care that he was talking very personal things in front of his men.

"Of course not, Philip, but there is an army here and we…" she stopped because he had stopped walking.

He turned to face her on the stairs, and his fingers lingered on her face. "Honey, I won't always be around. I am almost twenty years older than you, and the kids will still be young. Think about it." And he leaned forward and kissed her.

She did and he was right.

Now he held her hand and she noticed how close both Mac and Pauli were to them, one step right behind them. Something was going down she didn't understand. They walked into the lounge and there by the fireplace stood a robust suited gentleman, about ten years older than Philip, smoking a Cuban cigar and sporting scars down his face. Suddenly Emma was very scared and she clasped Philip's hand even tighter. He felt it, and whispered to her, and she nodded.

The larger man looked up, stubbed the cigar out in the fireplace, and moved towards Philip. At the back of the lounge stood Rossi and in the front of his pants was his gun.

"Philip. Good to see you again…" and Damien Vega stepped forward, bent his head and kissed the godfather's ring.

Emma felt sick and wavered just slightly. Philip let go of her hand and slid his arm round her back.

"Damien. This is Emma, soon to be my wife. If you or anyone near you ever touch her, I will kill you. I will end you personally. Do you understand me?" Philip was very calm and collected as he spoke.

"I understand you… I just came back to pack and then leave you all in peace." Damien's tone was very subdued.

"That's fine. Rossi will take care of you while you are in the house, and before you go and pack, I want to talk with you. Mac, take Emma to the pool. Find Patrick and have him stay with her, and then return here. Rossi, you and Pauli stay."

Emma was escorted to the door by Mac and it was very firmly closed behind her.

"Just business, Ms. Emma. Remember I told you it happens and Mr. Vega will seek you out later. For now, we will find Patrick and he will show you the rest of the house. That will please the boss." He watched the expression on her face. "I warned there will be times when you never know what he is doing… and you can't know it. Now let's find Mr. Patrick," and they walked to the pool area.

Emma could see the security so evidently placed in the grounds. There was no escaping it. Then she saw Patrick coming towards them.

"Emma… you brought your swim things with you?" he asked as he got a few feet from them. He had on Speedos and Emma could see a young Philip there. He was tall and well toned like his father. Very obvious whose son he was. Even the mannerisms and authority were the same as Philip.

"I don't have any, Patrick. I can just sit here today, and maybe you and I can talk." Emma sat down in a pool chair, and leaned back. This was all just a little too much for her, and it was beginning to tell. She was tired from the flight and the time difference; she ached from Philip's body on hers and now this. Mental stress. She had to be tougher and she knew it.

Patrick swam a little, climbed out of the pool, grabbed a towel, and then he sat down next to her on another chair. "So… what would you like me to answer for you? Things my father won't tell you?"

Emma raised her eyebrows. Straight to the point at least from his son. "Something like that, Patrick." She plucked up courage and took a big step in the dark. "Okay, here are my questions. One, what will your father do about Steven? Two, will there be other women in his life… I mean, like… a girlfriend on the side? And, what does he expect of me in the big picture? Oh… and why doesn't he like me talking to you, even though he sent me to talk to you?!"

Patrick stared at her. She wasn't just beautiful… she had brains.

"Wow, Emma. When you ask… you ask… Firstly… you talking to me is a test…you and I are pretty much the same age, and to be honest, you look much younger than twenty-five. He wants to see if you will go for younger men."

"But… I don't want younger men… I want him…" she protested.

"You and I know that, but he wants to be sure… and who better than his own son. My father knows how attractive he is to women… he's played the field enough in the last few years… not exactly like he has to… well, never mind… but it's a test. And no, he will not have a girlfriend on the side, if that's worrying you. Why would he when he has a woman like you? But to answer you… they don't do that anymore… which movies have you been watching?" He laughed at her. "He will never jeopardize the relationship with you. He obviously loves you, Emma. He has never introduced a woman to us and the twins, let alone as the future Mrs. Vega! As to your question about your husband… you might want to ask him for a divorce. Did you see him before you left?" Now Patrick was curious.

"No. Some story about he was busy… Philip made him stay away, didn't he?"

"Yeah, Emma, he did…or Mac or Alex did… one of them… From what I hear your husband isn't the best of men… file for divorce… now… tell my father that's what you want… tonight!" he paused. "Emma, did my father tell you what he deals in…" Patrick didn't say anymore. Maybe he had said too much…

"No, and I didn't ask…"

The second son smiled. She was doing just fine.

"Patrick, why is Donna, Marc's girlfriend, so quiet and why is Marc so blonde?"

"Because, although Sally is our mother, my father is not so sure that Marc is his son. When they married, my mother was already pregnant with quite possibly my father's child. He won't do a DNA test. Pride. And Donna… she is terrified of my father because of one reason or another. You see, Emma… with this uncertainty, when my father finally retires, as he has already told me, I will be the next Don."

Chapter 23

"**D**on't worry, Emma. Your's and my father's children will always have a rightful place here, as will you. On that you have my word, but I think he plans to live for ever and you will help him do that… give him more children, Emma, and whatever it takes, *please* keep him happy." Patrick laughed.

"Could we be heard?" Now she blushed.

"Yeah, you could… but in a good way. We could hear you guys laughing, and for that we all will be eternally grateful." Just then his cell phone rang, and he opened it. "Yes, Sir… yes, she is here with me. Would you like to speak to her? Okay. She should be ready at five… all of us… I will convey that to everyone. I will tell her, Sir," and Patrick hung up the call. "My father says to tell you he loves you and that he has some business to take care of and to be ready at five this evening as we are all going out to dinner. Oh, and he is going to get you a cell phone so that he can call you instead of me next time."

"He'll be gone all afternoon?" she looked quite surprised.

"Often… you won't know where he goes or with whom. You will never know. But he will always come back to you… and now, let me show you some more of the house and get something to eat." He reached for his jeans that lay on the nearby table and pulled them on, slung a towel round his shoulders and he and Emma headed for the great indoors.

They went to the kitchen first, and Emma thought she had walked into a restaurant. It was full of people. A chef and maids… he had maids? How much more was there? Her second day there and still she was finding out more.

"How many people live in this house, Patrick?" asked Emma as she looked around. The kitchen was all clinical white and solid steel. A good place to hide if bullets came your way.

"One more after this week, I hope…" he laughed. "Seriously, I have never counted. A good two dozen or so and more when my father is here. You will get used to it. We did, eventually. For now, stick to the rooms you know. His suite, correction yours and his… and the downstairs rooms. My room is on the next floor and so is Marc's and Donna's room. If you want anything, call Mac or me if my father isn't around. Tonight he will give you a cell… just in case. Now, I am going to grab a sandwich and a glass of wine as dinner seems hours away… would you like one?"

"No… no sandwich. I am fine. A glass of white wine, though, might be nice…"

Patrick knew she was having a hard time taking all this in. Later he would ask his father if he could stay here for good, help her out a little, but first he had to give his report. His loyalty was to Philip first and his report would be more than favorable. Emma was totally in love with Philip.

They found the wine and Emma had just a small glass and she also had some very red grapes and a slice of cheese. Didn't seem very much to Patrick and that he would mention that to his father. In the clothes she had on Patrick thought, like Philip did, that Emma was too thin.

She sipped the wine and looked around her. Just a few weeks ago she was in her own kitchen, now she was in this enormous place, not even allowed to get her own food. "Is it okay to sit outside on the patio…"

"Of course! You are not a prisoner here, Emma. One day very soon, you will be mistress of all you survey here. This will be your domain. Come; let's go sit in the sun for an hour. It's still nice and warm. Ask my father to get you a swimsuit when you go shopping tomorrow, then we can swim next time. I know he was taking you today, but that was before Damien." Patrick's look was like 'don't ask me about Damien because I can't tell you.' "Tomorrow, he will take you to Rodeo drive."

"To where??? I can't shop there! That's for rich people…" and Emma stopped. Philip *was* rich people.

They went back outside and sat down for a while. It was pleasant just talking to Philip's son. They chatted about growing up in this life, about the twins and about Marc. Emma learned a lot.

About three-thirty she asked Patrick if he would escort her back to Philip's suite. He duly did and left her there. She wandered round the airy rooms, this time on her own. As Philip had told her, there was a small gym, the famed Jacuzzi, a small bar in the lounge, complete with a rather large drinks cabinet and snacks, and then there was the bedroom of which she had already seen a lot of. She noted her clothes were now hung in the closets, the bed was more than made, and Toby sat on top of her pillow along with tiny mint chocolates. Her nightdress lay on her side and nothing lay on Philip's side of the bed. Emma was curious. She wondered if he kept a gun by the bed. He did. Inside the nightstand drawer was a .22. In the bathroom cabinet she found another one, and in his closet was a .357, his weapon of choice. She also noted all the clothes in his closet. They were immaculate. Leather jackets, the most expensive jeans, couple of Armani suits, and all kinds of boots. In the dresser drawers were an array of Polo sweaters. Notably scarce was underwear. It was there, but not much of it. Emma smiled. In her closet were more like old clothes and just the new jeans and the leather jacket she, rather Philip, had bought in England. She sat on the bed. She had just gone through his closets. Not an honest thing to do.Patrick had said out to dinner… what was expected of her to wear? She didn't have anything except the same old black dress. She pulled it out of the closest and held it up to her, looking through the mirror as she did. She laid it on the bed and was about to take a shower when she heard Philip enter the suite. His voice was very clear and then there was a second voice.

"So, Andrea, do I get to meet her tonight?"

"Yes, at dinner. I thought that was the best place. She is young, Mikey, but she is learning very quickly… all out ways…" and his voice was very masculine and dominant. "But before dinner, talk to Pauli… make sure that everything goes well with Barton's land. I want it and I will have it."

"Yes, Sir… and the casino that is giving us problems? You want that taken care of, too? Pauli has capos to do that, right?"

"He does… but we will try it your way first… okay, till tonight. I need to take a shower and change. Stop by the restaurant at six. I will have a place set for you. All the family will be there, even Damien. Then he will be gone from our lives for good." Philip shook his consigliore's hand, and escorted him to the door. As he did he heard a noise in the other room. He closed the door quietly, pulled the gun from the back of his jeans and moved across the lounge to the bedroom door.

Emma was frozen to the spot. Philip opened the door so fast she didn't have time to move. The first thing she saw was the gun in his hand, and then Philip grabbed her.

"Dear god, Emma, are you trying to get your head blown off? I had no idea you were there." He released his grasp on her, but let his arm linger on her shoulders. "So what did you hear, baby?" and he stuffed the gun back into his jeans.

She was going to lie, but there was no point. It had to be the truth between them or there was no future. "All of it… I wasn't eves dropping, Philip. I came to get showered. I didn't know what to do when I heard voices…"

"Baby. It's okay… so you heard. You will hear worse than that. Now, let's go get showered… together… I see the black dress on the bed. Tomorrow, Rodeo drive and new black dresses… lots of them. But I do have something for you tonight," and he let go of her and moved to the drawer in his closet. "Sit down a moment, Emma… before I give you this," and he glanced at his watch making sure there was time, "I want to tell you about the rest of what you heard. Then we will shower." He sat on the small whicker chair opposite the bed. Sitting next to her on the bed was too much of a temptation. "You know that everything you asked Patrick today came back to me?"

She nodded yes.

He raised his eyebrows. "Smart lady… well, I have to know, honey. He only did what I asked him to do. Everything he told you was true… everything. There will only be you… always. I don't want a woman on the side. Oh, I did, with Sally and she knew it. But I didn't know you then and I was still very young." He paused remembering. "Don't ask about Damien. After tonight, you will not see him again. Tonight you will meet Mikey. He is very important to the family as is Pauli. We do mostly land deals, Emma and sometimes *buy* casinos… Mikey advises me and Pauli takes care of the situation. You understand what I am saying or do I need to tell you more?"

"I understand what you are saying and it changes nothing. I still love you… but Philip, I have a confession to make to you. Before you came back into the room, I looked in your closets to see what kind of clothes you had. You have Armani suites, Philip, and look what I have?" She dipped her eyes. She had started so she would finish. "I… looked to see if you had other guns in the room. I'm sorry, I should not have done that… but this is so new to me… it's a whole other world, Philip…"

Philip stood up and reached for her, taking her in his arms, clinging to her, frightened he would lose her. The pearls he had for her could wait.

Chapter 24

The limo pulled out front at five. The twins were ready and waiting by the door, and Marc and Donna appeared shortly after all dressed in black. Patrick was there in his dark grey suit and black shirt, looking strikingly like his father. And then Philip and Emma emerged down the stairs. Like his son, Philip wore a dark charcoal Armani suit and a black shirt with high collar, no tie. Emma wore her black dress, very high heels and jet black stockings. Round her neck sat a row of pearls that Philip had just given her and in her hand she carried her leather jacket. Her hair was pulled high on her head, held there by very pretty slides.

Patrick recognized the pearls immediately. They were his grandmother's and now they were Emma's. Philip had crowned her queen and she glowed.

"Everyone ready? Mac, where is Damien?" Philip walked through the entrance way talking to Mac, but keeping a tight hold of Emma's hand.

"In the town car, Sir, with Pauli. Alex and Rossi are outside by the limo."

"Then let's go," and he ushered Emma outside in the warm September air. "I should have got you a wrap, Emmy." He turned to the other girl. "Donna, do you have a black wrap Emma could borrow?"

"Yes, Sir… I can run and get it for her," stated the young woman, hardly looking Philip in the eyes, and she was gone.

Emma watched with interest. The girl really was scared of Philip. She was back within five minutes and in that five, they were all seated in the limo just waiting for her.

An hour later saw them draw up at Gerard's at Malibu beach. The place looked magnificent with floodlights all round the grounds and parked everywhere were limos and cars with tinted windows. As Philip stepped out of the limo, the owner himself came to greet him.

"Mr. Vega. How very nice to see you again. I have the patio free for you just as you asked for, Sir, and this must be your lady. Ms. Emma, how very nice to meet you," and he took hold of Emma's hand and kissed it, just as he had done with Philip.

They were led to the patio where a huge table sat right in the center with black table cloths draped over it and red napkins made a slash of color. Fresh- cut white roses adorned the table, candles, champagne chilling and an ocean view to die for, all seen in the dimming lights reflected on the water. Emma gasped, her wrap almost falling from her shoulders, as she sat down next to her man.

With wine flowing and the food never ending, Emma found she could relax much more. Sitting to the right of Philip, it was easy for her to talk to him, until she noticed that Damien was staring at her, not so much at her but the pearls.

Philip saw it. "So… Damien, you all packed and ready for your new life? And, yes, those are the family pearls… you have a problem with that?" Philip rested his elbows on the table and leaned his chin on the back of his hands.

"No problem, little brother. None at all. They belonged to your mother, not mine!" and Damien's voice was not at all friendly. "And it is by your request I am leaving. Only room for one brother in this household, Andrea!"

Philip didn't even raise his voice. "Say goodnight, Damien. This meal is for family only," and he moved his fingers just slightly sending Rossi and Pauli to Damien's chair.

"Goodbye, Damien," and Philip turned his thoughts back to Emma and the twins, who were clamoring for their father's attention. Donna was trying to make them sit still and not succeeding.

"Daniel and Orry… did you not want to come to dinner again with your brothers?" stated their father.

There was an instant quietness from that side of the table. Then the little blonde child, with the toothy grin, looked at Emma and smiled at her. "I got another bruise, Emma, see?" and Orry lifted his knee high enough for Emma to see it right across the table.

Philip was not amused, but Emma jumped up from the chair and rushed around to see the child. "That has to hurt, Orry," and without thinking, she leaned down and kissed his knee.

Daniel saw it. "I have one, too, Emma… see mine?"

"Really, well, that gets a kiss, too," and she did the same for the other son.

Philip was more than impressed. She had treated both sons equally and he knew she would do the same with Marc and Patrick and their own children.

Marc watched Emma… where Donna had failed, Emma had succeeded. She had won both the twins over in two single meetings, just like she had won Patrick over and, very obviously, his father. He looked at Philip's face. He was watching her intently like she was an angel dropped from heaven. Emma was indeed a delight, far better than his girlfriend was… in fact there was no comparison… .and both women were the same age…

Philip never missed anything and he didn't miss the way Marc was watching Emma now. He thought he saw it last night, now he was sure. This could be a problem, one that had never occurred to him. It wasn't Patrick he had to watch for, it was Marc. He turned slightly in his chair and immediately Mac was there. Philip nodded towards Marc and muttered something.

Mac glanced up at Philip's son, whispered back to Philip, then stepped back into the shadows.

Emma returned to her seat completely unaware of the situation around her. She was glad Damien had gone and they seemed to be one happy family, except she wondered where he had gone to. She watched Philip smoking a Cuban cigar and Patrick had joined him, both powerful men in their own ways.

She turned her head. "Alex, I need the ladies room."

"Mr. Vega, Sir, taking Ms. Emma to the restroom…" Alex told his boss.

Philip nodded his approval, and as he did he saw Donna go with them. "Marc, would you join us? Mac watch the twins."

When Emma came back from the restroom, the little group was still there now joined by Pauli, only Rossi was missing. Cigar smoke wafted on the night air.

There were slightly raised voices from both Philip and Marc, and then it was calm as though nothing had happened.

Emma was learning that you didn't go to the men. You stayed in your place. She was thinking about this fact when she heard her name.

"Emma… Emma," and she looked up to see Mac there. "Mr. Vega would like you   to join him for a glass of champagne and take in the view." Mac pulled the chair back for her and she dropped the wrap on the chair moving towards her lover.

Philip stretched his hand out towards her and grasped it firmly in his. "Let's walk just a little way in the garden and take a glass with us."

Alex handed them both champagne, and then closed in behind them leaving the others at the table. Philip waited till they were far enough away not to be overheard. "Damien has gone and won't be back. He has, shall we say, hopefully seen the error of his ways. It took Rossi and Pauli to explain it to him. It's not how I wanted it, but I think he might try to hit back. Apparently in the car he mentioned Steven, something about he had called the house today looking to speak to you. Damien had answered the call but only just told us to-night. Steven is flying out here to see if he can get you back. Maybe it would be better if you left for the house in Colorado for a while till he goes back to England while I deal with the situation…"

"Or what, Philip… you get rid of him like you did Damien to-night? I won't run away and I am surprised you would even suggest that I would go to Colorado." She looked hurt.

"Emma, he will sue you, and me, for adultery and quite possibly end up with the house you own and the rest of any money you might have coming to you. Is that what you want to happen?"

"Let him have it… I just want out, Philip. I can talk to him… when is he due here?" She asked a babble of questions, suddenly feeling like she needed the champagne.

"Couple of days… maybe three… end of the week. He must need the money badly… and someone must have bankrolled him to fly here. Of course, Emma, I can put an end to him once and for all with one phone call… Just so we are clear on the point, I will never give you back, Emma, never! If he tries to take you by any means… I will kill him," and he sipped the champagne so matter-of-factly, his eyes looking into hers and never blinking.

Emma didn't answer him. She knew Philip meant it. She had to talk to Steven and get him to accept what she would propose, and she drank down the rest of the champagne, knowing full well why Philip was letting her drink it and what he expected from her tonight.

Chapter 25

"**E**mma, before we leave here, I want you to meet Mikey. He is running just a little late…"

Alex whispered to Philip.

"He has just arrived… Alex, have him come out here before he eats," and Philip put his arm round Emma and proceeded to share the view with her.

"Philip, this is one of the most beautiful places I have ever been and this evening is wonderful. You did arrange for the patio to be like this, didn't you, and that the whole family would be here?"

He touched her on the nose. "Brains and a body, too… words to an old Bee Gees song… yes… Emma, I can arrange anything I want to… just ask and it's yours… and when I ask of you, that's mine also," and he smiled, but there was a very serious side to the remark.

"Am I that easy?" she asked him half joking and half not, a little embarrassed.

"Actually, no… I would have slept with you the night I met you at the wrap party, or at least tried, but you didn't even give me the opportunity… now, well… I think you want me as much I want you…" and he felt her arm slide round his waist and onto his hips, her body pressing tightly to him. "Yeah… you do, don't you?" and he could see the look in Emma's eyes. "Limo is right through the gate…"

"There… really?" and they were about to shoot out the backdoor of the restaurant to the limo like two teenagers on their first date.

"Don Andrea…" Mikey's voice was deep and Emma recognized it immediately from the bedroom.

"Too late, baby… later," and he winked at her. "Mikey… this is Emma," and he introduced her to his consigliore, as she slid her arm back from round his waist.

"Ms. Emma… it is very nice to meet you." Mikey's accent was deep and very Italian. He was as tall as Philip, but with a much darker complexion.

Emma wasn't sure which man she was more afraid of… Pauli or Mikey. They were both very Italian, obviously family men and, more to the point, devoted to Philip over everything else.

Philip could sense Emma's nervousness. "Let's join the others and you can eat, Mikey. Did something keep you?" He saw Mikey look towards Emma. "This time you can speak in front of her. She knows Steven is coming, and she also heard us talking about the land deal."

Mikey nodded, and whispered in Philip's ear. "She doesn't know about that… Alex, escort Emma back to the table."

And it was done just because Philip asked it to be.

Philip and Mikey talked for about half an hour before they re-joined the table. The twins were tired and irritable, waiting to go home. Daniel sat himself next to Emma and Orry wanted to sit on her lap. Eventually Orry fell asleep, still on Emma's lap, and Daniel on Patrick's.

Pauli joined Philip. "You have a great family there, Sir… look…" and he nodded towards the table.

Philip turned to look and was delighted to see them, except for Marc who was visibly pissed off at the sight. This made Philip comment. "I think that Marc should go and visit his mother for a while. Have him take Donna with him, and the twins and Patrick can stay with me for as long as they want, maybe make it permanent."

"Yes, Sir… I think that is a wise move. You want them on a regular flight? Or the jet…" asked Pauli. If his boss wasn't happy then he wasn't.

"Regular, first class… tomorrow! Marc needs not to stare at my woman like that…" and it was arranged. Philip would not tolerate it. Shades of Damien.

As Philip moved back to the table, Pauli raised his eyebrows to Mikey. "Seems Emma being here is causing a split in the family.

Maybe good to find out who is on our side. Certainly not Damien and seems maybe not Marc," and he followed Philip.

"Damien go without problems?" asked the brains, and Mikey the brawn.

"Yeah… he did… surprised me, but I don't think we have seen the last of him. He knows Jack Barton very well and unlike our boss, Barton likes him. I may have to pay Barton a visit sometime this week, after Steven has been here. I need to be around. Steven is desperate, and desperate men do crazy things. I hear Mr. Sands is no match for our boss physically and mentally, but still… he needs security and so does the girl. And our boss pays very well. Sands makes no difference to me. I would just make him have an accident on the way from the airport… but Mr. Vega says Emma wants to talk to him first and he is gonna give her that chance… and then… bam… he will never know what hit him," and Pauli laughed while pointing his fingers in a gun-like gesture.

Mikey was eating spaghetti from the plate, and long strands hung from his fork as Pauli spoke. The strands slithered back to the plate as Mikey started to laugh. "I gotta admit, Pauli, our boss has great taste in both food and women! I'd have a hit put straight on the husband."

"He will… he will! Give him time!" replied Pauli watching Philip.

They all left the restaurant together. Philip tipped the owner several hundred dollars for such a great evening and the peace they had come to get at this place. As they left Emma saw the man kiss the now famous ring on Philip's hand.

In bed that night Philip told Emma that Marc was leaving for a few days. He told her it was on business. He also told her Damian was on a plane to Florida. He didn't lie to her, just didn't tell her all of it.

Emma had her day of shopping in Beverly Hills. A rare treat, accompanied by Philip who picked the clothes for her, paid for them and generally made her feel very comfortable... and that was the idea.

When they finally arrived home dinner was done and gone, and Emma and Philip ate on the balcony of their suite. Wine, salads, steaks and fresh bread, and Philip made her eat. No food… no Jacuzzi… and certainly no sex…

The next day Emma swam with Patrick and the twins. Philip could hear them from the office, so he left the high leather-backed chair to view them from the window. They were having a great time. The sun was more than warm today just topping ninety. It was a perfect September day. Philip decided next time, he would join them. Today, he could not.

The following two days were the same. One day turned into two, more sun, more swimming and much more sex. At the end of the week, Philip decided to join the party in the pool. Just clad in a pair of black Speedos, Philip left the bedroom and headed for the pool. He still sported the short-clipped beard and moustache that were growing nicely. He carried the towel in hand and made, with great haste, for the pool.

"Mac… come on, join us. You swim!"

"That an order, boss…" asked Mac, really not wanting to swim.

"Yeah, that's an order! I gotta have a bodyguard, don't I?" stated Philip, making it quite clear he wanted Mac there.

"Daddyyyyyyy," yelled the twins and scrambled out of the pool to meet him. Now Emma knew where the bruises came from as she watched Orry go the hard way over the side.

Philip picked them both up at the same time and Emma could see his muscles flexing, making it very obvious he used his gym and also confirming just how tough he really was.

Emma rose from her seat on the other side of the pool and wandered over to the side where Philip and the twins now sat, and slid into the water in front of them.

"Hey, baby, you have some good color today… how come I didn't notice that last night?"

"Maybe you had other things on your mind," laughed Emma, splashing water on him from the pool.

"Yeah, maybe I had, but I don't now…" and he dropped into the exquisite shaped pool next to her. "Come here, you…" and he chased her in the pool and the twins dived in, joining in the fun, chasing and splashing.

Patrick was laughing at them when Mac came over to him to tell him Philip had a phone call. Philip looked up and saw them talking, and he didn't look happy.

"What? It's not good by the look on your faces…"

Patrick leaned down to the pool as Philip swam to the side. He spoke in a low voice to his father.

"God damn it… the man has timing! Is he still at the gate? Fuck him!" and Philip smacked the water, not caring that the twins could hear him. "Emma… your husband is here! Go get dressed… on second thought, no don't… let him see us as a happy family… who gives a damn what he sees. You are mine, Emma, and he may as well know it right now and get used to the fact!" Philip was angry at the intrusion to his day off with the kids and he didn't care who saw or heard. "Let him in, Mac, search him and escort him to the pool!"

.

Chapter 26

Emma stood in the shallow end of the pool. She had to admit she was just as unhappy about Steven being there as Philip was, and especially in this situation. She would like to have been dressed and more in control and she knew that Philip would agree with that comment. Here they were out in the open and Philip could not carry out his threat. She watched her lover climb out of the pool and sit in one of the ornate poolside chairs. Now he was joined by Pauli and Mikey, and Emma knew he meant serious business.

Patrick appeared at the water's edge and slid in beside her. "My father said to stay in the pool with the twins until he or one of his men come to get you. Do what he says, Emma, please. It will make life easier for us all… and although you get a say in this, he wants to talk to Steven first…"

"But he said…" she tried to tell him.

"Emma… my father always gets what he wants. Please remember that. In our world, that is the only way," and he looked hard at her.

"Of course. I would always do what he says. I love him too much to disobey him." She floated back to the twins, remembering she had agreed to do what he said, now and for ever. She could not be seen to undermine him and she knew he would not tolerate it even from her.

It took several minutes for Steven and the cab to be searched at the main gate and let into the Vega compound. The cab dropped him at the house and Steven was led to the pool by the side entrance. He could see security everywhere as he walked along the stone path, and now he could hear laughing from children and a woman's voice that he knew very well.

Emma was getting a tan, looked a lot healthier in one week, sported a very sexy swimsuit, and generally looked like she was having a great time. As Steven turned the corner he saw Philip sitting in one of the chairs smoking a cigar. All he had on was his trunks and a towel round his shoulders. Behind him stood two men, all dressed in black and quite obviously not people you would mess with or in front of. Steven knew he had his work cut out. He glanced at the house, rather the mansion and grounds he was now in. Philip really could back all he said and as Steven looked harder, when Philip stood up, he could see he had a gun down the back of his Speedos.

Before Steven reached the table, Philip had made his way to the pool and called Emma to him. She rose up from the water, which was dripping down her body, making her look very sexy. She went to the steps, climbed out, and Philip leaned forward, kissed her hard on the mouth, making it very obvious where they stood. He slid his arm round her waist and whispered in her ear, causing her to look at Steven. Then Philip took her hand and led her away from the pool towards the chairs. The twins started to follow, but one word from Philip and then they stayed where they were.

"Mr. Sands… please sit and would you care for a cold drink?" Patrick asked him very politely.

"Thank you. Water is fine," and Steven sat his suited body down in a pool chair, completely out of place in the surroundings.

Philip and Emma approached the chairs, still hand in hand.

"Steven," and Philip sat down in the chair a few feet from Steven letting Emma sit next to her husband.

Philip noted Steven did not rise when Emma sat down.

"Steven," and she sat down next to him.

"I was hoping we could talk in private, Emma, but," and he looked at the entourage, and Philip, "I see we cannot."

"Anything you say can be said in front of Philip. We don't have any secrets."

"You two seem to be very close. You are still my wife, Emma. Is there something you want to tell me?" Now his voice became raised. "And no secrets… really… That's not what I have been hearing since I arrived… I asked in Hollywood about Mr. Vega, and the whole place clamed up. A movie star doesn't live like this…" Steven realized that this was only alienating his wife. "I came here to take you home. You are only on vacation, no visa. The passport only allows you ninety days…"

"Steven, I have only been here for ten days… plenty of time yet… and I'm having fun with the family…" She hesitated and glanced at Philip. "Anyway, where are you heading to? You didn't just fly to the States to get me… you didn't even say goodbye when I left England, so I am sure it's not just for me…" Now she was getting just a little bit upset.

Philip stood up, dropping the towel to the chair. "I think, Steven, that you are upsetting Emma, and she really doesn't need that. What she would like is a divorce…" Philip said it for her and laid his hand on her shoulder.

"So you speak for her now… is that it?" and Steven looked at Emma, who wasn't disagreeing nor objecting to his hand on her shoulder.

"Yeah, Steven, I do… I think you were asked to file for one before she left. Obviously, you didn't do it. So that should be the first thing to do when you get home, or Emma will file from here. I have a battalion of attorneys that will get it through very quickly… and then I want to marry her. And, Steven, what I want, I get…" He was looking down on Steven.

"Just who are you, Mr. Vega… I asked you that once before." Steven tried not to show fear and stood up to face Philip.

"And like I told you the last time… you really don't want to know. But what you might like to know is that Emma and I are sleeping together, so that's why she needs a divorce and fast. I want more children, with Emma! Do you get the idea yet?" Philip was being very rude and extremely arrogant.

"What?! How can that be… she is still getting over the accident… Emma, is he telling the truth? Are you sleeping with him?" he looked down at his wife.

She raised her head and looked up into her husbands face. "Yes, Steven, I am."

"He made you, didn't he? I mean you haven't slept with me for months… tell me he made you…" Steven was obviously upset and looked from one to the other.

"What the fuck do you think I did, Steven… forced her into bed?! I don't think," and Philip paused, "I have ever had to do that with any woman in my entire life, and especially not your wife… maybe if you had been more of a man, she wouldn't be in my bed now!"

Emma didn't wait for Steven to say anything, stood up and took over. "He did not make me sleep with him. Philip is more of a man than that. I went to him on my own volition. I love him, Steven, and have done since the first moment I saw him!"

"And before you ask me, Steven… I love Emma and I would die for her… could you say the same?" Philip's eyes flashed at the other man, showing him total disregard. "You stole from her… pretended you were working, when you were not… What kind of *man* does that to his wife?" Now Philip was firing on all burners. He dropped the cigar onto the floor and Pauli stepped forward and stamped it out under his boot.

Mikey moved to Philip and spoke very slowly and quietly into his boss's ear. "No… not yet. We'll try this way first." Philip turned to his mistress. "Emma, have you said what you wanted to say, baby?"

"Yes, Philip… except Steven, just give me a divorce… please. You don't love me. You haven't for years. I was just a teenager when you married me, nothing like the person I am now… you can keep the house, sell it, or whatever you want to do with it… I took the money out of my savings account…" she couldn't say anymore and turned to Philip's arms both for comfort and protection.

"I think, Steven you have your answer, and now I think you should leave her in peace. Pauli and Mikey will stay with you a moment while I take Emma indoors. Then I will return and you will leave…" and Philip encircled her with his arms, protecting her like one of his children.

"What are you going to do, have me beaten up?" Steven was almost mocking Philip.

"Not this time… Patrick, with me…" and Philip and his son escorted Emma into the lounge where Mac was waiting by the door. "Keep her here and stay with her."

As she left Philip, Emma looked back one last time at her husband, a time never to be repeated.

Philip picked up his checkbook on the way out of the room, and grabbed a pen. He paused at the table and wrote the check. He ripped it out of the checkbook, left the book there and walked back outside, handing the check to Steven.

"Now, go! If there is a next time, my associates here with me, will be escorting you out of the back gate… and you will never be coming back… in one piece, that is!" And with that Philip turned on his heel and walked away, into the house and closed the doors very tightly behind him, leaving Steven standing there knowing completely who Philip Vega was.

Chapter 27

Emma was upstairs in the suite watching from the window by the time Philip got back inside the house. She watched as Steven stuffed the check into his jacket pocket and she knew it wasn't over. With her heart in her mouth she went into the shower losing the swimsuit as she did. Not only had she left her husband, but also her country and it had just sunk in what she had done. There was no going back. She turned the water on and stood there, her tears mixing with the water like pearls in the rain.

Philip could only just hear her. "Emma… you there, baby…" and he knew what he had done, what she had given up for his love. "Damn you, Steven… you will not get away with this!" and he entered the bathroom, laid his gun on the dresser, stepped out of his Speedos and into the shower with her.

She looked up at him as water cascaded down them both. He pushed her hair from her face.

"Baby, don't cry… he will be out of your life… I promise you, we'll go up the coast, take a small vacation just for a few days. Just you and me, no kids… go in the jet, us and the bodyguards…"

"I can't run every time, can I? I am a grown woman, not a child, right…" she asked him.

Philip looked at her body…"Yeah, baby, you sure are…" and he pulled her tightly to him. "Emma, I love you more than my own life…"

"I know, Philip. I love you, too… god help me, but I do…"

"God won't help you, but the family sure will," and he leaned down and his mouth covered hers, the water running down them both and once more they became one.

After Steven's visit, security was increased. Philip had a feeling that the money was not enough to buy him off, and he was right. Philip's men kept tabs on Steven, wherever he went, they knew about it. They were there in the airport when he caught a flight to Florida. Coincidence that that's where Sally, Marc and Damien were... Philip didn't think so... okay if he stayed there, but he didn't.

It was a week before they were able to talk more about the promised vacation, and now it was October. Philip wanted to take her to Tahoe. The twins wanted to go. Philip didn't want the twins to go. He wanted time alone with Emma, a lot of time. He also wanted to get her away from the house, knowing she had been too confined there, jogging with Patrick or shopping with him... and a bodyguard or two. Philip didn't jog... he worked out, every day in his gym. Sometimes Emma would watch him and they would end up, yet again, in the shower together.

The pain pills stopped, mainly because Philip threw them down the toilet, causing their first fight. The whole house heard the argument and the making up.

Finally the trip came about; almost six weeks after Emma arrived in Philip's world. From a private airstrip near LAX they would fly to Tahoe in Philip's private jet, with flying time about an hour and a half tops. From there to the destination that Philip had arranged... and one that belonged to his friend! The household had their instructions. No one was to come and no one was to leave... not upright anyway.

They left at noon on the Wednesday afternoon, telling the twins they'd maybe be back by Sunday, maybe not. The flight was fast and Emma was intrigued with the jet's lavish interior... all the comforts of home, even down to a bar with both champagne and scotch on board. The seats were plush red, fluffy red blankets and white pillows, magazines, chocolates and real food, even if it was brought with them... and guns. And that was why they flew in the jet and into a private airstrip owned by Philip's close friend, owner of the best vineyards around and his mentor, Don Alehandro.

This time only Mac and Alex were going with them. Emma noted that Mac went everywhere with Philip. The landing was good but

Emma felt nauseous, trying hard not to throw up. She didn't say anything to Philip keeping the fact to her, but did notice Mac watching her very intently, and she saw him say something to Philip when they touched down. The sickly feeling passed as quickly as it came.

There was a welcoming committee at the side of the runway. Don Alehandro had sent his *associates* to meet Philip with a car and driver, and an invitation to supper, one they could not refuse.

Only ten minutes from the airstrip, the house loomed into sight, the most beautiful hacienda Emma had ever seen. She marveled at the sight, peering out of the window of the car as they got closer. The hacienda, standing tall in the vineyards, was resplendent in the sunlight, looking like a fiesta was in full swing.

"We're going there?" she whispered to Philip.

"Yeah, baby… we are…. you can swim, horseback ride, eat, drink," he dropped his voice, "make love till dawn… you name it, we can do it. These few days are just for you."

"Haven't you done enough for me, Philip?" she asked, looking up into his face.

"Not yet, baby… there is much more to come…" and he stopped almost giving his and Mac's suspicions away.

She snuggled into him not even realizing what he had implied.

The car pulled up at the door of the Don's hacienda, and he stood there, a man in his late fifties with his wife, a very elegant woman maybe late forties with long dark hair turning a slight shade of grey. She was devastatingly stunning, and she knew it, and most of all she was a very confident woman, alongside a very prosperous man.

The car stopped and Philip climbed out into the arms of Don Alehandro.

"My god, Philip. It is so good to see you. It's been a long time and you look wonderful. Your new lady must really agree with you," and the older Don peered towards the car.

"Don Alexis Alehandro… I would like you to meet Emma, hopefully soon to be my wife… and give me many more children," and he took Emma by the hand and helped her out of the car.

Today Emma sported a very expensive form-fitting black pantsuit with a white T shirt underneath. Her hair was pulled up tightly on her head in a little plait. Philip kind of liked it like that, because it made her look even younger than twenty-five... good for his ego. She stepped out onto the concrete path and stretched her free hand to Alehandro, who was immediately captivated by her charm.

"Sir, it is my great pleasure to meet you, having heard so much about you." She hadn't heard that much but it seemed the right thing to say, and she felt Philip squeeze her hand. She half glanced at him, with his now full beard and great-looking moustache. His hair was longer and he also sported black... a black Armani suit and black shirt. Now she knew why they were so dressed.

"Emma, the name is Alexis and this is my wife, Gabrielle."

At the sound of her name, she stepped forward. "Emma, it is very nice that Philip brings you here to see us. Would you like to see your suite before dinner, also freshen up?" and Gabrielle, after flashing her eyes and a huge smile, ushered Emma away from the men folk, with Mac right behind them with the luggage.

"She is beautiful, Philip, and so young. You are a very lucky man. When will the wedding take place?" He glanced after Emma.

"When she is free of her husband, which by the way it's going, will be very shortly!" replied a dominant Philip.

"Ah... you have a slight problem. Nothing that you cannot fix though, correct?"

"Nothing at all... and I think, soon, we may have another addition to our family..." and Philip flashed a devilish smile at his friend.

Alexis slapped his friend on the back. "Really? Now, let's go join your lovely lady and have some wine. My vineyard has produced some very wonderful grapes in the last few years and brought in a very handsome profit for us."

"That's why you have such high security, Alexis? I noticed it on the way down the driveway." Philip glanced around him. It was like a fortress, even on the shingled roof of his home. He wondered if Emma had noticed.

"Partly, and partly because of my son... he wants to take over from me... only I am not dead! He is being a punk and running with the mob from Vegas who see a profit here. But that's not for this weekend. How are your sons?"

"Three of them are fine… one *likes* Emma a little too much! And that I won't tolerate, my friend, not even from my own son!"

"I assume that the son is not Patrick…" and he offered Philip a glass of his famous red wine from his vineyard.

"No, Sir, it is not. It's Marc… the one I don't think is my real son… and who will never be heir to the Vega dynasty. But Patrick will and he already knows it."

"Wasn't there some incident with his girlfriend a couple of years ago? Didn't something happen between you and the girl?"

"Yes… we had all been drinking and she made a play for me. I had gone to get a bottle of wine from the kitchen and she followed me. She kissed me and … I kissed her back before I realized what the hell was going on, and it ended up with me yelling. I told her if she wanted to stay in the household to keep out of my way and I wouldn't tell Marc. Wish now I had… I do think someone told him, but I'm not sure," he was totally sincere in his statement, and sipped the wine, nodding his approval of the excellent quality.

"Does Emma know what happened?" asked the wiser Don.

"No. I should have told her. I know she wonders why Donna is so afraid of me," muttered Philip, kind of disgusted with himself.

"You should tell her, my friend. If she finds out another way, she is going to wonder what else you are keeping secret…"

Philip knew he was right. He should have told her and now he didn't know how to.

And Philip and Alexis walked into the house to taste more wine, complete with a bodyguard for each man and one for good measure, not knowing that Emma had been at the bedroom window and heard every word.

Chapter 28

Emma held her breath. Now she knew the reason that Donna would not speak to her and she was glad she had gone from the house. She had no doubt Philip was telling the truth... but Donna worried her and Emma, too, had noticed Marc taking more than an interest in her. She had said nothing to Philip about it but was glad they were all gone. She also knew she was splitting the family, and that wasn't so good. As much as she loved Philip, maybe she should not have come into his life. Perhaps she should think about that fact.

She was sitting on the bed contemplating these things when the door opened and Philip entered, his jacket slung over his shoulder.

"You feeling okay, baby... you look kinda flushed," and Philip sat down beside her on the very Spanish-looking quilt, and he felt her forehead. The room was warm and he glanced towards the open window. He had a feeling she had heard them talking earlier. "Nice view, Emmy..." and he stood up and walked towards the window. It was familiar countryside to him and he loved it there with rolling hills and trees... lots of trees, and vineyards. One day he would build a house on some land he had come into near there years ago... one day, and retire with Emma and their children. He came back to the present, and turned to face her. "What did you hear; Emma... was it about Marc and Donna? In a way, I hope you did."

"No, I was..." No good lying "Yes, I heard. I believe you, Philip. I watched her at the house. She is terrified of you like you are holding something over her head. And I knew Marc was watching me far more than he should have been. But he is your son... no, I guess maybe he's not, is he?"

"I don't think he is. I just didn't want to face the fact. He is too much like Sally to be my loyal son, even if he's not by birth." As fast as he started the subject, he stopped it. Tall and proud, and dangerously dark, gun still in the back of his pants, and jacket thrown casually over the chair, Philip moved back towards her. "Nice room, right? I have stayed here many times, and no, not with anyone, just me… when I wanted to be alone to think. Emma, you have to promise me something…"

"Anything, Philip. You have given up so much for me. Anything you want…"

"Promise me that we won't have to wait till we are married for a child?"

She was taken aback. Even she wasn't totally sure yet. "You have my word, Philip. We will not wait," and she giggled, trying to take the tension from the moment. "Why don't we take a nap before dinner… well, christen the bed anyway…" and she slipped off her shoes, kicking them across the floor and she leaned back provocatively against the large Spanish headboard.

Philip sat down next to her, leaned over her and his mouth covered hers. She could taste the wine on his lips from the drinks he had had with Alexis. His hand slid to the front of her pants and reached the zipper.

As he did the phone rang by the bed. "Damn. Like a dinner gong! Rain check, baby, right after dinner. Meet you back up here, whatever happens. I want you, Emma and I need you," and Philip stood up, slid back into his jacket, straightened the front of his pants slightly and walked to the door. "You ready, honey?"

"Just one minute," and she ran to the wall mirror and looked in it. Her hair was still in place and her makeup was just fine. The only telltale sign they were about to make love was her flushed face.

Alexis and Gabrielle were already seated at the huge table, along with two other guests. When the one saw Philip, he jumped up from the table and rushed to him.

"Don Andrea… Alexis did not tell me it was you that is their guest. I am so happy to see you," and he leaned down to kiss Philip's hand.

"Don Giovanni… my pleasure and it's Philip in this company," and Philip straightened the old gentleman up and hugged him to him, kissing Giovanni on each cheek. "Maria. How nice to see you!" and Philip hugged the lady to him like she would disappear, her long hair dropping over his arms.

Emma found she was quite jealous of the much older woman with long gray hair and the olive complexion. She could have been his mother and yet Emma was still jealous. As if sensing it, he brought Emma into the picture.

"Don Giovanni and Maria, this is Emma…"

There was a glow about her that none of them could miss. She was radiant, and when he spoke her name she moved forward and one at a time, both Maria and Giovanni kissed her cheeks.

Alexis bade them be seated and dinner was served. Mac and Alex stayed at the back of the room with Don Alehandro's men who were very obvious, like they were expecting trouble.

Everyone ate till they could burst. The spaghetti was beyond comparison as well as the wine was from Alehandro's own vineyard. Emma had two glasses and she lost count how many Philip had. Then he had scotch. Cuban cigars graced the table and the smell this time made Emma feel sickly.

She whispered to her lover and asked could she be excused outside for a moment. Philip clicked his fingers and Mac appeared on cue. "Take Emma just outside the door… no further. Bring her back when she feels better. If for any reason I am not in here, escort her to our room."

Mac nodded, and pulled the chair back for her. Philip also stood, as did the other men at the table and waited till she left.

"She is very beautiful, Philip and very young. Where did you find this angel who is so obviously proud of you?" asked Maria sipping her wine.

"At the wrap party for my movie, 'Angels and Kings', and then again in England, when they thought she would die after a very bad car accident. It's like I have been waiting for her my whole life," mussed Philip, staring at the scotch in his hand.

"I think, my friend… the lady feels the same," remarked the older Don. "I think you should see if she is feeling better…"

Philip stood up and bowed his head in respect to the other men. "I shall do just that, but also it has been a very long day for us, and I have been drinking too much of Alexis's fantastic wines. I will see you all in the morning. Please excuse me," and Philip left the room with Alex in tow.

"I think," commented Alexis, "that I have seen him drink twice as much as that… and be here all night! He wants only the company of his mistress, and I cannot, for one minute, blame him!"

Philip left the French doors to their bedroom open on purpose as he and Emma lay in the sprawling bed. It was a tad chilly at night, but they didn't seem to notice. Nothing could stop the way they felt for each other. Finally after a couple of hours they fell asleep, Emma curled up in Philip's arms, and blankets pulled around them.

Philip woke first to the sound of a gunshot, then another. He leapt from their bed, pulled on his pants, grabbed his gun and yelled to Emma. "Go into the bathroom and lock the door! Do not come out till you hear my voice… or Mac's. You understand me?!"

"Yes, Philip," and she grabbed his silk shirt and ran into the room, locking the door as he had asked her to do. She was shaking. Two minutes ago they were locked in each other's arms; now she was locked in the bathroom and Philip was brandishing a gun. She looked at the window which was open and hurried to close and lock it, even though they were on the second floor. She could hear Philip yelling to Mac and Alex and then more shots. She cringed behind the shower doors, hoping no one knew she was there. This was real, almost too real. This was the life she had become part of.

"Mac… where's the gunfire coming from?"

"Downstairs in the kitchen…" replied Mac, gun in hand. "Don Alehandro went down there about fifteen minutes ago…" and he raced two steps at a time down the stairs accompanied by Philip.

As they turned into the hallway, all hell seemed to let loose. Philip sent Mac one way and Alex the other.

"Tell Don Giovanni and Maria to stay in their room… do it Alex!" and when Alehandro's men saw Philip they followed his instructions. "Where is Alexis?"

"He is down, Sir, in the kitchen. Gabrielle also. I think he is dead…"

"What?! How the fuck did that happen... how did they get to him? Is it his son?"

The lieutenant nodded his head. "My boss said to let him in whenever he came here... I was following his instructions and went for the Don, but he wasn't in his room... next thing there was gunfire."

"Where is he now? Still in there..." and without even thinking of his own safety or standing, Philip charged to the kitchen door calling Alexis's name.

There was no reply as he knew there would not be.

"You in the kitchen... show yourself, you fucking son-of-a-bitch!" Philip yelled, still not knowing exactly who was in there. He tried to see, but the kitchen light was dim.

"Don Andrea... it was an accident. I would not have killed my own father... I came to talk to him and he was angry... it was Tony who shot him..." and Alexis's son gave up his own man to save himself.

"Throw your guns on the table... do it... now! Both of you. Tony and you, Frankie... where is your mother?"

Philip could hear her crying as she cradled her dead husband on the floor, his head in her lap, blood seeping across her nightshirt. Now her son stood there, wetting his pants, fearing that Philip Vega was going to take him out. But Tony was arrogant, this not being his first kill. He didn't want to drop his gun even though the only way out of the kitchen was in a body bag. He had a better view of people outside the kitchen, and raised his gun firing one clean shot. It hit Philip in his left arm. Straight in and straight out, but enough to distract him, and to hurt like hell.

Now Frankie was terrified. "Nooooo... ... ..." he screamed. "Mama, don't let them kill me. It was Tony..." and he dropped to his knees praying for forgiveness. "It was not meant to kill Papa and you, Don Andrea... I am so sorry."

Philip flipped on the light-switch outside the kitchen. The sight that greeted him was not tolerable. His best friend and his wife lay on the floor. She alive, Alexis very dead.

Now all the soldiers could see Tony. His shot had killed one Don and harmed another. En mass they leveled their guns at Tony ready to kill him and also at Frankie's head. Philip stood there never flinching. Blood dripped down his arm, his gun in his right hand poised and ready to execute a man, when he heard a disturbing noise behind him.

"Oh, my god!" and Emma clasped her hands to her mouth, Philip's silk shirt hanging from her body.

Turning slightly, Philip could see her. "Didn't I tell you to stay upstairs... didn't I?!" Philip yelled positively venomously at her, unhappy she was seeing this and that all these soldiers could see her dressed like she was, the shirt barely covering her backside and black lace underwear glaring at them.

"Yes, Sir..." and Emma was scared of him and what he stood for. Then she saw the blood on his arm. "Philip, you are bleeding..." and she stopped as she knew exactly what was going on. "You're going to shoot him, Philip..." and she looked at him like she feared the ground he walked on.

"Yeah... he's going to kill me, little miss... to prove he can do it... a rising Don..." and Tony laughed crazily. "He could get one of his men to do it, but he's a killer..."

"Mac... get her out of here... NOW!" and as Philip said it, he watched Mac lift her, his arms round her waist, and physically carry her out of there. Philip raised his gun and shot Tony just once through the forehead, a job he did not need to do, but his anger and the death of his friend was too much not to make the hit personal.

Chapter 29

"Gabrielle... the decision is yours... does your son, live or die?" and Philip meant it as he watched the despair that she was now in. All he could think of was Emma, and one day this could be her cradling him on the floor. He should not have brought her into this world. His world.

Gabrielle screamed. "Please Andrea, do not kill my son... I cannot lose both my husband and my son in one day. Let him live," she murmured.

Philip lowered the gun; and stuffed it in his pants. "You... take over from here. You are his lieutenant. Sort out his son! I will stay here and arrange the funeral and see he is buried in the manner he should be. I am sorry to be here for this day. Gabrielle," and he reached down for her, helping her up, her nightdress soaked in his friend's blood.

"Thank you for sparing my son. I will never forget that kindness," and she clung to Philip, tears flowing from now redden eyes as he led her away to her room, Alexis's blood staining his chest as he did so.

Alex followed them up the stairs speaking low to Philip as they went.

"Are they still in their room?" asked Philip, clutching his arm.

"Yes, Sir... should they come down?"

"No... I will go to them. Ask them to wait. First, I have to go see Emma. I think, Alex, I should not have brought her into this life... take Gabrielle to her room and stay with her. Do not leave her for any reason," and Philip excused himself by his own room.

Philip did not know what to expect when he opened his room door, but he knew what he must do. He must return her to her own world.

Emma was sitting on the bed just staring at the door, and Mac stood by her, having no idea what to say to her.

"Mac..." Philip moved past him and happened to look into the mirror. His chest was blood red and his arm hurt. To him it was a scratch. To Emma it wasn't.

She jumped off the bed. "Philip, let me look. You are bleeding. There is a hole in your arm! And your chest... it's covered in blood..."

"Emma... calm down. It's just a scratch. Mac will take care of it for me." He was shutting her out... on purpose. He looked at her. Whether he was wounded or not, he wanted her. "Emma, you should not have come down there. I told you to stay in the room and you didn't. Why? You could have been killed down there..." his tone was cold and he tried to be uncaring.

"I heard you yelling and I could hear gunfire and I was scared for you..." she blurted out all in one go, looking up at him with tearful eyes.

"But I told you to stay... I think maybe you should go back..." but he heard her say '*for*' you.

"Back where? To Los Angeles?" she asked, not understanding.

"No... to England. This is not the life for you. Mac, will you help me here?" and he grabbed a towel from the rack to help stem the flow of blood.

For a moment she didn't speak. "To England? I can't go back! You took that right away from me the first time we made love... and why would I leave you, Philip? I love you... and you love me, right?" She didn't care Mac was standing right there.

And Philip didn't answer her.

"Philip... you do, right?" she screamed at him, almost throwing herself at him, not believing this situation, wanting to hit him and kiss him all in one go.

Still no answer and Emma ran into the bathroom and threw up.

"Boss. Mr. Vega. I know what you are doing. Don't send her back. It will kill her. She's..." Mac stopped, worried maybe he was way out of line, but also concerned for Emma.

"Pregnant? I know she is. I got her that way. Even more reason for her to go!"

"Mr. Vega… there is something else you should know. The spare gun that you always carry on trips, I found it. Emma had it under your shirt that she was wearing. It was tucked in her underwear. In her eyes, she was coming to help you."

"What?! Emma? She can't use a gun…" Philip was horrified and didn't want to know how Mac knew where it was. He trusted him.

"Yes, Sir, she can. Better than some of the men. I taught her. Not so much taught her, just brushed up a few things for her. Her father actually taught her! Emma is much tougher than you think she is. You told her husband you would die for his wife. I think, Sir, she would do the same for you!" Mac had said exactly what he was thinking. Right or wrong, it had to be said.

Philip sat down on the bed. This was all too much of a night to take in. By now it was getting light and streaks of early rays of sunlight reflected through the windows and onto the sheets. "I can't let her stay, Mac. If anything happened to her, I would die."

"I know that, Sir, and I will protect her with my life. You need to tell her you know she's pregnant. She's confused, Sir. She doesn't understand some of this…" Now he knew he was way out of line and Mac knew it. "Let me see your arm."

Philip held his arm out. It was far worse than a scratch. "You need it cleaned and stitched. That's a pretty big hole. Doesn't it hurt?" asked Mac, grimacing a little.

"Now that you poked at it, yes, like hell… just clean it and wrap part of a sheet round it. There are more important things than my arm to check on," and he looked towards the bathroom.

"Emma," called Philip. "Come on out, baby. Emma…" Philip stood up and almost lost his balance. His arm was far worse than he had let on. The bullet had gone in and out the other side, but he was also losing a lot of blood.

"Mr. Vega, Philip…" and he tried to catch him as he fell backwards onto the bed. "Emma, get out here now!"

She rushed back into the bedroom, and saw him lying there halfway out of it. "Oh, god… is he okay?" and she looked down at him.

"I've seen him looking better. It's not the first time he's been shot and it won't be the last, but he is losing a whole lot of blood. Must have struck an artery somewhere. He needs a doctor. Emma put your hand there where the first hole is. Press hard on it. Can you do that? We need to stop the flow of blood. I'll call downstairs and find out where the hospital is."

"No hospital…"whispered Philip half conscious. "You do it. You know what to do."

"Boss, I can't do that! What if it's not right? You need a hospital, Sir…"

"Get Alex and couple of Alexis's men." He looked up at Emma. "Baby, I didn't mean what I said. I was just trying to protect you… I would die without you," and he was out cold.

"Philip… Philip… I know you didn't." She looked up at Mac. "What's happening to him? I can't stop the flow, Mac… what's wrong with him?" Now she started to panic.

"Mac… do something… what does he want you to do…"she was all but yelling, a frightened look on her face.

"Cauterize it! I need help. Stay right here with him. Do not do anything. I'll be right back," and with that he was gone out of the door to find Alex and some kind of flat iron.

Emma held her hand where Mac told her to. There seemed to be blood everywhere now… on the quilt, the sheets, her.

"Philip, don't you dare die on me… I know you love me… I know why you said those things… I saw what you did for your friend, Philip…" and tears streamed down her face.

Mac and Alex rushed through the door inside five minutes. "Ok, Emma. We'll help him now. Go shower and put a robe on. Don't shut the bathroom door so we can hear you… He's not going to die, Emma. We just need to get him fixed up." Mac helped her up from the bed and ushered her into the bathroom. "Shower, Emma…" and she turned to see them taking his blood-soaked pants from him and redressing him in sweats.

She nodded. They wanted her out of the way so they could so men's work. Dropping the robe by the door, she stepped into the shower. Even with the shower water running, she heard him cry out when they sealed the wound with a burning hot iron. She clasped her hands to her ears trying to shut out his yells. She failed miserably and felt herself sliding down into the water, and heard voices calling her name… felt someone lifting her from the water, wrapping towels round her and carrying into the room. She could see Philip lying on the bed wrapped in blankets and his arm covered in bandages. He was alive and that's all that mattered. Maybe God had helped her after all. She remembered someone giving her brandy. It tasted bitter and she tried to spit it out.

"Drink it, Emma… it won't hurt you or…" and the person stopped speaking, and this time Mac tipped it to her mouth, not taking no for an answer. "He's gonna be fine, Emma. He just needs to rest and we gave him something to take away the pain. Here, lie at the top of the bed," and he pushed pillows under her. Sleep for a while. If he wakes, I'll wake you."

Emma slipped into an uneasy sleep, her face turned towards Philip. The sun had now completely risen, and its rays shone through the patio window.

Mac and Alex sat on the side of the giant bed.

"He's still asleep. How was the rest of the house?" whispered Mac.

"Quiet enough now. Gabrielle and her son are talking in the bedroom, along with two of Alexis's lieutenants. Maria and Don Giovanni will stay also till the funeral. They thought our boss might need some help. By the way how much did you give him for the pain?" asked Alex, a little concerned, as Philip seemed to be right out.

"The tiniest amount. He left that habit behind him years ago and I don't think he is about to start again, not now…" and Mac stopped mainly because only his boss and he knew. "By the way, I called Patrick. He is on his way up here with Mikey and Pauli. Mikey can make the funeral arrangements with Mr. Vega."

As they sat talking in a low voice, Emma moved her arm across the pillows towards Philip as if she was searching for him. As she touched his right hand, he groaned in his sleep and as they watched, his hand tightened round hers, and she smiled. Now they knew nothing short of death would divide them, and maybe not even then.

Chapter 30

Noon saw much more activity in the household. Alexis's body was removed to the wine cellar before his daughters arrived to await funeral arrangements. Tony's burial was away from the house, a grave without a marker.

A private car from the Alehandro's picked up Patrick and his two bodyguards from the airport. Patrick had simply chartered a private flight up from LAX, which wasn't difficult when you had the money and the power that the Vega's had.

Alex let them in, shaking hands with both Mikey and Pauli and being very dutiful to Patrick, knowing one day he would be *the boss*. Patrick sprinted up the stairs to his father and his mistress and Mac let him in. He was not prepared for the sight. Emma was still asleep curled up in a little ball at the top of the bed with her hand still touching Philip's. Patrick looked at his father, who at the sound of voices, appeared to be waking up. He was wrapped in blankets, his arm swathed with a bandage and the smell of burning flesh still lingering in the room.

"You do that, Mac?" asked Patrick hoping it was Mac, the only one with experience.

"He didn't give me any choice, Patrick. He wouldn't let me get a doctor and certainly no hospitals. Your father is one tough son-of-a-bitch!"

"Yeah, I know he is. You did the right thing. And Emma? She okay?"

"She's fine. Not the vacation she was expecting," and Mac turned to his boss as he came back to the land of the living.

"Mac…" Philip's voice was low and the looks to him were dark.

"Here, boss… what do you need? Need some more…" asked Mac very quietly, fishing in his pockets.

Philip stopped him saying it. "No! I don't. Patrick, who is with you?" gasping for his voice.

"Mikey and Pauli. They are downstairs talking to Alexis's men and Mrs. Alehandro."

"Then we should go down… help me up," and Philip struggled to sit, trying not to let go of Emma's hand. "Wake her gently, Patrick. She must know that I am fine…" and then he let her hand slip from his.

"Boss, you aren't fine. You were shot!" Mac tried to make him see sense, while pulling blankets around him.

"*Was* being the operative word. You did a good job, Mac. Hardly even hurts."

Both he and Patrick knew he was lying for their benefit, but they helped him sit up straight on the bed. The blankets fell from him revealing his suntanned body just clad in a pair of sweat pants… and the bandages.

"Help me up and into clothes, at least into jeans and a shirt. I can hardly make a formidable impression dressed in a pair of sweat pants, now can I?" and Philip tried to laugh.

"Dad, you make a formidable impression whatever you do and whatever you are dressed in…" and Patrick was serious. Since a child he had been scared of Philip, all the children were, and so were the people that worked for him.

Philip stared at him. "Good! That's how it should be. The only one I don't want scared is Emma, and Mac, she is not to carry guns anymore, for any reason. You understand me?"

"Yes, Sir… I didn't know she had it till I picked her up…" He was trying, without success, to explain.

"I don't give a fuck… she had it… and she doesn't carry a gun again… got it?"

Patrick looked from one to another, not knowing what was going down here.

"Philip," she spoke up. "Don't blame Mac… he didn't know. If you want to blame someone, blame me…" and she stumbled off the bed and stood next to him, her robe hanging off her, staring him in the face, defiant, a different woman. She had seen him kill someone right in front of her and now Emma was changed… for life. She knew her lover was a killer and she also knew she had to be what he wanted her to be if she intended to keep him. "I will go down with you," and she leaned towards him and kissed him on the cheek.

Philip slid his good arm round her waist and pulled her to him. She was more desirable than ever, seeing a side he had not observed till just. He wondered how much was bravado and how much was real, but he appreciated her support all the same. He whispered in her ear and she nodded, grabbed clothes from the closet and left for the bathroom to get dressed.

"Patrick, there are some black jeans and shirt in the closet. Get them for me."

His son duly did what he was asked to do, and the two men helped him dress. Mac handed him his gun and Philip tucked it in the front of his jeans and pulled the shirt over the top of it, but left it visible in the open shirt. As he did Emma emerged from the bathroom also in black jeans and a tight black low-necked sweater just as Philip had told her to do. She slipped on black high heels and fluffed her hair out. She had donned more makeup than usual and now she looked more like Philip's mistress.

Patrick saw the look on his father's face when she stepped out of the bathroom. He hoped that sometime in the near future he would look at a woman like that, and he also hoped she looked like Emma. He had no doubt that tonight they would make love again just like every night at the house, whether his father had a bullet hole in him or not.

They went down the stairs together. Philip straightened up at the bottom step and was greeted by Pauli and Mikey, who had been reminded by Alex not so shake their boss's hand. He let go of Emma and he stood there totally empowered and in control. Tony had been right. He was a rising Don and he had no intention of letting anyone see he was in pain. Philip also had no intention of letting Frankie go. He had told his mother one thing, but something was going to happen to Frankie. Now Pauli was there it would be taken care of and

Philip's hands would be clean. Pauli, the enforcer, would take Frankie outside later for a drive and Frankie would never come back. Tomorrow they would tell Alexis's wife that Frankie had left on a business trip. Eventually she would understand why it had to be like that. It would take a while, but she would understand.

In front of Philip stood the older Don Giovanni and Maria, along with Gabrielle and Frankie, and a whole bunch of the Alehandro men. They were waiting for Philip to act and it was time to.

Philip was ready to speak, and the dining room that last night had housed a beautiful dinner, fell silent. He wasn't about to wait for the two daughters to arrive. "This morning we lost Don Alehandro by foul means," and he looked straight at Frankie, who positively cringed under Philip's stare. "It has been dealt with and the offenders are no longer with us," he stated, still looking Frankie in the eyes.

And Frankie knew he was not spared, that it was just a matter of time before he joined Tony. His mother could beg for him all she wanted, but it would not work. He knew it wouldn't be the Don himself, but someone, somewhere would end him and by the look in Philip Vega's eyes… it would be soon.

Pauli knew it, too. He knew his boss would have him do it. That's what he was paid for, and he, too, knew it would be soon. Somewhere on a dark road… a bullet to the back of his head, even a car accident, or maybe a long drop from a tall building. But happen it would.

As Philip finished speaking the door opened and two of the most beautiful girls that Patrick had seen came into the room. There was a man with them, a few years older than himself. He had his arm around one of the women, but the other seemed to be a free spirit until she looked at Philip, and the mood changed like she knew he was judge, jury and executioner, and that's exactly what he was.

Chapter 31

"**D**on Andrea..." and the oldest daughter walked to Philip. "May I speak with you in private, Sir?" She was very matter of fact considering her father was murdered that morning.

"Whatever you have to say, Felicia, you can say it in front of my family," said Philip with a tolerable air of arrogance.

"Are you sure you want that, Philip?" she said, as she painted her lips with her finger, and flipped her long black hair back as if to impress him.

"Yes... and as I told you a year or so ago, what you and I had is long over, and I believe that is your new husband with you, correct?" Philip looked down on her, much as he had done when they had the affair.

Patrick looked totally shocked. Twenty-seven-year-old Felicia Alehandro... and his father? When and where had that little affair gone down? He looked at Emma, who didn't even blink. What was before her was before her and not her business, and if he was hiding anything he certainly wouldn't have said that in front of her.

Philip reached his hand to Emma, who took hold of it. "Felicia... this is Emma, soon to be my wife."

Felicia stared at the woman with Philip. She was younger than she was, but she had to admit to herself that Emma was very stunning and completely complemented her man. Felicia acknowledged her with a nod of her head and a smile, and turned her attentions back to her ex-lover.

"Very well. I would like to talk to my brother in private..." she didn't get to finish the sentence.

"No…" Philip said so matter-of-factly.

"What?" Felicia stated very indignantly staring at Philip.

"No… you may not. Not now and not ever. He is going on a little trip away from here and your mother. The estate and his territory will be run by Gabrielle and myself for now. In time you and your future children, along with Alexandria, will be able to take it over. Your father said that they were being threatened by someone from Vegas, and we cannot allow that. Tony, I believe, was from Vegas, along with Frankie here." Philip looked towards Frankie, a deep hate in his heart and then he looked back to the girl. "The answer stays the same… no, so don't ask again." Philip looked away from Felicia to the other sister, Alexandria, just turned twenty-one… a bright, beautiful girl who aside from the olive color of her skin looked a lot like Emma.

There were tears in the girl's eyes. Philip glanced at Emma and squeezed her hand. Emma nodded very slightly and let go of his hand. She moved to where Alexandria stood by the door, and for some reason she did not understand, she put her arms round the girl's shoulders. Alexandria looked into Emma's face and she leaned her head on Emma's arm and sobbed.

Both Philip and his son saw Emma in a whole new light, so did Philip's people. If there was any doubt that she could handle the future as Don Andrea's wife, they were dispensed with here today.

Emma led Alexandria to Philip and he put his hand on her shoulder. He spoke very quietly to her so only the three of them could hear, and then he called Patrick to them.

"My son will look after you. You need anything… he is there for you," Philip thought that Patrick would be only delighted to look after the old Don's daughter, especially the way he was looking at her.

Philip decided that the business there was almost concluded. "Gabrielle will live here, of course, and perhaps Alexandria would like to move to the house…"

The girl nodded yes, her long black hair flopping on her shoulders and her deep brown eyes switching from Philip to his son, and Philip handed her over.

Philip looked to Don Giovanni and spoke with him vey briefly, and then he called Pauli to him with very specific instructions. He and

Mikey were to take the trembling Frankie out to dinner tonight and discuss his future with him. In other words they were to make sure he never came back. He would make up the business trip thing over night and tell Frankie's mother tomorrow. And now, he was tired and in pain, and he needed Emma. He looked to Mac who took the hint.

"Don Andrea, you should eat something and so should Miss Emma. They have laid out food for you in the lounge," and he pointed to the other room.

"Will you join us, Don Giovanni and Marie? Patrick, you also, and please bring all the ladies!" and he took off to the lounge with Emma in tow, and found himself a very comfortable couch to sit so he could rest his aching arm. What he really wanted was his bed in his own home and that wasn't going to happen anytime soon. He wondered what Emma was thinking. Her face betrayed nothing. She had seen him kill someone, watched him conduct business and then met one of his past lovers all in the space of a few hours. She would have every right to leave him, but somehow he knew she never would; especially now that she was pregnant. Had she figured it out? Everyone else had. He was doing a lot of thinking as he sat in the great room of the house. Alexis had always done business in here, and now he was gone, and not only did Philip have his own territory, he now had another to maintain.

"Philip," Emma tried again. "Philip would you like something?" she asked very tentatively. Emma had gained a new respect for her lover since last night, not fear, just respect.

"Yeah... you!" He wasn't so quiet about it.

"You can have me later... ," she whispered, blushing slightly. "I meant food."

"I know what you meant and I know what I want, and it isn't on the table... yet!"

"Philip..." now she was really embarrassed. "What did they give you for pain, because I think it's gone to your head?" Emma had a good idea and now he was about to drink red wine. "Philip... don't drink..."

And Philip gave her a look that said it all. 'Don't tell him what to do, but you better be ready later' look. "Mac... pour me a glass of wine..."

Mac agreed with Emma, but he couldn't tell his boss that. So Emma solved it for him. Mac poured a glass of wine. Philip took a sip and set it on the table in front of the couch. By now the room was busy with people, so Emma picked up the wine and sipped it slowly. She hated red wine but anything to stop Philip drinking it. Each time he took a sip of it so did she till it was gone.

He knew what she was doing, but her concern for him was more than attractive. She stood up to put her now empty food plate on the table. He had eaten also, but not too much. His appetite was for other things. As she leaned over the table he smacked her on her backside, and Emma turned and glared at him. He looked at her like he dared her to say something. She didn't.

"I think, Emma, we should go upstairs. My arm is feeling the worse for wear," and he rose up from the couch.

"Need any help, boss," asked Mac.

"I think I can manage this on my own," and he raised his eyebrows at Mac. "You have the room next to mine, right?"

"Yes, Sir…" replied Mac, thinking he might want to turn the TV up for a while.

Philip nodded. "Let's go, Emma," and he set off up the stairs, not even bidding the rest of the room goodnight.

Philip didn't even wait to get through the bedroom door. He leaned on it, kissing her at the same time, and then somehow, with only the one arm, he managed to get her inside and close the door behind them. He freed himself from his shirt with a tiny bit of help from his lover. All he had on now was his jeans. She kicked her shoes off and undid her own jeans, stepping out of them as they moved across the floor to the welcoming bed. It was all changed and brand new… and beckoning them.

Emma lay back on the bed pulling Philip with her. He lay on top of her, a very urgent need to satisfy both himself and her. She bent her legs and his hand moved quickly up them to the long tight sweater pushing it out of his way. Now it revealed what passed for black lace panties and a black bra. Philip dispensed with them pretty much in one go.

Sweat poured down his chest and she could see he was in pain. She could also see he wasn't giving up, and he rested his left arm on the sheets. He had tried to move his hand once or twice and the pain shot through him. Whatever they had given him before, he needed again. But now was not the time and certainly not the place. He needed his jeans gone and he seemed angry with them for even being there.   Emma undid them for him and with her feet pushed them down from his body until he was able to kick them off.

They were as naked now as the day they were born. Philip rose up slightly to look at her in the failing light from the windows.

"I'm a killer, Emma. It's what I do best. The father of your child is a killer!" and with that statement he thrust inside her declaring once more she was his.

She tried to breathe through it all and spoke in a low key. "I know, Philip. I know. I knew it in England. I think I'm pregnant, Philip. You knew that though, didn't you?"

"Yeah, baby… I did know. I tried so hard to get you that way." He paused. "Today I took a life and I got one back!"

Chapter 32

It was approaching November now. Police came and police went. The Vegas mob formed an uneasy truce with the Vega's, fearing Don Andrea's long reaching fingers, and a war was not on the cards. Don Giovanni and his family attended the funeral, as did the Vega's.

From the first time Emma and Philip had made love Emma was pregnant. The only clue was the glow about her and if you missed it, you had to be blind.

At the funeral she stood with Philip, hand in hand, as always by his side. She wore a very expensive black woolen dress, black high heels, her hair was plaited neatly and like the rest of the family she wore shades. Philip was dressed by Armani again. Patrick escorted Alexandria and they seemed very comfortable in each other's company. Philip allowed Felicia and her husband to come to the funeral and to sit with their mother, a still grieving widow. No one asked where Frankie was, no one needed to. He'd taken a road trip. Security was very much in evidence just in case Vegas did have ideas.

As the priest read over the coffin that was lowered into the ground, Philip looked around him. One day this would be Emma standing like this, watching him departing for a better life. He shivered. She felt it and glanced at him. He squeezed her hand and shook his head just slightly from side to side, a slight smile on his face reassuring her. Limos brought them and took them home.

It had gone well as funerals go, and then Philip decided they should leave in the next few days, having been there a month longer than anticipated, and head back to Los Angeles and the twins. He and Patrick left the group and with Mikey and Pauli excused themselves to the study. Philip wanted to talk business and he took chair central.

His hair now met his shoulders and his facial growth deep and dark. Sitting in Don Alehandro's chair had become his responsibility, one he wasn't sure he wanted. He had another child on the way and he had a need to marry Emma well before the child was born. He also knew Steven had not returned to England, Mikey had informed him of that and tabs had been kept on the situation.

"Emma and I will be leaving end of the week. Patrick, I would like you to stay here, run the household on my say so. Mikey will also stay for a few more weeks with you, just to guide you. Pauli, you will return with us as will Mac and Alex. I will send some of the men from the house to join you so that they are not all Alehandro's men here. Felicia will be gone tomorrow and I will not allow her to return for a year or so, not until she shows she can conduct herself properly. Patrick," and Philip paused not really caring that the others were in the room, "how do you feel about Alexandria?"

Patrick had been expecting the question from his father sooner or later… apparently it was to be sooner. "If you mean, have I slept with her, Sir… yes, and maybe when the time is right I will ask her to marry me."

Philip stood to his son. "That's the answer I was hoping for. Thank you, Patrick. That will join the houses together, and that makes me very happy!" Philip hugged his son to him showing how proud he really was of him. "You have my blessing, Patrick… when ever you decide. Just let Emma and I get married first…" and Philip laughed. Humor had come back to the Vega's.

That week Philip, Patrick, Emma and Alexandria shared breakfast together on the patio for the last time.

The plane was ready and the day was bright and clear. The flight was just as good, except on landing Emma was sick. Home was a very welcome sight for both Philip and Emma. As they entered the gates in the limo, Emma now felt she belonged there, and when they arrived at the door the twins greeted them, and so did news for Philip. After the very brief welcome home, Rossi and Anthony escorted Philip to the study. Emma wanted to follow. Mac stopped her.

"Best you go to the suite, or stay with the twins. Here… let's a take a walk by the pool with the kids. I am sure Mr. Vega won't be long. He's been away so many weeks that they need to catch him up on plans…"

"What plans?" asked Emma, irritated that she was left out. "Why can't I go in?"

"Because it's *family* business, Emma, you know that… I'm sure Mr. Vega will tell you later… let's go to the pool with the twins. Then I will escort you to your suite."

Emma knew she was beaten and she knew Mac was right. She walked in a man's world. Secretly she hoped the child she was carrying was a girl and she knew that's what Philip wanted.

Emma was tired and after the pool excused herself to their suite. She lay on the bed hugging Toby thinking how life had changed in just a few short months. It was a little cooler at nights and she felt she needed a blanket. Getting up from the bed she went to the windows to close them and could hear Philip's voice from the study. It was loud.

"And what's more, she doesn't need to know! I pay you to take care of such things… right? Isn't that why I pay you, Pauli? And you, Rossi… you have men to do this kind of work. I should not even have to be involved… god damn it. I come home to this? Get the land deal done. Find out why it isn't just straight forward. I want that land and I will have it. It's right next to the house in Denver. Maybe for Christmas I might want to take the family there and Emma can have the baby in that house. And why am I explaining this to you? Because apparently you didn't understand what I said the first time…" Philip was yelling at the top of his voice… way more than just angry. "Pauli, just take the guy out! And why are you all looking so surprised? Yeah, she's pregnant… didn't Mac tell you? I guess not by your looks…"

Then she could hear another voice, but not as loud, and couldn't hear exactly what they were saying. She could hear congratulations and then the conversation continued at the same tone as before.

"Damien is with Jack Barton? When did this piece of astounding news come about?" He waited for the reply. "Am I surrounded by idiots? Get Mac and Alex in here, and Pauli, you better find Steven, too; because I have a suspicion that where one is the other is… when they spoke on the phone before Steven arrived here, I am sure they stay in touch. They both hate me for different reasons… and probably both would like to see me dead."

Emma's blood ran cold. Steven and Damien together… how could that be? And were they all in Denver? Seemed a very strange place for them to be. L.A. or Florida, yes, but Denver? Now she was confused. She and Philip had only just returned and there seemed to be chaos and she knew by now what that meant.

Then she heard the phone ring and Philip's very loud voice. "He's what? Where? How do you know? Which hotel? On my way! Make sure he stays there!"

Suddenly she heard a door bang and from the area of the garage a car start. There was a huge revving noise from one of the cars, but an unfamiliar one to her. She ran through the suite and to the other window where she was able to see the driveway and the very tip of the garages. A black Ferrari sped out of the garage and down the drive-way. She didn't know till then Philip had a Ferrari. The gates opened very reluctantly at the end of the driveway and she heard the horn on the car blasting away, and a very impatient Philip wanting to be let out of his own estate. Then another car followed right behind it, a black SUV screaming out of the garage at full speed after their boss.

Next was a voice yelling at her door. "Emma, get out here, now!" It was Mac's voice. "That was Mr. Vega in that car you just heard! He is furious… and I think you are the only one that can calm him down." Now Mac was banging loudly on the suite door. "Emma, can you hear me? Emma? He needs you and so do we!"

Emma ran to the door and let Mac in. She had on jeans, pulled on a very skimpy T shirt, grabbed a denim jacket that lay by the door and followed Mac down the stairs.

"What happened down there? I could hear him. Who upset him like that? I've never heard him that mean… was it something to do with me?" She was talking loudly as they ran down the stairs.

"Yeah, Emma… it was… Steven is here in the Los Angeles area… he left briefly and then came back. One of the men called Mr. Vega to tell him. Rossi had them keeping an eye on your husband since he left this house. They thought he had followed Damien to Florida, but apparently not. Then the boss gets a call right when he didn't need it and both Damien and Steven are here in LA. It's a dangerous situation, Emma. Mr. Vega has a violent temper where you are concerned. The boss has at least two guns with him, maybe more in the car, and he won't let this rest now till it's finished. The SUV, with three men in it, is behind Philip. There is a car outside for us and you and I have to catch up to both cars. They are heading to the freeway and then up the coast road. If either Steven or Damien makes a break for it, your lover will kill them!"

Chapter 33

Emma couldn't get in the car fast enough. She flung her jacket on the seat and jumped in beside Mac, who, while fastening his seatbelt, took off at breakneck speed up the driveway and through the gates. Rush-hour traffic was bad, but Mac knew back streets and where they were going.

"Emma, try calling him..." urged Mac.

"What?" and she fished in her jacket pocket for her cell. "I left it in my purse back at the house... you have your cell?"

Mac handed his to her. "Only problem, he'll think it's me calling, not you... damn! He probably won't pick up," and Mac thumped the steering wheel. "We thought he was coming up the stairs to you and instead he just took off on his own in the Ferrari... it's always gassed as he hardly uses it, and he never goes anywhere on his own... ever!"

"I didn't even know he had a Ferrari... what other 'toys' does he have?" Emma said, almost frightened to ask.

"Helicopter... couple more cars, but not here. They are in Denver. An SUV of his own and a Lotus Elite..." Mac glanced at her, seeing quite obviously Philip had not imparted this information to her. "Emma, Mr. Vega is a very, very wealthy man, both in money and property, but what he lacked was a 'you'... to him, money was not enough. And then he found you and he set out to get you, Emma." Mac glanced at her stomach... point made.

"I had no idea, Mac... all I saw was the movie star Philip Vega. I didn't care if he was an out of work actor. The moment I met him, I fell in love with him... and now I carry his child. I hope, Mac, it's a little girl... I can see what Patrick is going through... I... well, never mind...

why did he go on his own? Why didn't he send someone? There's men there though, isn't there?" She was really concerned.

"Only a couple of men that were keeping an eye on Steven. If Damien is there, he will have guns with him. Money can buy almost anything in this line of work… what's wrong, Emma?" The GPS was showing him where to go.

"Mac, maybe I shouldn't have come into his life… I seem to be splitting his family in half and now this…" she was getting upset.

"Don't even think that, Emma… he would die for you…"

"That's just what worries me…" she interrupted him and looked out the window at the failing light.

They were through the traffic and onto the coast road where there was not so much traffic nor was there light. Mac turned on the headlights and picked up speed.

Emma tried his cell number again… this time a very angry voice answered.

"What the fuck do you want, Mac?" and Philip switched to the speaker phone. "I don't think I want to talk to you right now…"

"Philip, it's Emma… I'm with Mac…" and she had their phone on speaker.

"Mac!" he yelled. "I hope to god you are at the house, because if you are following me, you will be looking for a new boss…" and Philip shifted gears to gain more speed.

"The SUV, with Pauli and some soldiers, is following you. We are behind them… a long way behind… I thought that…" pleaded Mac.

"Do I pay you to think, Mac… do I? Get out of my fucking way, you idiot…"

It was obvious Philip was yelling at someone on the road ahead of him. They could hear the car horn blaring away and the screech of tires.

"Philip, please calm down… and slow down… please. I need you alive for our child…" and she stopped, thinking it was useless to talk like this.

"Yeah, Emma, and I need you to be alive to be my wife and to give me our child and more children… you hear that, Mac… you keep her alive whatever the cost! You understand… because if anything happens to her, I will kill you... on that you have my word!" and Philip dropped the call.

Emma was shaking. "He means it, doesn't he?"

"Yeah, Emma, he does... I gave him my word that if he would let you stay, I would protect you with my life... and I will..." End of conversation, and Mac focused on driving knowing they were almost at their destination. He could see the SUV parked in the lot of the very small hotel, and he could see the Ferrari, headlights still on and the doors wide open.

Emma saw the cars at the same time and in the headlights she could see the tags reading V1... and she froze.

"Emma, stay here. Do not get out of this car. Lock the doors behind me. In the glove box is a .22. You know how to use it! If anyone tries to get near you, shoot. It's loaded," and Mac jumped out of the car and locked the doors behind him.

Emma flipped the glove box down just to make sure. It was there just like Mac said. As she was looking she heard someone yelling. It sounded like Philip. Then another voice and this time she recognized Steven's voice. She let the window down just slightly and as she did a gun barrel appeared through the crack.

"Out, Emma, now! Open the door! You will make a very good hostage. You for Damien and your very own husband."

"Who are you?" she asked staring down a gun barrel, trying desperately to see a face in the bad lighting.

"The name's Jack Barton... and Don Andrea, or should I say Philip to you, wants my land in Colorado and I came to meet my friend Damien Vega to discuss things... and lo and behold your husband is here. What good fortune."

"How do you know who I am?" Still she could not see clearly.

"Obvious, right... Philip has his Ferrari right there and two cars behind him with V2 and V3 on. Not hard to figure who you are, young lady... so, again, out!"

Emma reluctantly opened the door of the car and climbed out.

"Damien was right... you are very pretty," and Jack eyed her up and down. "Philip is a very lucky man... Now, let's go find him. He is after his brother, I think... and also your husband. Philip likes things his way and when he doesn't get them, he just has them taken out… but I am sure you know that by now, and your husband, he is in Philip's way right now! He's not going to divorce you, Emma, so Philip will have no choice…"

"Philip bought him off…" she stopped. Bad move to admit that.

"Really, news to me… but then Philip tries to buy everyone off. He offered me a lot for my land, and I refused. So now it's his way! Maybe we should go find your lover…" and he grabbed her arm, pushing her down the steps to the hotel, a hotel that was very close to the edge of the cliffs.

She tried to pull away from him and her T shirt tore under the strain. Emma could hear gunshots, two, maybe three. All she could think of was Philip's safety.

"You, young lady, are going to talk to your lover… your life in exchange for us… that he leaves us alone, and spares both Damien and Steven. A guarantee, or else you aren't going to make it out of here in one piece! We'll… not so concerned about Steven…" and Barton laughed.

"He won't do that! You know he won't. He has his men here. He will never let that happen, not even for me." It was then she felt something cold in her back and she screamed, and a hand slid across her mouth.

"Shut up, for Christ's sake. I want you where Philip can see you, not giving the game away…" and he had put the gun away and was pushing a knife just slightly into her back so she would know exactly what it was. "Don't make me push this any further," and then he saw Philip about to confront Damien, and Barton quite calmly maneuvered Emma towards him. Damien slid his arms round her neck and took the knife from Barton. Then he laughed and pushed it into her.

"Say something to Philip…" said Damien.

"Philip, help me…" and her voice was quiet.

Philip could hardly see her in the bad lighting when suddenly, what light there was was brighter as Philip's men turned headlights on from all the cars.

Philip could see her clearly then, his young and pregnant mistress held firmly round the shoulders by Damien, a knife stuck so close to her waist that not even a breath of air could pass between them. Damien held her there, his fingers gently caressing her face, pushing her long blonde hair out of his way, as Emma visibly cringed.

"Let her go, you bastard! It's me you want, not her," and Philip took a step forward, dropping his gun to the hard ground, with his spare gun in the back of his jeans, and his hands raised as if to surrender.

"Really? I think it's both of you we want," and another, only angrier voice emerged from the darkness into the lights. He, too, carried a gun, but seemed not quite sure how to use it.

"You! What the hell are you doing here with these people anyway? Didn't I pay you enough for you to disappear from our lives?" yelled Philip.

"Money can't buy my wife! All you think of is money! That, and her… She's sleeping with you, so she can die with you!" Steven Sand's voice was shrill and echoed on the evening air, his face contorted in hate for the older man that he was looking at.

Philip was franticly thinking of ways to get her out of there. In the beams of light he could see the glint of steel, but he knew that no on else could. If anything happened to him, his men had orders to kill anyone left standing. Anyone!

"Emma… are you hurt, baby?" yelled her lover.

"No… I'm fine," she replied in a desperate tone, her eyes betraying her real feelings.

"And the baby?" Philip continued yelling to her.

Steven glanced at his wife, and just for a second he took his eyes from Philip. It gave Vega time to pull the gun from the back of his jeans. His .357 loomed in the darkness like a canon ready, positioned on the battlements. He was very much in control now and between two hands aimed it straight at Steven.

"Now… tell Damien to let her go. NOW! Yeah, Steven, your wife is pregnant with my child. Shocked? The look on your face says you are. Why would you be? Like you said, we have been sleeping together… Tell him, Steven, or I will put a bullet in you right where you stand…"

"You wouldn't do that in front of Emma… then she would know who and what you are…" Steven laughed nervously, looking from one man to another, the gun wavering in his hand…unsure of what to do.

Philip Vega laughed an almost cruel laugh, and then he stared point blank at Steven. "She already knows, Steven! She's known the whole time!"

"Have you, Emma… did you know exactly what he is?" His eyes questioned her.

"Yes, I knew…" and she looked him straight in the face.

Steven turned towards her aiming the gun at her stomach. "I won't let you go, Emma! I won't! He can't just buy you…" and all she heard was the click of the hammer.

In slow motion she felt the knife go in her even further, more in panic from Damien than anything else, and she closed her eyes waiting to die.

And Philip pulled the trigger, killing Steven dead on the spot.

Chapter 34

Steven dropped to the ground and all hell let loose. In desperation, Philip grabbed Emma's hand and as he did, she fell forward into his arms. Behind Damien and Jack Barton, Pauli and two men appeared.

Jack Barton raised his hands to surrender, and Pauli pulled the gun from Barton's waist band. But Damien went for his gun, dropping the knife as he did. Even though Philip had Emma in his grasp, he pointed his gun at Damien. On the fingers of his hand holding her, he could feel something sticky.

"You god damn bastard! She's bleeding! You cut her," and Philip yelled to Pauli and without any hesitation said..."Bring him!"

Philip didn't wait to see what had happened. He stuffed the gun in his jeans and picked Emma up in his arms, and carried her to his car. He didn't seem to notice he was carrying her uphill. All he thought of was getting her out of there.

Mac came circling round shocked at what he saw, and rushed to help his boss.

Philip glared at him.

"I told her to stay in the car, Mr. Vega... how did she get down there?"

"It wasn't his fault, Philip. Barton... he forced me..." and she blacked out in his arms, her head flopping backwards.

"Need to get her to a hospital... now..." and he could feel the sticky mess running through his fingers. He reached the Ferrari... and slid her into the seat, pulled of his shirt and stuffed it behind her to absorb the bleeding. There wasn't time to look to see how badly she was cut. Philip knew instinctively it wasn't good. He slammed her door shut, and ran to his side of the car and jumped in, starting the engine immediately. "Mac, follow us… going to UCLA…"

"Mr. Vega, wouldn't she be better in the SUV?" he yelled above the Ferrari's engine.

"My car… faster…" and he slammed the car door shut and took off at the fastest speed Mac had ever seen him go. He tore out of the parking lot and onto the coast road ignoring the blaring horns from the cars that moved out of his way. His speedometer read ninety and then a hundred passing everything on the road. In the distance he could hear sirens. Hopefully they were not for him, but far back at the hotel where he knew by now someone had reported the disturbance. Maybe he should slow down a little… and maybe not.

Emma came round just slightly and realized she was with Philip. She moaned.

"Emma, baby. I have you. Taking you to the hospital…"

And she nodded, not quite sure what was wrong, only knowing she was in pain and she could feel something wet on her back. She slid her hand to her jeans and pulled it back out, letting out a scream as she did.

"It's okay, baby… Emma. You were cut…" and then Philip realized it needed to be dealt with now and the house was closer than the hospital was. Emma was about to go into shock and that wasn't good for the baby. He hit the button for the speaker phone.

"Yeah, boss, pretty much behind you…"

"Change of plan, Mac. She's going into shock. Heading for the house. Call our own doctor. Get him there now. About ten minutes away. Do it!' and Philip disconnected the call. Still he passed everything on the road and amazed himself that he hadn't been stopped by the police.

Ten minutes was right, and Philip pulled into the driveway to open gates. He could see another car ahead of him and hoped to god it was the doctor. The Ferrari screeched to a halt, headlights still on, and Philip leapt from the car to Emma's side, picking her up and straight out of the car. Men came pouring from the house headed by Anthony and cleared a path for his boss.

"Doc's in the lounge, boss…"

Philip carried her to him… she was hardly breathing, definitely in shock. He laid her down very carefully on her side on the couch. Her blood was now on his T shirt.

"Doc…" and Philip acknowledged his presence.

"Don Andrea. Sorry we meet under these circumstances. This is your d…"

"My fiancé… and we believe she is also pregnant. I think the shock of what she just went through is too much for her. My half-brother cut her…" and he lifted her T shirt to reveal exactly that.

By now Mac had joined them and both he and Alex were in the room and they closed the door behind them.

It was worse than Philip first thought. The cut was large and needed stitches. "Shit… that's got to hurt like hell…" and he bent down next to her. "Baby… Emma… can you hear me?" He felt like he had been there before. "Mac… give me a hand with her." Philip removed her T shirt, exposing her bra. He undid her jeans and lowered them just slightly. Nothing Mac had not seen before on her. And the doc was the Doc, and one who was also going to make sure the baby was a baby and that it was okay. "You want her here or upstairs, Doc?"

"Upstairs would be better, and then she can be in her own bed," the young doctor decided.

"Mac…" and Philip and Mac picked her up gently, wrapped a blanket round her and Philip carried her up the stairs to the bedroom.

Mac opened the suite door and Philip carried her in laying her on her side on their bed. This time she cried out in pain.

"Philip…" and she yelled out his name, raised her arm to try and reach him.

He grabbed her out-stretched hand and hung on. He knew she was so close to breaking and he leaned over her, protecting her from the world. Tears flowed down her face and she clung desperately to Philip. He turned and looked at the Doc.

"Make this right…" and Philip's look was such that the Doc had a feeling that if he didn't, Mr. Vega would shoot him.

"Would you remove her clothes, Sir?" Doc asked tentatively. Doc was used to dealing with wounds in men not women, and not a woman that belonged to the Don.

"Yeah…" Philip pulled her jeans off very carefully and then unhooked her bra, slipping it from her body.

"Mac… hold her legs," and Philip held her arms together and looked into her face. "It's gonna be fine, baby… Gonna hurt when he touches the cut. He needs to stitch you." He looked at the Doc. "Can you give her something to freeze or deaden the pain?"

"Yes, Sir, morphine… okay?"

"Go ahead, and do it… I don't want her in shock…"

Doc plunged the needle into her arm, and she screamed out loud.

"We have you, baby. Look at me, Emma. Look into my face… into my eyes. I love you, Emma, dear god I love you! You will come through this and we will have children, maybe two or three. Hey, Emmy, how about we go to Denver for Christmas? There's snow, Emma and you can make snow angels with the twins and Patrick will join us. Mac can come, too…" and he waved his finger in front of her, and she was out cold…

The whole time the Doc was working on her back. Damien had cut her in two places, one much worse than the other. One would heal in a few days; the other would take a good week and, mentally, a lot longer.

"She's going to have scars, Don Andrea… I can't do anything about it… I'm sorry…"

"I know that, and only I will see them… and my brother, possibly … before he dies!" his voice filled with venom

Mac didn't like the sound of that. He had the feeling it would be by Philip's hand only. Man to man… and Philip was good.

The Doc's hands had blood on them from Emma. It was also on the sheets they piled under her side. Philip looked down at his T shirt, one that was covered in her blood, pulled it up over his head and threw it onto the floor. They could be tossed in the trash much like Damien.

"Bathroom is through the door, Doc…" and Philip slid down on the floor next to the bed. He watched her face and gently moved long blonde strands of hair from her cheeks. She was still out cold and he hoped she stayed that way for a while. He glanced at the clock. Ten p.m.

"Mac, call Patrick. Tell him to leave Mikey there. Tell him the jet will be up there for him first thing in the morning. I want him back here. He can bring Alexandria if he wants to. Send about six of the men there to the winery and maybe Rossi. Pauli stays here. I want... no, I need my son here. I have something to carry out... and also a wedding to plan!"

While Philip showered, Mac watched over Emma. If he had had a sister, he would have wanted someone like Emma. He watched her resting even though the Doc was still with her

"Tell Mr. Vega I will be back first thing in the morning. She needs to sleep. Rest is the best possible thing. Mac, as your boss is in the shower... he says he thinks she is pregnant... is she?"

"She thinks she is... you best ask the boss... I would be shocked if she wasn't..." and Mac stopped, now was not the time for such comments.

"Tell him tomorrow we'll find out. How long have they been together?" Doc was packing up his bag.

"Almost three months..." Mac was considering that was correct.

"You think a lot of her?" Doc smiled and finished up.

"She's like a kid sister, and she is more than capable of becoming the Don's wife, young as she is. She has more guts than a lot of men I know," and Mac thought of at least two incidences.

"Yeah, she does, doesn't she, Mac..." Philip had reentered the room clad in tight sweat pants and towel-drying his hair.

"I was just saying how..."

"I heard, Mac... all of it... and yes, she's pregnant, Doc. We just want to make sure the baby's healthy... especially now, after tonight..."

"She had surgery recently, Mr. Vega?" A logical question from the Doc.

"Over four months back she was in a car accident in England... problem?" asked Philip, a little concerned.

"No... shouldn't stop anything. She should rest okay now. I will leave this for you to give her... just in case she wakes. She will be in pain, a lot of it... May I suggest," and Doc hesitated, "that you sleep somewhere other than your bed tonight, Sir. Just in case she moves..."

Philip smiled. He knew what the Doc was saying.

"Mac and I will take turns sleeping on the couch over there…" and Philip pointed to it.

"Nasty scar, Mr. Vega… recent also? Bullet hole, if I am not mistaken…" noticing the scar on Philip's arm.

"You are not… Very recent…" Now Philip felt Doc was prying. "So we will see you first thing?"

Mac knew Philip was cutting the Doc off. Enough questions.

"Can you find your way out, Doc? There is a check for you downstairs. Anthony will see you get it. I already signed it. Just fill in your amount for your services."

Anthony was positioned outside the bedroom door and as always could hear pretty much what was said. That was his job.

Philip waited until the Doc was out of earshot. He glanced at Emma, confident she was still asleep, and wrapped in a clean robe, he asked Mac. "So… where is *he*?"

"Mr. Vega… I…"

"Mac. I will ask you one time only… where is he?" Philip dropped the towel onto the chair. Mid forties he may have been, but he was in great shape, and he was ready to kill… with his bare hands.

Chapter 35

In the semi-dark and dank wine cellar Damien had time to think about his transgressions. He knew that Philip would come for him. He had hurt Emma and Philip had already promised him that if he ever touched her, he was a dead man, half-brother or not. Damien didn't think it would end like this. He thought he would walk away with some of the Vega fortunes. They had been making plans at the small hotel, himself, Jack Barton and Steven Sands. They would kidnap Emma and hold her for ransom, but true to his brother's good luck, his men had found out first, and now any chance of survival had gone. He wondered where Jack Barton was. Probably swimming with the fishes by now.

Damien sat alone in the basement with no chance to escape, not a one; Philip's men had made totally sure of that. He could tell by the light through the grilled basement window that it was still night; other than that he had no clue. He was surprised Philip had not come for him by now. He figured Emma must be worse then he had thought. He knew that had been a stupid move to stick a knife in her, but then again it was no more than they had planned for her in the future.

Then he heard voices on the stairs and the door opened shining light in from the outside landing. Damien squinted in the half-light. He could see the shapes of three men and he knew that Philip was one of them by the build.

Someone turned the light on and Damien's suspicions came true. In the middle of the three men stood Philip... bare-chested and ready for blood, furious-looking, with his fists clenched by his side. Mac stood one side and Alex the other side of their boss. Damien had no doubt that Philip had other men with him.

"How is Emma?" asked Damien. It was a risky question with his half-brother in this mood, but one he needed to ask as it would determine his fate.

"Why would you care? You stuck a fucking knife in her... the girl's pregnant! You stuck a fucking knife in her, you bastard..." and Philip moved forward. "Untie him. Let him find out what it's like to be on the other side..." and Philip stood there never so angry as he was right now.

Mac undid the ropes round Damien's wrists, and watched him as he rubbed them. If Philip didn't finish him, he would.

They stood there then, two brothers by one of the same father. One almost ten years older than the other. One fighting for his freedom and one for the woman he loved... and to bring his dominance back to the Vega dynasty.

Philip landed the first blow. Damien reeled back not expecting Philip to be so powerful. Philip's strength was fueled by his anger. Damien came forward and he hit Philip just once on the jaw, causing instant bruising. Philip went again, bloodying Damien's nose and mouth. Damien lashed back, missing his target and Philip went at him, hitting him over and over again till he sent his brother sprawling to the floor. Damien's face was bloody, with one eye closed and he lay there on the dirty floor trying to pull himself together. He was no match at all for Philip.

Philip's knuckles were bleeding from hitting his brother so hard. He didn't feel guilt, only the satisfaction of knocking the shit out of him.

Damien rubbed his face. "So finish it little brother... you can't do it, can you? Because after all we are blood! And Emma is not!" and Damien spat blood onto the floor.

That was all Philip needed. He grabbed the gun from the back of Mac's jeans. This one had a silencer attached, pointed it at Damien's head, and he didn't hesitate. One bullet, that's all it took to end that line of the Vega's. Philip dropped the gun and it made a clanging noise as it hit the floor, and he turned his back and walked away. Both Mac and Alex followed their boss leaving the body on the floor for other men to clean up and dispose of.

Philip climbed back up the stairs to Emma. Anthony had stayed there while Philip took care of business, and now it was done. Philip checked on her, and then went into the bathroom, leaving Mac by the bathroom door. Philip could hear him telling Anthony it was over.

Philip washed his hands and looked into the mirror to see his face bruised down one side. He knew Mac was watching from the doorway, knowing it had to be hard to deal with this. First Steven and now Damien.

Philip leaned on the washbowl for support. He was the Don, and one could not show weakness. All he wanted right now was to comfort Emma, show her he cared. The faucet was still running and he washed his face in the clear, cold water, splashing it on his head and neck. He slung a towel round his shoulders, turned off the tap and walked back into the bedroom to look at her.

She was sleeping peacefully, which would be more than he would do tonight. He sat on the couch realizing just how tired he was. Turning to Mac, he said, "I'll stay here with her. Just leave the bedroom door open so you can hear. By the way, where is Barton… swimming, I hope…"

"Yes, Sir, swimming," and Mac left the room.

Philip didn't sleep much at all. Just dozed, and woke to the sound of cars outside. He went to the window on the garage side of the house and could see Patrick getting out of the limo with Pauli. He glanced at his watch. Seven a.m. already. Later than he thought. Patrick would come up there at any minute. Philip moved away from the window and into the lounge… he realized that Emma didn't even know that all three of them were dead. Had she seen him shoot Steven? He didn't know. He would need to find out when she awoke.

"Sir…" a voice at the door interrupted his thoughts.

"Son…" and Philip hurried to the door and wrapped his arms round his favorite child, and Patrick reciprocated the gesture, and each for their own reasons consoled one another.

Philip held Patrick back and looked at him. Something was wrong. He looked into his son's eyes.

"I didn't bring Alexandria with me, Sir. I think… well… maybe I take more after you. One woman isn't enough, not till you meet the right woman, like you met Emma. You just know, don't you, Dad?"

"Yeah, son… you do. I'm sorry, Patrick… really, I'm sorry. But better to find out now, not like I did with your…" and Philip stopped. 'That wasn't bright!' he thought. "The good things that came from that marriage were you guys! The bright spots in my life… till Emma," and Philip looked back into the bedroom and motioned his son to join him.

"How is she? Does she know exactly what happened yet?"

"No…" answered his father. "She will."

But Emma did know about Steven. She could remember Steven turning a gun on her and Philip firing and she remembered Barton and Damien standing there…

"Philip…" her voice was very low. "It wasn't your fault," she whispered.

"Honey… how do you feel?" And Philip sat on the side of the bed, felt her forehead. It was warm and she was flushed.

"I'm fine," and she tried to sit up, her back hurting like hell.

"Not so fast, young lady. You need to lie still, at least till the doctor returns."

"Need the bathroom, Phil…" and she tried to make a face at him. "Patrick…"

Philip pulled back the covers and slid his arms under her, picking her up in one go and carried her to the bathroom to pee.

Patrick knew his decision was right not to bring Alexandria. Now he knew that's how his father was so certain Emma was the right woman. He would do anything for her and had proved that in the last twenty-four hours.

Chapter 36

The doctor came and went, did tests and checked on Emma. While Philip talked to him, Patrick stayed with Emma.

"She'll be fine, Sir. Just needs to rest. Pretty sure she is pregnant. Her first child, right?"

"Yes. Let me ask you…" and Philip led the doctor away from the suite. "She fit enough to get married?"

"No problem at all. If you mean is she fit enough for sex… the answer is yes…" and the doctor laughed just a little until he looked at Philip's withering stare. "Right. I'll be on my way…" and he was gone.

Philip motioned Mac and Alex to him. "How are the plans going for the wedding? Anything I need to check up on? Church, cars, flowers? You know about the flowers right? And the catering at the house?"

"Yes, boss, we know what to do…" replied Mac somewhat amused at Philip. His boss was never this flustered, but then again he'd never seen him get married before.

"This week, hopefully, we can take her to look for wedding dresses. Doc says she will be fine and the wedding isn't for two weeks yet. By the way, is the house in Denver fixed up yet? I think we should all go there for Christmas. I'll take her somewhere nice after the baby is born… but for now Denver would be good… Snow, trees, log fires… and all of you guys!" and Philip laughed, the first time he really had in days.

December twenty-first was the wedding date, and then they would all fly to Denver the next day.

The tests came back confirming she was definitely pregnant. By the wedding she would be four months and still the only clue was the glow about her. Philip discussed the deaths of her husband and Damien with her. Philip tried to make it easy for her… in fact, he tried to make everything easy. He gave her straight answers to her questions, omitted to tell her about killing Damien in the basement, but generally it was for real.

The week after the drama died down Patrick was still in the House of Vega; Philip sat him down in the study for a talk, along with Rossi and Pauli.

Philip lounged in the big leather chair that once was his father's and his grandfather's before him. One day it would be Patrick's, but for now Philip took centre stage.

"Patrick, you should go back to Alehandro's Vineyard and make sure everything is secure. I would go but I don't want to leave Emma right now. It would be very bad timing for her. You can take Rossi with you or Anthony, or both. I don't expect any trouble here, not now. Vegas are quiet enough. They are too busy fighting with some folks to the north of them." He paused. "Of course, if there is some reason you don't want to go, Pauli and Rossi can go." Philip looked his son in the eyes. "Is there, Patrick? Is it Alexandria?"

"No, I can take care of that situation. I owe her an explanation and hopefully we can still be friends. I'm a grown man and what I told you still stands. I can't be with just one woman… not yet. Maybe when I am your age… and with someone like Emma," and Patrick smiled at his father. A carbon copy looked back at him.

Philip couldn't argue with that statement. It had taken him years to find Emma. "You want me to ask her if she has a sister?"

"Yeah, would you? One that looks just like her…" Patrick joked. "Seriously… I will go back. I'll leave tomorrow and just make sure the place is still standing. I'll take Pauli. No need for lots of folks, as I will only be gone for a few days. I don't foresee any problems and I think you might need some help back here." Patrick turned serious. "Sir, Marc called me today. He heard about Emma and he wants to come home for the wedding. I said I would ask you for him… Donna will stay in Florida, if you prefer…"

Philip looked surprised. "I didn't know you knew what happened with Donna…" and Philip stood up, walking to the window. He pulled out his cigarettes and Rossi was right there with a light. Smoke rings floated to the ceiling. Philip thought it was chilly even for the beginning of December in Los Angeles. He needed to keep the temperature in mind for the wedding arrangements.

No one spoke. Patrick watched his father thinking. Philip turned to face them. "Marc tell you?"

"No. Donna did. She felt terrible about it. She knew how drunk you both were, and I do know how sorry she was. She and Marc had been fighting before the party… well… you know the rest! I'm not sure Marc knows. Does Emma know?"

"Yeah, she does. Marc can return end of this week, and I will leave it up to Emma about Donna. One thing though… if Marc returns, I want a paternity test done. Clear that little detail up once and for all!"

"I think that's very fair, Sir. I will call him later. Will you let me know what Emma says?" Patrick inquired.

"You can ask her yourself. Let's go see her…" and Philip disbanded the meeting, swung his arm round his son and marched him off to see Emma.

Philip and Patrick joined Emma in the lounge where she sat with a dozen bridal magazines strewn on the floor, the twins at her feet helping her to select a wedding dress and outfits for themselves to wear.

Philip stopped his son in the doorway and they watched her with the twins. Philip smiled, and looked at Patrick.

"Yes, Sir… that's exactly what I want in a woman… she fit right in from the start. You knew that didn't you, at the wrap party?"

"Yes. The instant I saw her come through the door, and even if I had known the cost, I would still have pursued her… whether that's right or wrong in God's eyes."

"Daddyyyyyy," and Orry ran to greet his father on a rare treat of him even being in the room with his younger children.

Philip hoisted him up in the air, and Orry laughed as Philip ruffled his blonde hair. Then the dark-haired twin wanted up, too. With his other arm, Philip lifted him into the air. All three started to collapse the couch in fits of laughter.

"Emma," yelled Orry. "Look at us…"

"That's not Emma anymore, Orry. She is going to be our new mommy!" Daniel said it with such finality that Philip almost dropped him.

"Say that again, Daniel…" asked his father, his face a total study.

"Emma is now our mommy and when the baby comes, she will have five children… and you will too, Daddy."

"Hey, *mom*," yelled Patrick from the doorway, "welcome to the family," and he was thinking how that was not going to go down with his mother… it wasn't, and to be honest he didn't care. The twins were happy, his father was most certainly happy and he himself thought the world of Emma. Perhaps Donna should stay in Florida and he hoped to god that Marc turned out to be his father's son, or Marc might be gone to Florida for good.

Chapter 37

"So, Emma, the doctor says your back is looking good, baby… a few more days and no one will even know, and anyway, only I can see your back… ." And he sipped his glass of red wine.

He set the glass down on the patio table, pulling her onto his chest as they sat on the large pinstriped couch on the balcony taking in the last rays of sun. She smelled good to him and he ran his fingers through her long hair. She had been leaning on him and raised up, turning towards him. As he looked into her eyes, he was so serious, his long dark lashes and those deep brown eyes seducing her yet again. She reciprocated the look, flashing bright green eyes at him, dipping them just slightly and pushing her hair back out of the way. She undid the buttons and slid the shirt down from her shoulders till it dropped almost to her waist. She turned her back to him and he could see the scar and he leaned forward and kissed it and then again, a little more passionately. Emma's head tipped back and let herself be seduced by this man, his arms encircling her, and then holding her hand, he stood up taking her into the bedroom. She leaned back on the bed and Philip pushed her shirt out of the way, his mouth kissing their unborn child, then up her breasts to her mouth, and she returned those kisses most passionately. He wasn't wearing a shirt and only his jeans stood in the way.

"I love you, Emma. I will always love you and our children… I thank God you came into my life, and I will never leave you," and his mouth closed over hers till she could hardly breathe.

It seemed like an eternity of delight for Emma. Each time they made love it seemed to be better and Emma could not understand what she had done to deserve such a man like Philip. And now she had a surprise for him. She was going to wait till the wedding, night to tell him but could not contain her joy. She waited till he lay back on the sheets and pulled her to him while moonlight streamed across the bed.

"Philip… I have some news about the baby. I was going to wait till the wedding, but I think you should know… Philip, when I was at the doctors yesterday, he had news…we are expecting a little girl…" Emma said the last part with such enthusiasm.

Philip leapt up from the bed. "Are you sure? Really?"

"Yes… I was hoping for a girl for you, but I wasn't sure… are you pleased?" Her eyes were glowing.

"Pleased? Pleased? Do you have to ask? I am ecstatic… this calls for a celebration… Patrick is home and Marc arrives tomorrow. Emma, it's late, aw… what the hell. Can you get dressed? Do you mind?" his thoughts racing along with happiness.

"Of course not, Philip. Only you would ask was I happy… give me five minutes," and she ran to the bathroom and threw on a huge sweater and her jeans.

Philip grabbed on jeans and waited for Emma…"Emmy… come on, girl… let's go down. We can celebrate now. You can have a glass of wine…"

"Philip…" and she threw her arms round him as she came out of the bathroom, looking up into his face.

"I didn't ask you, little Emmy… are you happy?" he looked down into her face, brushing her hair with his fingers.

"Of course, Philip… I am carrying your child." Now she was excited just as much as he was, and very happy that Philip was so pleased.

He opened the bedroom door and grabbing her hand whisked her down the stairs, picking her up in his arms as he went. Emma was squealing with delight and Philip's enthusiasm as Patrick ran out of the dinning room, while Mac and Alex appeared from nowhere.

"Everything alright, Mr. Vega?" asked Mac peering at the two of them.

"Everything is just great… we are having a little girl!" Philip almost yelled the fact.

"Way to go, Dad..." and Patrick laughed as he smacked his father on the back. "And you, Emma. You really listened to me... *mom...*" and as Philip put her down to the floor, Patrick hugged her.

"Break out the champagne. Get Rossi and the rest of the guys... everyone gets to drink... give the boys a very small glass, and for Emma... she gets one or two... right Emma? Champagne, baby?" And Philip laughed a mischievous laugh that everyone in the room got the gist of.

Emma blushed profusely. They had just had sex and Philip wanted more. Much more before the night was out.

They drank champagne, then wine and smoked cigars. Philip realized Emma was not in the room. She had stepped outside in the cool and less smoky atmosphere.

"Excuse me, gentleman..." and Philip found her out by the pool. "You feeling okay, Emmy? I am sorry; I got carried away in there. I am just so happy, Emma. You have given me a reason to live!" Philip was so effervescent.

Emma was overcome with the statement, and burst into tears.

"Hey, come on... why the tears... is something wrong? Did I say something to hurt you?" and he cradled her in his arms, his fingers brushing away the tears.

"Oh no, Philip... you just said the most wonderful thing that you could ever say to me. A reason to live... .you gave me that, too, Philip... and now you have given me more. You have given me a life here inside me..." she looked up into his eyes. She didn't care what he was; only that he loved her. He had taken her pride and respect, but given her the thing she craved the most... his love.

"Oh, Emma, my sweet baby... I have something for you, too..." and he let go of her fishing in his jeans pocket. "I was saving this till for the right time, and I think this is it." Philip pulled a box from his pocket, a very tiny box and flipped the lid open. Inside was the brightest diamond ring she had ever seen.

Emma stared at it in total amazement. Hadn't he given her enough?

Philip prized it from the box and took hold of Emma's left hand, dropping to one knee as he did. "Emma Sands. I never officially asked you. Will you become my wife? Will you marry me?" and he slipped the ring on her finger.

"Yes, Philip, oh, my god, yes, yes…" and more tears flowed from her eyes… tears of joy, and she flung her arms round him as he stood up.

Everyone from the house had rushed outside; amazed Philip would get on one knee to anyone, but also to congratulate their boss, their father… and the Don's official fiancé.

And the next day was wedding dress day.

"Sir, you can't see her in her wedding gown… nor can you see the twin's pageboy outfits. Emma wants to surprise you…" Patrick insisted.

"She did that last night!" and Philip laughed. "Okay… I need to get a suit. Alex, you and Pauli take me shopping. We'll meet back here at six for dinner. Patrick, look after her. I know she is tired. She can't not be, and make her eat something before six, okay?"

"Yes, Sir. Dad, the ring you gave her, it's so perfect for her. She hasn't stopped smiling or talking about you all morning. All she thinks about is you and how to make you happy like you are on some kind of a pedestal. Don't ever betray her, Sir… please… not ever," and Patrick turned and walked away to find Emma.

Philip thought that was a very strange comment from his son and left him wondering exactly what he meant. It was a statement that would come back to haunt Philip in his later years.

The long day turned longer as Philip couldn't find what he wanted. He had set his mind on a very pale grey suite and a dark grey button-neck shirt. No tie, and grey snakeskin boots. Traditionally it should be black. But Philip wasn't a traditionalist, and he felt sure that Emma's dress wouldn't be either.

"What do you think, Patrick? Think Philip would like this one…" Emma was in the best bridal store in town modeling the dresses for his son. She watched his face and then Mac's. She had a feeling Mac would like anything she wore.

"If my father doesn't like you in that, I will marry you myself…" and Patrick sat forward on the slick leather couch admiring the slightly off-white strapless gown that Emma wore. "Turn around, Emma…"

She turned slowly showing every angle of her. The shape of the sides panned away to pearly buttons all down the back of the dress. It was exquisitely designed with very tiny pearls woven into the fabric. It was floor length and a perfect fit, almost handmade for her.

"That's the one, Emma... don't look any further. It's perfect..." 'Like you,' he thought.

Mac watched Philip's son, and waited till Emma left them alone. "How long have you been in love with her, Patrick?" and Mac sat on the arm of the couch and waited for the answer. "That's why you didn't want to stay with Alexandria, right?"

Patrick laughed. "You are a very smart man, Mac. Emma's like your kid sister, isn't she? I can tell... and you are right. The first day she came to the house with my father, I was amazed by her. She is like a ray of sunshine in the dark world we live in. I won't ever get married, Mac. I will always be in love with her, but I swear to you, I will never tell her or my father and I will give my life for her if needs be, just like my father would. I ask you one thing... never tell either of them... whatever happens! Neither of them must ever know!"

"It will remain our secret, Patrick... whatever the cost they will be happy together. Whatever it takes..." and Mac breathed a heavy sigh.

Chapter 38

Marc arrived home two days before the wedding and he and Philip, plus security, departed for paternity testing. Philip had to know if Marc was his son or not, and they knew by going now the results would not be back till after the holidays. It also gave Philip time to talk to Marc in private. That night, as they lay between silk sheets, Philip questioned Emma.

"Nervous, baby?" he asked her as he moved strands of hair from her face.

"Honest answer… terrified…" as she played with the hair on his chest.

"Why? You know almost everyone coming to the church. Maybe not here to the house, but just stay with me and you will be fine. There will be more security than usual. Tomorrow we have the rehearsal at the church. Nothing to be nervous about. I have everything arranged. All you have to do is show up…" and he laughed. "You will show up, right?"

"Of course, I will. I know Philip this is a big step for you, getting married again as it is for me, but you understand your world… I am still learning…"

He lay on his back thinking about that statement, and Emma lay across him nestled into his chest.

Emma broached another subject carefully. "How did it go today with Marc?"

"Fine. Won't get the results till after the holiday. Between you and I, baby, I don't think Marc is my son. I am prepared for it. If that's the case, then so be it. I won't turn him out, but I also won't have him here. He will go back to Florida and live there with Sally. Just a gut feeling… and it's not going to ruin anything, especially not tomorrow… or the holidays. This holiday is going to be your best ever, baby, and I have some surprises for you in Denver," and he turned her on her side and tweaked her nose.

"I can't take anymore from you, Philip… that's just plain greedy."

"You'll be my wife, Emmy. You can have anything you want, baby, and I mean anything…" and he flashed mischievous eyes at her.

"Ice cream and some chocolate… maybe a Popsicle…" and she laughed precociously. "But tonight, I just want a man named Don Andrea… have you seen him around here?"

"Emma Sands… I do believe I have…" and he turned out the bedside lamp.

Morning came all too soon and so did the rehearsal. Emma wished they were having the service at the house but Philip had insisted they got married in church.

As Philip stood at the alter of the magnificent old Catholic church waiting for Emma, he could hardly believe he was doing this. He had said he would never marry again… until Emma. He didn't really think he would have more children… until Emma, and at one point he didn't want to come out of the drunken and mob related life… until Emma. Now here he was at the rehearsal, getting married again, and was very happy.

And today was here. Philip had said goodbye to her at the bedroom door, holding her close whispering in her ear, telling her how much he loved her and then he was gone to Patrick's rooms to change.

Emma stood in front of the mirror as Donna and the twins entered the room. The boys were already dressed in charcoal pants, grey shirts and little black waistcoats with shoes to match. They waited patiently while Donna stepped into the bedroom to help Emma into the gown that awaited her. It wasn't an easy task doing up fifty pearl buttons, nor was it going to be easy getting her out of it. Philip had his work cut out for him. A partial veil covered her face, a face that sported just enough makeup, with big green eyes sparkling from under it. She looked back into the mirror. Was that really her standing there in this finery... and laughed at the thought that if Philip didn't like it Patrick would marry her.

Two little voices at the door disturbed her thoughts. Orry spoke first. "You ready, Emma. We shouldn't keep daddy waiting..." and he stopped. The next words were in unison with his brother. "Wow... Emma. You look like a model or a film star or..." and they couldn't take their eyes off her, still staring and talking.

"Thank you both, and no, we shouldn't. How nice you two look," and she ushered them to look with her in the mirror... two little cherubs.

There was a knock on the door and Mac appeared resplendent in a very dark gray suit and grey shirt. He was elected to give her away, and honored to do so.

"Ready, Emma... Mr. Vega has already left for the church with Patrick... and Marc." He changed the subject slightly. "Emma... Mr. Vega asked me to give you this gift and requested that you wear it today. And here is your posy to go with it. He said you'd like white roses."

Mac handed her the present and she opened the box. It was a bracelet to match the necklace she was wearing. Pure pearls. She looked at Mac, who just smiled at her with brotherly love, and Emma leaned forward, throwing her arms round this totally loyal family man. Mac was surprised with the gesture and in his eyes Emma swore she could see a tear.

"Come on, Ms. Emma... let's not keep the boss waiting... today or any day..." and he laughed, a joke between him and the soon to be Mrs. Vega. He ushered them from the room and escorted his charge and the two sons down the stairs and into the waiting limo. She had no time at all to see either the dining room or the lounge; in fact he got her into the car so fast that she didn't see anything.

Emma shivered in the December air. Maybe it hadn't been so smart to get a strapless dress. Even with the bright sunshine and the long veil round her it was cold.

The limo pulled up outside the church. It was glorious. It looked nice yesterday... today it glowed, its tower spiraling to greet the sun-sprinkled heavens. As the car door opened and she stepped out, she could hear organ music seemingly blasting out of the church through wide open doors. There were light bulbs flashing everywhere and police on motorcycles. She was shocked.

Mac was immediately on her left and Alex appeared on the other side of her, as Rossi took charge of both boys.

"Mac, what going on? Why are…" and then she realized. Philip Vega, American movie star, was getting married. Suddenly a world of things fell into place. Why she never went out on her own, only with security or family. Why the twins were schooled at home, why shopping was always done like it was and why dinners were always in secluded places.

She hurried up the steps of the Catholic church. Something she would have to get used to, not that Philip seemed to be a regular visitor at this particular establishment. Mac and Alex made sure that both she and the boys were safely inside, before they closed the heavy wooden doors.

As the doors closed, with a not so quiet thud, most of the congregation turned to look for the bride, and Philip was no exception. He stood there then, looking at Emma, a vision, his angel waiting for the right organ music to play so she could walk down the aisle to start her new life. Pregnant with his child, almost twenty years his junior and entering into a world she hardly knew. Yet somehow, she did.

As he stared at her, he smiled, and dipped his head just slightly to her, then winked, and Patrick saw the bond that was between them.

Mac walked her up the aisle. She didn't see anyone on either side of her only Philip. waiting for her, and he stepped out into the aisle to meet her. Mac let go and Philip took her hand in his. His eyes looked her up and down, both in respect and admiration, and she blushed unashamedly under the veil. He glanced down at his twins who had dutifully followed their new mother up the aisle, and Emma turned to them handing them her posy of white roses.

Now it was just their time, Philip and Emma, as they stepped up to the priest to become man and wife, knowing that till death do they part… and maybe not even then.

Chapter 39

When Philip was told to kiss the bride, he flipped up the thin veil that covered her face. Underneath he could see tears in her eyes and with loving care he brushed them away with his fingers, and gently kissed her. The couple turned back, hand in hand, to their waiting audience and together, as man and wife, they took the journey back down the isle. Posy in one hand and Philip clutching the other, Emma was radiant as they stepped outside to the loud cheers of Philip's adoring fans, and Emma swore she could hear one of her favorite songs playing, 'Wedding Day'. She looked at Philip.

"Yeah, baby… you hear right…" and he laughed as they posed for a couple of photos on the church steps. Once more camera bulbs popped and Philip whisked her, and the twins, off to the waiting limo back to their home.

The gates opened and the limo, followed by half a dozen cars, made their way into the awaiting arena of caterers and photographers. The limo stopped and Mac, Alex and Rossi were there to open the doors for the family. Philip stepped out first and reached his hand in for Emma. As he did, he noticed how nervous she was, and held her hand very tightly to him.

"Mrs. Vega," and her husband helped her out of the car and into the proceedings. Now was the time for confetti and rice and they seemed to be drowned in it.

The sun shone, enhancing the photos of the couple taken at the pool and in front of the house making for a perfect backdrop. All the doors to the residence sat open, guests seemed to be everywhere and Emma hadn't a clue who most of them were.

Marc and Patrick watched from the sidelines, united today by their fathers wedding, and joined by Donna and Alexandria Alehandro, a young lady who had come to terms with Patrick's decision.

Patrick watched carefully the respect the other bosses had for his father and his new bride. One after one they paid their tribute to the bridal couple, handing her small envelopes of money and kissing her on the cheek as the Don's wife. He also thought how today Emma looked particularly young next to his father, a father who even Patrick had to admit was an exceedingly attractive man on any given day and today he had excelled himself.

As always Mac and Alex were behind the pair and security was the highest that Patrick had ever seen it as the house. Music played in the background and both champagne and wine flowed showing Philip had spared no expense for this wedding.

Philip whispered to Emma. "How are you feeling, baby? I keep forgetting you are pregnant… me of all people," and his eyes shined at her. "Are you hungry? Let's get something to eat? Maybe you should sit a while before the dancing…" and he clicked his fingers and they were whisked inside the house.

It was there the dining room greeted her. It was resplendent with flowers, balloons, and the table was covered in food. Emma gasped. No wonder she hadn't been allowed into the rooms earlier, and she could hardly take in everything around her. "Is the whole house like this Philip? The lounge…" and she stopped as she saw the twinkle in his eye.

"What did you do, Philip?"

"You wait till later, baby… just you wait… but first you eat… and then we dance…"

"You dance? Really?"

"Yeah, baby. I do… forgot to tell you that… at these kind of weddings we dance… but we dance on full stomachs…" and he took a plate from the server and filled it full of Emma's kind of food, food he thought she should eat. They retired just temporarily to the lounge where the twins came to join them, as did Mac and Alex, who closed the doors to anyone else while the bride and groom ate.

"Emma, before we go back out there… you look so beautiful, baby," and he leaned a little closer to her, "and I love you so much…

don't ever forget that!" and he kissed her, a long lingering kiss that promised so much for later. "Ready, Emma…"

She whispered in his ear.

"Sure, you can… but not upstairs, baby…" and Philip called Mac.

"Mrs. Vega," and Mac led her to the downstairs bathroom and waited outside the door for her.

Philip sat alone, except for Alex and the twins who were running round the table trying to pop balloons. "Kids… if you want to play, go outside… not in here. Alex take them to Patrick…"

"Sir, I can't leave you on your own…" Alex looked staggered that his boss would suggest this.

"I'll be fine. Rossi is right outside the door with Pauli. Send them in on your way out." Conversation ended, and Philip continued to eat.

"Yes, boss," and Alex grabbed a twin in each hand.

Philip sat playing with the matching wedding band on his finger… bands of very expensive gold with both sets of initials engraved in them. As he waited, the cell in his pocket vibrated. He took the call recognizing the number.

"Yes, this is Philip Vega." He listened to the voice on the end of the line. "This fast? You rushed it through before the holiday… thank you. And thank you for the news." Philip closed the cell.

And then Emma was back, just as Rossi and Pauli came through the patio doors.

"Good… you are all here together. Emma, sit for one moment, then we will go outside and dance, and take more photographs…" and Philip changed his mind. He couldn't ruin the wedding. This wasn't the time to tell anyone the news.

"Everything alright, Sir," asked Pauli. He knew that kind of look on his boss's face.

Philip replied way too fast and directly to Pauli. "Fine. Why wouldn't it be?" Then he turned to his wife. "Emma, are you back and ready to dance?"

Philip's reply was stilted and Emma knew that something was wrong. "Are you asking me to dance, Mr. Vega?"

Philip stood up to her. "Yes, ma'am, I am… will you do me the honor of dancing with me on the patio?" and he bowed to her.

"Indeed, Sir. I will," and she allowed herself to be whisked outside amongst the cheers of the guests. Emma could see Alexandria and Patrick talking with Marc and Donna. And then it struck her. Was there time for the results to come back? Something had clouded Philip's afternoon. He was hiding it well, but she was now beginning to understand him and his moods.

Philip held her tightly to him and as he did 'How deep is your love' started to play over the PA system…

"Ladies and gentleman… I give you Mr. and Mrs. Philip Vega… Don Andrea and Emma Vega."

Philip swirled her round and held her even closer. "Listen to the words, baby… might have been written for you," his arms round her waist and back, while Emma slid her arms up and around his neck. "Gotta make a speech, Emma… don't be shocked when I do."

"Why would I be shocked, Philip," and she thought maybe she knew. "Whatever it is, Philip, I am right behind you."

"I know that, baby… one of the reasons I married you, another one is inside of you, and the most important one is that I love you…" and he leaned forward, not caring where he was, and kissed her very passionately.

The music stopped and the guests fell silent at Pauli's request. Philip held her hand and then he started to speak.

"Firstly, thank you all for attending my wedding to this lovely young lady here… Emma is the light of my life, as I am sure you can all see. And my wife and I thank you for the lavish gifts that have been bestowed on us tonight." He glanced towards the house as the lights came on and showed his home and patio to perfection. The caterers had done a magnificent job. Flowers, balloons, and lanterns decorated the whole place only surpassed by the elegance of the attire the family wore and the obvious wealth the Vega's had. "Secondly, as some of you know, and now everyone will, Emma is four months pregnant with our baby girl…" This was received with mostly rounds of applause from the gentlemen. "Thank you, and thank you all for coming. My family thanks you, especially," and Philip's hand tightened round Emma's, "my son's thank you, all of them…" he couldn't say it, not now. "Now eat, drink and dance… in our home."

Now Emma knew what the secret was. He had received news on Marc's status and he didn't want to tell them right now. She looked at him, resplendent in his manhood, Philip Vega, movie star, and more importantly, family head.

He could feel her eyes on him. "Anything wrong, honey?"

"Nothing, Philip. I was just thinking how lucky I am..." and she was interrupted.

"Sir, may I steal your wife for a dance with me?" and Patrick put his hand out to her.

Philip slackened his grip on Emma. "You may, as long as you don't steal my wife..." and Philip didn't smile. He let go of her hand and offered it to Patrick.

Patrick took her very gently in his arms, and held her close, but not too close, knowing that his father was watching every move he made. "So, what's it like being Mrs. Vega, *mom...*"

"Patrick, I don't think I can ever be your mother..." and she laughed at the idea.

'*You have that right*,' thought Patrick. '*My wife, maybe*,' and he pushed that thought away from his mind. She was married to his father and that's how it was. Patrick felt ashamed of himself for even thinking like that. His father was making him heir and one day all this would be his, and he loved his father more than his own life. And this had to stop, right now, this infatuation for Emma. "Emma, is my father alright?" He felt her stiffen in his arms.

"Of course... why would you think otherwise?" and she knew that Patrick had seen it also. She changed the subject. "Are you bringing Alexandria to Denver with you?"

"No. She is flying back home with her mother. I think it's best that way. Seems I am more like my father than I thought..." and Patrick stopped because he was getting in too deep, and also the music had stopped.

Philip was watching on the sidelines, now surrounded by other bosses... some for business and some for pleasure. Now they smoked Cuban cigars, and he received the congratulations with great delight, but his eyes never left his wife.

Darkness fell quickly over Los Angeles and the house sat resplendent, ablaze with the lanterns and lights from inside the building.

Music filled the air and the dancing carried on late into the night.

Finally Emma realized how tired she was and rested against the lounge doors. Mac stood with her.

"Mr. Vega is very proud of you, Emma. You do know that, right?"

"Yes, Mac... I do, and I of him... he is everything I want in a man..." and she stopped, blushing and now very tired.

"You want him over here, Emma?" Mac asked her, a little concerned that she had been standing way too long.

"Would he mind?" she asked quietly shifting from one foot to another on her very high heels.

"Of course not. I think he needs an excuse to leave them all and what better excuse than his new wife!" and he called to Alex to go tell Mr. Vega she needed him.

"You okay, baby... I'm sorry, they wouldn't let me get away... you want to say goodnight to them and we can go and get rest... well, we can go to the suite anyway..."

Emma glared at him and then laughed. "Yeah, I'm tired, Philip. Need to lie down," and she whispered in his ear.

"Really?" and he bent down as if to pull up her dress.

"Not here, Philip!" and she started to run from him.

He caught her, and laughing, turned towards the audience of guests, and picked her up in his arms. "Ladies and gentleman, my wife has a present for me... **upstairs**! So I bid you all goodnight and again... thank you." And with that he carried Emma into the house and up the stairs... alone!

Chapter 40

Philip pushed the door open with his foot and held his wife in the doorway. Emma wasn't prepared for the bedroom. It was resplendent. Gone were the black sheets. In place were pure white silk ones, countless pillows, white roses everywhere, and as she looked harder at the bed there sat a big white fluffy teddy bear. Toby still sat on the pillow in his usual place but the new bear accompanied him. Next to it was a silk nightdress and a large card, one that proclaimed Philip's love for her. That one could not be missed. Champagne glasses at the end of the bed and a giant bottle of the bubbly stuff just for Emma.

She turned her head and looked back at Philip's face, and clung to him. "This is too much, Philip... today is too much... I feel like I've died and gone to heaven..."

"Don't say that, Emma... ever..." and the harsh look of the man was there for a second and then it was gone. He slid her to the ground. "You need some help getting out of that dress..." and his fingers started to undo the buttons one by one, with him never taking his eyes off her.

Emma woke at dawn as the first rays of the rest of her life shone across the bed. She turned over to look at her husband. He lay on his back, his chest rising and falling in the cool air. She snuggled into him and, even in sleep, his arms automatically encircled her. Emma glanced at the bedside table and there, as always, sat Philip's gun. She shuddered. She had a very strange feeling that one day she would look at that gun in a very different light.

Philip sensed there was something wrong and whispered to her. "It's okay, baby... you are safe... whenever you are with me, you are safe," and he kissed her very gently.

It was then the main line phone rang.

Philip let go of her and answered the call. "Yeah, okay. Get the boys ready. Our cases are just inside our suite. Have Mac get them. Emma and I will be ready in about a half hour. Is the jet fuelled? Okay. Have them put some fresh fruit and bagels or something on the plane. We'll be outside at nine a.m. What's the weather like in Denver? Snowing? Great!" and he hung up the line. "Come on then, Mrs. Vega. We have to get up and dress so we can take you to make snow angels…" and he pulled her up on the bed and carried her into the shower.

"You said nine a.m., Sir…" stated his son.

"Yeah, sorry," Philip said sarcastically. "We got a little side-tracked…" and Philip looked back towards the front door.

Emma emerged from inside the house as if on cue. Patrick had never seen her look so beautiful. She glowed and was dressed in the same color jeans and leather jacket as his father. Her hair was pulled into a ponytail and anyone only half awake could see she was unbelievably happy. She slung her purse over her shoulder and seemingly bounced along the ground till she reached Philip. He slid his arm round her and she round him… and the two became one.

"You ready, baby… fancy distracting me like that… and you a married woman…" and Philip kissed her forehead and ushered into the waiting car.

The plane left from Philip's friend's landing strip outside Los Angeles and didn't take but a couple of hours to get to another friend's airfield outside Denver. It was indeed snowing… and very hard. Emma was thrilled and so were the twins, even if the landing wasn't the best.

Philip allowed Marc and Donna to come with them and still he held the secret from them all. It was Christmas and also the day after his wedding. There was a time to bring this up and this was not it. It was not a long drive from the airfield and, as the house loomed into sight, Emma could see it was an enormous log home with smoke pouring out of the chimney. Giant fir trees surrounded the buildings along with white picket fences that enclosed horse property. On a strip near the house sat a helicopter ready and waiting, in case of emergency. By the time they reached the door the snow was falling hard. They had flown in just in time. Another few hours and the trip would not have happened.

Everyone was ushered inside the large oak doors and the car stayed parked under the eaves of the house. Luggage in the rooms, Philip took Emma to show her their suite, but not before he introduced her to his permanent staff of a housekeeper, two maids and two security men.

Upstairs in the amazing bedroom, a large fire sat ablaze in the grate, with logs in copper bins. Boxes of Swiss chocolates lay on the table near the bed and a basket of fruit and cheeses sat next to them. Fresh white roses adorned the room and the bed was covered with a huge white comforter and white pillows. Philip led her into the bathroom where the giant Jacuzzi took central stage and pine paneling complemented the room.

"That's for later, baby," and he glanced at his watch. "We'll just go down and have dinner and then come right back, jump in the Jacuzzi and stay up here till Christmas.... tomorrow anyway, and then Christmas Eve we put up the tree and decorate it… been a custom for years with this family and now you will be part of it…" He said it with such pride. "Come on, baby, as I, for one, am hungry. We haven't eaten properly since yesterday… and you, you have one extra to feed… you sure you're pregnant? You can't even tell…" and he looked mockingly at her.

"You should know, Philip. You should know! It's all your fault…" and she fell back on the bed and threw a large pillow at him.

She was too tempting for Philip…

Everyone had made it to the house. The twins, Patrick, Marc and Donna, Mac, Alex, Pauli, Mikey and Rossi. Only Anthony had stayed behind with the staff to lock up the house for the winter.

Finally Emma and Philip made it downstairs. This time he didn't feel the need to make excuses. In the lounge the fire blazed relentlessly and Emma wandered around the great room looking at the family photos on the mantel. The twins took great pleasure in pointing themselves out in every photo to their new mother and dragged her by the hand to inspect anything they could find that pertained to them.

The housekeeper, a jolly rounded person, brought them all hot chocolate and fresh baked scones to keep stomachs from grumbling till dinner.

Patrick joined in the fun, feeling a certain joy at being there, leaving Marc to sit at the back of the room with an air of gloom hanging round him fearing this was his last Christmas with this family. He was correct… it would be. He was not Philip's son.

Chapter 41

Christmas Eve was upon them and putting up the tree. The twins were so excited they did not eat till the tree was in place. Emma had never seen a fir like this one, cut from Vega stock and stored outside till now. It had taken all the Vega men to shake the snow from it and drag it inside, even though it had had shelter from the eaves of the snow-laden roof. Now it stood the only place it could, at the bottom of the stairs, one place that could house its ten foot height.

She was standing staring at it when Philip approached her from behind, sliding his arms round her shoulders. "Penny for them, Mrs. Vega?"

"I was just thinking how different this Christmas is to the last one. I mean there was no you, just an unhappy life. Certainly no Christmas tree or presents…" and she stopped mainly because she knew she was about to cry.

Philip kissed her hair and let his hands slide down onto her stomach. "Nor the little girl that we made together. Emma, I am so happy it's a little girl… so happy…"

The twins ran from the lounge following their father and Mac had stopped them, letting Philip have some very personal time with his wife. Patrick also stopped in his tracks. How he envied his father right then. Mac saw it.

Alex came through the doors with a giant box of ornaments.

"That's a big box of stuff, Alex…" Patrick commented, as he walked by with them. "You need some help putting them on the tree?"

"Sure could… and the twins are going to help. What about you, Emma?" asked Alex.

"Go ahead, baby… just watch she doesn't do any lifting and climbing…" added her husband.

"Philip, stop fussing… I'm pregnant, not disabled…" and she laughed at him. She turned in his arms and reached up to kiss him.

He let her go and nodded his head at Mac implying he needed him. They left by the side door into the garage.

An hour later, and a tree decorated to the enth degree, the whole gang stood back to admire their work. Alex obtained a ladder and put the brightest star on the top of the tree. Gold lights were everywhere and very expensive ornaments hung from any branch that happened to be sticking its fingers out. It looked phenomenal and the twins could hardly wait to show their father. Alex made a call to Mac to let him know that the kids and Emma were impatient to view their handiwork, knowing that would get him back. He was right.

Philip was through the door in less than five minutes, along with Mac and Pauli in tow. Emma didn't seem to notice who was with Philip. Patrick did and he had a feeling he knew why. He hadn't seen Marc and Donna very much since they arrived in Denver, and knew his father was hiding something.

"So, who wants the lights on then?" and Philip covered his ears while the twins yelled at him. "Emma does? Okay, if my wife does, that's different…" and he went to flip the switch and stopped, turned to Emma, and handed her the control for the tree "You do it… this is the first Christmas with us and the first as my wife… When I turn the main lights off hit the button."

The look on her face told everyone in the room how happy she was to be asked, and as the room went dark, she flipped the switch… and a thousand lights glowed on the tree.

Philip slid up behind her. "Merry Christmas, baby… Merry Christmas. It's tradition with the family to give one present on Christmas Eve from the head of the family… so that being me…" and he addressed the kids, Patrick and Emma. There was no sign of Marc and Donna. "Mac, ask them to join us… please."

Mac knew who the 'them' referred to and he left the room to find them.

"Okay guys. Emma doesn't know what to do. Who will show her?" and Philip sat himself on the large brown patchwork couch that had been there since he was a kid. He put his feet on the matching stool showing very expensive snakeskin boots under his black jeans which had a slight trace of white on them.

Emma had never seen Philip sit like this before. She looked closer and watched the white rim disappear. It was snow, yet he told her they couldn't go outside. She thought that strange. As she was thinking about this and following the kid's instructions, Marc and Donna appeared.

"Hi, guys… didn't you remember we do the tree thing on Christmas Eve? Then the family present and then dinner waits…" Philip sat upright in the chair. He had been joking and now was instantly serious. "And it's also rude on Emma's first Christmas with us not to be in the room!" and Philip smacked his hands on the arms of the chair in disgust.

"I am sorry, Sir… we were talking with…" and he went to say his mother, "with Sally…" and Marc sat down opposite his father right next to the door.

"Really! What did she have to say?" he reached for a Cuban cigar. Mac was there with a light.

"She congratulated you on your wedding and she asked when the twins would be going home…" Marc said hesitantly, his eyes darting between Philip and Patrick.

"Next time you talk to her, say thank you… and they are not…" and Philip glanced at the twins who looked like they were about to burst into tears at the thought of going back to Florida. "You're not going back, guys, neither is Patrick… Let's do the present thing so we can all eat." He had changed the subject nicely.

Now Patrick was sure his father was unhappy and trying hard not to let it ruin the holiday.

"Orry and Daniel… on the first floor landing… Patrick…" and he handed him a small box… "Emma…" and he gave her the same kind of box… wrapped in red ribbon… and the last gift was for Marc and Donna.

The twins disappeared up the stairs and came back down screaming with delight at two brand new watches similar to their father's.

Patrick opened his and there sat a gold Rolex exactly like Philip's. He shook his father's hand. Then it was Emma's turn.

She pulled the ribbon from the box, opened it and there was a set of car keys. Her eyes were wide. "I get to drive one of your cars? Really?"

"No, baby… you get your own! But you can't see it till tomorrow. It's only a little car and you only drive it here in Colorado and while you are pregnant only with me or Mac with you. Never on your own…"

"I can't see it now?" She was shaking. "Philip? Please?"

"No, but I can tell you it's black and it has your own tags on it…"

"Really??? Really??? Oh, my god…" She hugged him till she realized everyone was watching. "I've never had a car… ever…" and she began to cry. Her life had changed so much in six months.

Philip stood up and held her to him; his face nestled in her hair. She wasn't so tough after all. He glanced up at the tree. It was majestic like he was, and on the top sat the star. Maybe it would have been more appropriate to put an angel, and as he looked down the tree and back to Emma, he caught sight of the look on his son's face… and then he knew.

Chapter 42

Dinner came and went with much hilarity and amounts of food fit for kings. Philip almost gave in a couple of times to his wife, especially when she ran her toes up inside his jeans leg as they sat at the table. Still he said no to the car, but yes to an early night and alone time with her…

Christmas day came in at six with two very eager young men banging on their father's door and then, without waiting for his voice, came bursting into the room. "Emma, mom, Emma… Santa has been…"

Philip rose up from under the covers in a less than happy mood. "Out! Now! You know you never come into my bedroom…"

The twins stopped dead in their tracks and backed out of the room.

"It's Christmas, Philip. They are just excitable boys… anyway what did Santa leave me…" and she pulled herself from his arms and jumped out of bed, running to the window. All she could see was snow piled on the ledge. "Philip, come on… I want to see what Santa left me…" and she was attempting to get him out of bed.

He slid on jeans and boots, and a thick sweater as he ran out of the door behind her. She had grabbed her sweater dress and pulled it on.

"Emma," he yelled, seeing her backside in full swing. "Underwear!" and he threw her some sweat pants.

She stopped long enough to pull them on and then ran barefoot, two at a time, down the stairs to the lobby. Philip could not keep up with her and yelled to Mac to stop her till he got there.

"You gotta wait for the boss, Emma… don't spoil the surprise…" and Mac picked her up like she weighed nothing and held her there till Philip arrived. "Emma…"

She slid to the floor and stood there waiting for her husband, who was right down beside her, carrying a pair of boots.

"Okay, now we can go… into the garage. All of us…" and Philip grabbed her hand and in the other one he held the car keys.

As he opened the side door, they were met with glowing lights, the twins, and all the security. There in front of her, with a giant red bow on top of it, sat a Mercedes and the tags read EV1.

Emma stared at it not quite knowing what to say. He said a 'little' car and this wasn't a little car. It was a Mercedes, jet black with a black interior, and tinted windows.

He was watching her face. "You like it?"

"Like it??? Are you joking… it's wonderful, Philip… my god… I am shocked," and she tried the door. It opened and she climbed in and sat behind the steering wheel.

Philip realized they would need to get the seat adjusted for her as she could hardly see over the top of the dashboard, and he tried very hard not to laugh at her. At least she couldn't drive it with three feet of snow outside. He watched as she ran her hand along the side of the black leather. He could also see her shivering in the cold. Sweatpants and a woolen dress were not the best things to be out of the house in this weather.

"Okay, baby… let's go back inside the house. Too cold for you out here," and he helped her out of the car, much against her will, as he ushered her back into the warmth of the house, dropping the boots by the door.

It was now way past seven and everyone in the house was awake, even if a couple of them were still bleary-eyed.

"You missed the surprise, Patrick. Emma was delighted…" and Philip thought that Patrick looked like he used to look and wondered if he was drinking.

"Patrick, anything you want to tell me?" mussed Philip, stuffing Emma's keys in his pocket as he spoke.

His son froze. Had Mac told his father? "Yeah… there is," and he just happened to look at Mac, who was moving his head side to side.

"This is a great Christmas… and maybe I had too much to drink yesterday. Think I am picking up your bad habits, Dad," and he smiled with the same sultry looks as his father.

"That's what I thought. Don't drink like I did, Patrick. It's not good. By the time I was your age I was married and had a son…" and Philip stopped because that wasn't quite true. "I'm not the best one to give you advice on drinking or women."

Then they both glanced at Emma. She was the reason there was no more women.

They were saved by the bell from saying anymore as the housekeeper called them all to breakfast, and everyone scrambled into the dining room to enjoy the first meal of Christmas day… ham, scrambled eggs, fresh bread, juice. Emma had eggs and pushed them round the plate. Philip whispered in her ear and she ate them down like a refugee.

"Such power, Dad… How did you do that?" asked Patrick, wolfing down ham.

"Trade secret, son. Worked though. Now she gets more presents… and so do I!" and he winked at his son, and he also watched Patrick's face. Philip finished his meal and nodded to Mac, and saw the look that passed between Patrick and Mac.

"Just going for a cigarette, baby… be right back…" and Philip was gone and he went out the side door with Mac in tow.

He waited till they were in the garage. "How long?" and Philip pushed his hands deep into his pockets, and looked his bodyguard straight in the eyes..

"Sir…" asked his bodyguard, knowing exactly what his boss meant.

"How long has Patrick been in love with Emma?" Philip was straight to the point. "Did I send the wrong man away?" He didn't say son and waited for the answer.

"Since you brought her to the house. He asked me not to tell you. He gave me his word that he would never tell you and especially never tell Emma… and I believe him. He only wants her to be happy and he knows she is with you. He will never do anything against you. He idolizes you, Mr. Vega." Wasn't that the truth.

There was silence and Philip knew Mac was right. "I know he does, and I think that's the problem. Did you know he's drinking?"

"I wondered, boss. He's taken right after…" Mac stopped, very abruptly.

"After me? Yeah, he has. Mac… if anything ever happens to me, tell Patrick to look after Emma. I know she would be safe…"

"Safe, boss, but devastated… she only lives for you." Mac couldn't imagine Emma without Philip.

"I know that, too. Quite heavy shoulders I have, Mac… Gonna step outside a minute in the snow. Don't let anyone else out, okay?"

"Right, Mr. Vega… Sir?"

"Yeah," and Philip stopped, turning slightly to look at Mac.

"What are you going to do about Marc?"

"Only thing I can. Wait till after the holiday and send him and Donna to live with Sally. He's not a Vega and never will be…" and Philip opened the garage door and stepped into the falling snow.

Patrick could just see his father through windows piled high with snow. Had Mac told him… no… had his father guessed… probably. Would he be angry… he doubted it. Did he have a lot on his mind… absolutely. Patrick made a decision. He would go back to the Vineyards and live there. Do the work his father had asked him to. Was it close to alcohol, of course… but for now he could control it. And the women? There he could have a different one every night or he could go back to Alexandria… that wasn't fair to use her. One every night would do… just like his father had.

Chapter 43

In bed that night, Philip lay on his back and fingered the gold chain that Emma had given him for Christmas. It hung tightly round his neck and sat there resplendent, the links shining in the lamplight. He glanced across the room at the gifts and their wrappings piled in the corner. Clothes, books, stuffed bears, jewelry, wine… and Philip thought about the day. When he found out about Patrick, he wasn't angry, in fact he was glad. If anything happened to him he knew that Patrick would be there for her. His mind switched to Marc, a twenty-five year old man who was not his son. He couldn't blame him. He didn't know he wasn't a Vega, but Sally must have known who the father was, and when he returned to Florida, it would be for good. It would be a wrench for both him and Marc but necessary. He had handed Marc an envelope, with a check in it for Christmas, a very big check of 50,000 dollars. If that wasn't a clue to Marc, nothing was, but Philip had not told him yet.

"Baby, you okay in there?" Philip turned on his side and called to Emma in the bathroom.

Emma knew Philip's mood wasn't good, so she picked out one of the cute pieces of lingerie he had bought her and was now pulling it on. She didn't know how long it would stay on but he would appreciate the gesture. She opened the bathroom door and Philip looked up. His eyes started at the bottom and worked their way up. Emma stood there, painting her lips with her finger, and then letting her finger slip into her parted lips. She watched Philip's smoldering eyes take in everything about her and she could feel the sexual tension between them.

He flipped the cover back on her side of the bed and she could see his still tanned naked body ready and waiting for her. Now she had to change his mood and that she would gladly do. Slipping in beside him, she leaned over him, her hair hanging on his chest and she kissed him over and over until suddenly he turned her over in one go, his need becoming very urgent, almost desperate to take what was his. This time she cried out and Philip held his hand gently over her mouth, while his eyes questioned her.

"I will always love you, Emma… I will never leave you, come what may… not even in death…" He didn't know why he said it. He just did.

She looked into his troubled face. "What's wrong, Philip? Something is worrying you… I'm not going anywhere, not ever. Where you are, I am… for life. You are my everything, Philip…"

"And you are my angel…" and once more they sealed the bond between them.

But still she knew something was wrong. She knew that Marc was not his son. Philip hadn't told her, she just knew. She also figured that he would let him go, and that's just what happened. Philip couldn't keep it till New Year.

It stopped snowing briefly and Philip decided that this was the day Marc and Donna should go. He didn't want Patrick to go yet. Patrick had not seen a change toward him from his father, none at all, but he had noticed Philip was much more distant towards Marc, especially when he caught him still looking at Emma. Patrick knew his father would not tolerate that.

Philip made sure that Emma, the twins and Alex were outside playing at being snow angels and he called a meeting, something he never did on a vacation, demonstrating the gravity of the situation.

Seated in the lounge, Philip sat on the most prominent chair he could find. Alongside of him stood Mac and on the other side of him… Pauli. Now Patrick knew it was serious, and more to the point so did Marc. When Patrick and Marc were seated, both Mikey and Rossi positioned themselves by the door.

"I am sorry to do this today but in two days we go into another year, and I need life to be back to normal for all of us." He stopped and

looked at the man he had called son for twenty-five years. "Marc…
you are not my son. It's not your fault that you are not, and you have
always been a good son to me… but still you are not a Vega. You
will return to Florida today. Seats have been reserved for you and
Donna on the last flight of the day from Denver. Pauli and Rossi will
drive you to the airport. First class tickets are waiting for you both
and I gave you money for Christmas… and here is another check for
100,000 dollars, to either find a place to live or whatever you want.
You can keep everything you have, the cars, clothes, anything you
have in Florida, except your inheritance. That will end first of the year.
You never wanted to be in my position and that honor still goes to
Patrick." Philip was choked just slightly. "I will miss you and I would
like to hear from you now and then, but not from Sally. You should
go and pack and anything else we will send on to you. Tell Donna, I
forgive her…" Philip stood and put his hand out to Marc.

Marc stared at him. "Do you really think I am going to shake
your hand? You bastard… I was a good son… and now you are just
turning me out…"

"Stop right there!" and Philip raised his voice. "I am not the bastard… you are! And secondly, I don't want a man in my house letch-
ing after my wife! First your girlfriend makes a play for me, and then
you start looking at Emma like you want to get her into bed…" Philip
was now yelling at Marc.

"So what… **Mr. Vega!** Donna told me ages ago, said it was your
fault, and my mother told me I wasn't your son months back…" he
lied. "Your *real son* here is in love with her, too… or don't you know
that? Everyone else knows it, except Emma, and that's because she
can't take her eyes off you!"

Patrick didn't wait. He turned and hit Marc as hard as he could
on the jaw, and Marc went sprawling back onto the couch. If Patrick
hadn't done it, Philip would have.

"Now get out, Marc! Get Donna and your things and leave… and
don't ever let me see you again!" Philip turned back to his seat, sat
down and waited for Marc to leave, his hands gripping the side of the
chair. He was furious and nodded to Pauli to take over… and it was
done. Marc was escorted from the room.

Patrick shook his fist. It hurt and he turned to his father. He could see the look on both Mac's and Mikey's faces. "I…"

"Don't say one fucking word, Patrick. I know… that's all that counts. You betrayed yourself, no one else did. Promise me one thing. If anything happens to me, you will look after her for me."

"You have my word, Sir, and you also have my word I will never touch her for any reason, now or in the future. I would die before I would betray you…"

"I know that, Patrick… I know," and he put his hand out to his son who bent down and kissed his father's ring.

And now Emma knew. She had come into the hallway, feeling just a little cold and was looking for anyone… and couldn't find a soul… she hadn't meant to listen, but when Philip raised his voice, everyone heard. She didn't love Patrick. He was like a little brother to her and she never would love him. Her heart belonged to Philip and she tried to slip away into the kitchen before anyone knew she had been there. But as she moved she knocked the picture on the wall next to the door. She froze. They had to have heard her.

The door opened and Mac stepped out. "May we help you, Mrs. Vega?" He was all business. Family business.

"No. I was on my way to the kitchen. Needed something to drink…" she replied in her mellowing English accent.

Philip's voice echoed from inside the room. "Let her in, Mac… I am sure she heard most of it…"

"No, I saw Marc and Donna on the stairs with Pauli…" and she walked round the corner into the room, "Are they leaving?" She knew full well they were, but she didn't want to let on she had heard the rest of the conversation. She looked straight at her husband and for the first time she lied to Philip. The worst part was, he knew it and she knew that he knew. But some things were left better unsaid.

Chapter 44

New Year's Eve crept around. Now Emma was the only female in the family and Philip regretted that. A brand new year and a brand new life. Emma sat on the couch watching the flames in the grate. A roaring fire lit the room and she sat thinking about the baby inside her. She wanted a glass of wine. She doubted Philip would let her have one. Champagne yes, wine no. She felt his hands on her shoulders and immediately she reached up to touch them.

"You feeling alright there, baby?" and he kissed the top of her head. "Emma, I want to apologize for the last few days. It could have gone better..."

"Philip... come and sit by me, would you? Just hold me..." She looked up at him, almost pleading.

"Nothing wrong with you or the baby is there?" and he slid round beside her and pulled her to him enveloping her in his arms.

"No, Philip... nothing. I was just thinking..." and she almost said what she was thinking. Would Marc try to get back at Philip? "Was just about the baby and wondering if we were going to stay here or go back to Los Angeles for her birth."

"What do you want, Emma?" he questioned her, also watching the flames in the grate, like the Phoenix would rise up.

"Los Angeles... because that's where I first met her father..." and she smiled a rich smile at him that she knew he could not resist.

"L.A it is, baby. Would you like a glass of champagne, Emma? It's almost midnight. Patrick is bringing the twins down to wish you a happy new year."

"I'd love that, Philip, and then maybe you might let me seduce you?" and in the firelight she flashed her eyes at him, ones that she now used very well.

In January the snows melted just a little and they took that chance to leave Denver and fly back to LA. She was five months gone now, and at last her baby bump was there. Philip wanted to show his new wife off to his friends, which he did with much frequency on their return. Patrick left for the Vineyards, and the twins took up permanent residence with Philip. Life settled down for the Vega's. The twins turned nine; Philip turned forty-six and Emma became a year older, too.

Life continued on an even keel and Philip acquired another casino to his list of already Vega controlled establishments. Patrick visited once in a while to Los Angeles. Each time he had a different girlfriend, and each time they resembled Emma.

Lying on the bed one night, Emma was talking to Toby. Telling him how her life had changed and of all the good things in her world, especially Philip, when suddenly she had contractions. Shrieking out loud, Philip heard his wife, and ran upstairs to their suite to find Emma sitting on the side of the bed almost doubled over.

"Emma… is it time?" he rushed to her.

"I think…" she gasped, "it's your daughter…" and another contraction hit her.

"Mac…" yelled Philip, "get the car… we gotta get her to the hospital!"

"Philip…" shouted Emma, "I don't think there is time…" and she was wide-eyed.

"Breathe, baby, like they taught us. Come on, you can do it… one, two… breathe."

They made it to the hospital like Philip knew they would. Emma gave birth to Philipa Emma Vega late evening on May third, a bouncing bundle of a child with very dark hair and deep brown eyes, but with Emma's cute nose and mouth. There was no doubt she was a Vega, all seven pounds of her.

Emma and baby Philipa returned to the house three days later. Philip had the limo bring them home in grand style with himself and three security guards. Emma looked tired but very happy, and Philip was more than ecstatic. He celebrated the night before her return with all the men including his son. Three bottles of champagne and three of red wine went down in a couple of hours. Philip didn't remember getting to bed; fact was he didn't remember much till nine a.m. the next morning and his son banging on the suite door. It wasn't the first time Mac had put his boss to bed and he doubted it would be the last.

Philip hired a nanny, an older lady with years of experience. Emma didn't want a nanny but she didn't get the luxury of a choice. Philip became fiercely protective of his family and no expense for security was spared, even installing more security cameras and baby monitors.

The day of the christening saw them back at the same church where they were married. This time there was no rehearsal. The limo took them to the church, dropped them off and parked with security still in the car. Philip was very aware that this would be a good place for any vengeful acts to take place. He knew Marc had remained in Florida, but he also knew that he was very unhappy at the treatment that the Vega family had handed out. He had started searching for his real father and unbeknown to Marc, so had Philip, who now had a good handle of who it was.

But today was family day. Patrick and Mac were godparents, both men devoted to Emma and the family. Emma thought that Patrick looked more like Philip today than ever. Both dressed again by Armani and in dark grey suits, and both stunning men. The twins also wore suits and she couldn't help notice how they seemed to be growing. Emma wore a very lightweight grey form-fitting dress, and she had managed to get most of her figure back already, much to her husband's delight. She once more wore dark grey high heels, and her hair was neatly plaited on the top of her head. To look at Emma one would hardly know she had had a child. She had herself back in shape very fast, both for herself and for Philip, looking good for his image, and mindful that he would only be patient with her in bed for so long.

Philip held his daughter in his arms, his hands protecting her head… hands that could hold this child could also kill … as Emma very well knew.

"Don Andrea, may I have your child please?" asked Father O'Reilly, an older priest who had known the Vega's for years.

"I baptize this child Philipa Emma Vega, daughter of Philip Andrea and Emma Vega. Who is the godfather of this child?" and the good Father made the sign of the cross on baby Philipa's head. She gurgled and her brown eyes stared at him.

"I am," replied Patrick, the first son.

"Welcome, Mr. Vega," and Father O'Reilly dipped his head just slightly to Philip's son.

"And I am the other," added the blonde haired, blue-eyed Mac Hunter.

"Sir," answered the Father.

With the sign of the cross blazoned on the little child's head, Father O'Reilly proceeded. "In the name of the Father, and of the Son, and of the Holy Sprit, I give you Philipa Vega…"

Emma could hear him and she could see her's and Philip's child. She felt Philip slide his arm around her shoulders and pull her gently to him. She also realized that Orry was pulling just slightly on her arm, as nine years olds do. Then baby Philipa was back in her arms, cradled there in her long flowing traditional christening dress of white with tiny pearl beads hanging from it.

Shortly after that they left for the house, where family and friends had gathered, a party in full swing there to celebrate the birth of Philip's new family. He held the baby in his arms and showed her off to his friends, Emma by his side.

"Emma, take our child, and please excuse me for a short time. There is some business I have to attend to…"

"Now?" she asked him.

"Yes, Emma. I will join you later…" and his look was serious.

Philip, Patrick, Mikey and Pauli, along with two men Emma had never seen before, disappeared into the library. Emma stood silhouetted in the doorway, Philipa in her arms, watching them kiss the Don's ring and the door closed in front of her. She knew then she would never be included in the Don's private world, only in Philip Vega's personal bed.

Chapter 45

Summer passed quickly, and Emma enjoyed the time with the children. Philip seemed to be busier than ever in the daytime, but was always there for dinner and in his and Emma's bed every night. She never doubted his fidelity, and she knew he loved her more than ever, but she knew something was amiss.

Patrick came down to visit in late October, this time on his own. No women. Philip had asked him to come and this time Emma was to be included in the meeting. A first. It rained that day, not too much, but enough to keep the children in the house. They were restless as was most of the household waiting to be summoned to the library. A meeting that wasn't to take place till nearly four.

Patrick had had breakfast with Emma in the baby's room. He had played with his step-sister and she had responded well to him. Patrick was never sure if Emma had heard everything that day Marc left or not and he really hoped she hadn't. They had finished breakfast and 'Pip', as her father called her, was fast asleep, when Emma ran into the baby's bathroom and promptly threw up.

Patrick waited a couple of minutes and then went to the door. "Does my father know you are pregnant again?" 'Stupid question,' he thought. 'It's his child.'

"No. He has enough on his mind. I was planning on telling him tonight until he called this meeting. Any idea what it's about?" and she straightened her bright blue T shirt up a little.

"How far are you?" Today Patrick thought she looked stunning. Just the plain shirt and tight fitting jeans, and if his father couldn't see she was pregnant, he was a fool and that was something his father was not.

231

"Eight weeks. I wasn't totally sure till two days ago, and don't change the subject! Do you know?" She switched the light off in the bathroom and moved back to her baby.

"I have an idea. Only two reasons he would include you, Emma. Either he is sick and going to hand the Vega dynasty to me, which I know is not the case… or it's my mother and Marc." That was enough for her to know and he moved away from the bathroom.

"Sally and Marc… why would that be…" She didn't understand.

"I heard that one of the Vegas boys was not too happy about Tony never showing up again. Frankie, they didn't care about, but Tony, a different story…" and he sat down on the chair near the baby. "Tony's brother is now a lieutenant and Marc may have stirred the pot."

"But that was over a year ago… and Tony had it coming that night," and she stopped speaking, knowing that wasn't her place.

Patrick had forgotten that Emma was there the night when his father ended Tony. But none-the-less, he saw the fire in her eyes when she said it. What he did know was that it made Emma a different woman from the one that had first come to their home. She was tougher and she had had to be to deal with his father. And now she was pregnant again. Kind of bad timing. He knew that his mother blamed Emma for the split in the family and she and Marc had recently formed an alliance with Tony's brother from Vegas. Marc had turned out to be not so nice after all and neither had his own mother.

"Emma, you have to tell my father you are pregnant before the meeting. If I am right and it's my mother and Marc, my father will have you protected day and night till this in ended, and I mean that. You will not be able to move without someone knowing where you are."

"Then I won't tell him. If he doesn't know he won't worry. And you will give him me your word that you will not tell him." Emma glared at Patrick. "Please!"

"I can't do that! My loyalty is to my father before anything or anyone else…" 'Wasn't that the truth!' Here he was with his father's wife knowing she was pregnant by him and backing his father yet again. Patrick had the feeling Emma knew how he felt and right now was using it to her advantage.

"Emma… don't ask me to do that! Your husband is my father. I cannot betray him and I won't, not even for you…" and he stood up towering over all five feet of her, his voice very raised.

"I am not asking you to! I am asking you not to tell him. I don't want him worried about me all the time. He has more important things in his life than me, Patrick… you, the twins, Pip and his empire. They should come first! He has worked for what he has. His men respect him and so do all the other families. I watch, Patrick, how they treat him. They all show him such respect. This man from Vegas is nothing. Your father will deal with Marc and Sally his way… without him knowing about me…" and now she was yelling back at Patrick.

The door opened and Mac appeared. "What the hell are you two yelling about? You can be heard halfway round the house. Mr. Vega wants you both down in the library… now! Meeting has been brought forward. Go Patrick!" and Mac waited till he had left the room. "Are you okay, Emma? You know about Patrick, don't you?"

"Yes, I overheard that day, and what did you just hear, Mac? Never mind!" and Emma stormed out of the baby's room and down the stairs into the garage.

Mac followed her down to see where she was going. "Emma…" he yelled to her through the kitchen door into the garage. "Come back here… your husband wants you…"

It fell on deaf ears. She continued to the car, any car.

Mac opened his cell and speed dialed Philip's number. All he heard was 'keep her there.'

The next thing Emma knew was Philip yelling as he came through garage to the car. Security had kept her from even getting near the car and Mac stood over her like he was going to kill her.

"What the fuck do you think you are doing? I asked you to come to a meeting and all I can hear are you and Patrick screaming at each other… and then Mac is calling me to tell me where you are… what's going on, Emma?"

Emma looked up into Philip's face. It was red with anger and his pupils were pinpoints. She had never seen him like this with her, and she thought any minute he would pull his gun and shoot her.

"I'm waiting, Emma, and I am fast losing patience with you and Patrick..."

And there it was. It was Patrick he was angry with, but he couldn't say that.

"I want to go for a ride out of here and they won't let me..." and she pointed at two gentlemen, with guns, of Italian descent that stopped her from going anywhere.

"You want to what? Fine! Let's go..." and he grabbed her hand and led her to his Ferrari...

Now she was terrified. She knew how he drove that car. "Later. We can go later..." she begged.

"No, Emma Vega! We go now. Get in! There is obviously something on your mind," and he almost pushed her into the car, slamming the door behind her.

The garage doors went up and the Ferrari shot out of there and down the driveway with Mac in the SUV right behind them. Like a bolt of black lightening through the rain, he powered out of the gate and down onto the freeway towards Mulholland Drive. Emma was clinging to the seat, tears streaming down her face as they weaved in and out of the traffic to get on the Drive. He changed gears twice to get more power as he climbed the steep hill to the top.

"Philip, please stop... Philip..." she was begging him.

But Philip didn't stop till he got to the top, then he parked the car and locked both doors, turned off the engine and looked into Emma's face. He grabbed her by the shoulders and let rip.

"So you heard that day... you heard Patrick say he was in love with you, and today, I heard you telling him you are pregnant, yet you haven't told me! And you asked him not to tell me... because why? And crying doesn't work on me!"

Emma raised her hand and hit him hard across the face. As her hand made contact he pushed her against the door, pinning her there.

"If you were a man... I would kill you for that!" and his eyes narrowed at her.

She realized what she had done. She had hit Don Andrea, and he was having a hard time to not hit her back.

"Can I finish? If you had waited to see what I was going to say... Because you think you are in the way? Taking up my time instead of ending Sally and Marc's friend? Did Patrick tell me? Do I think what? I know it's my child, Emma... is that why you hit me? You think I was going to accuse you and Patrick of having something going? I know you far better than that. I know you would die for me. You already proved that at the Vineyard. And I told Patrick that if anything happens to me, he looks after you and our children. Sally wants the twins, Emma. She wants to see them... says she is sick, dying... and Marc has teamed with Tony's brother... that's what the meeting is about. And how do I know what you both said... the baby monitor was on! That's how!! Our own child gave you away!"

Chapter 46

Emma slumped down in the luxurious soft leather seat giving way to the strong grasp Philip had on her. She had been crying almost hysterically and stared at her handprint on Philip's face. His hand flipped down the glove compartment and he reached for tissues. A .22 fitted neatly in there as Emma could see.

"Dry your eyes, Emma," and he handed her a bunch of white tissues, sliding his other hand onto her face and then into her hair, holding her.

As she took the tissues from him, his hand was on the other side of her head, and there was a look in his eyes that Emma had never seen before. He was so close to her that she could feel his breath on her face.

"Baby... you're afraid of me... please, don't ever be afraid. I would never hurt you. Dear god... never..." He kissed her so forcefully that she gasped for air. "Emma..." and he kissed her neck and down to her breasts.

She reached for him, her hands sliding into his jeans, and they made love right then and there in the black Ferrari with the tinted windows on an empty lot on top of Mulholland Drive.

"This is why you love me, baby, because my life is exciting to you. It's dangerous and daring... like you."

And now Emma realized that she was not only his wife and lover but also his mistress, but she also knew Philip was right. He had seen something in her that she had not... till now.

He started the engine up, flashed his headlights to Mac in the SUV, and then took off down the hill, yet again at breakneck speed.

He happened to glance at Emma and realized she was still terrified of the way he drove and he slowed the pace, as the rain poured down.

"Emma, we have to have this meeting and I would like you to be there. Sally and Marc have to be dealt with, baby. I will be leaving for Florida first light to see what is going on..." He could see her face, and he knew she was about to disagree with his decision. "Please don't argue with me, baby. It won't do any good. Patrick will stay at the house with you, as will Mac and Alex and the house security. You will be safe."

"Will you, Philip? Will you be safe?" Emma murmured just loud enough for him to hear her above the noise of the engine.

"Yeah, baby. I'll have all the men with me..." he paused. "I'm afraid that my ex-wife and Marc may not be so safe, though, before I return..." and he stopped aware of what he had said. He was going there to threaten them... and maybe more.

They pulled into the driveway at normal speed, and he slowed right down near the door. "Emma, I am very happy about the baby... however, I found out. I am very pleased and tonight I will show you just how much," and he winked at her.

The meeting was held, just later than Philip wanted it to be. It was tense, very much so. It included Pauli, Mikey, Rossi, Mac, Alex and, of course, his son... and Emma. She felt uncomfortable being there, the only woman in a stronghold of men, very powerful men and she sat bolt upright on a chair fairly near to Philip, displaying the fact.

"I know some of you are surprised at my wife being here." He nodded towards her. "She knows most of the situation from one source or another, mostly from me." Philip took the blame. "Tomorrow at first light myself, Rossi, Pauli, Mikey plus our travelling security will be leaving for Florida. Patrick, Mac and Alex will remain here at the house with Emma and the children. And while we are on that topic of children, Emma is pregnant again..." Philip looked pleased... in fact, he looked delighted.

There were unanimous congratulations to both Emma and especially Philip, and then the meeting continued for a good solid hour. At last it was over, just in time for an early dinner.

"Patrick... a word," and Philip stopped his son while he spoke to Emma. "Baby, I will be right out. Seat the twins and you..." and he waited till the door was closed. "She knows, Patrick, she knows how you feel about her. She overheard that day in Denver. Doesn't make any difference. She thinks of you as a brother, and that's what you need to be to her. She's tougher than she thinks she is changing the night she saw me end Tony. She's a smart woman who has grown up so much in less than two years. I am very lucky to have found her, Patrick, and I can never lose her… that's why this has to be dealt with and now. Patrick, if your mother or Marc steps out of line… I will kill them, just like I did Damien. You understand?"

"Yes, Sir," and Patrick bent his head to his father.

Dinner was pleasant, on purpose. Emma had Pip at the table with her, something never done at the Vega's. She knew what Philip was doing, just like she always knew.

Bed came early. Bed, not sleep. Emma watched Philip as he checked his guns, and she watched as he laid jeans and sweater out for morning, clothes to die for, and after a long night of pure love and lust on both their parts, Philip left her lying in silk sheets.

"I'll be back, baby… tomorrow latest. I love you…" and he was gone in the early morning light and the mist of rain.

She ran to the lounge window just as the cars pulled out of the garage and she waved him goodbye. She didn't think he could see her, but she waved anyway, and then she cried.

Philip could just make her out, standing there, and he pulled his long leather round him against the cold. Worst part of the trip was the flight, an endless monotony of time without Emma, and his disposition reflected that. He sat at the back of his plane, could not doze and was generally unsociable towards anyone who approached him.

Early afternoon saw Philip's jet arrive in Florida. They were met with the usual limo that took them directly to Philip's old house.

Philip climbed out of the car into warmer weather. "Sally still in the house?"

"Yes, Sir. Soldier says both she and Marc are there. Some other guy with them. Maybe the guy from Vegas is there and some girl."

"Good enough. Let's go do this and get back home!" and he wanted that so badly.

The soldiers went to the door while Philip stayed in the background. When the door opened, Sally stood there in dirty sweats, more shocked than anything else, till she saw Philip.

"We were expecting a visit from you, *Mr. Vega...*" she yelled at Philip. "Do you really need an army?"

Philip moved to the door . "That depends, doesn't it? Who you have in the house..." and Philip pushed past her and into the hallway along with Pauli. "Marc... get out here!"

"Why?! You are not my fucking father..." Marc's rude reply was more out of frustration than anything else, and he sauntered into the hallway.

"No, I am not, boy... but I know who is ..." Philip came right back at him.

The statement took every bit of wind from Marc's sails and he stopped dead in his tracks. Dressed in torn jeans and nothing else, he looked like a beaten man. Behind him stood a pregnant Donna, almost cowering in the shadows.

"Yours?" he asked Marc not so quietly, staring very pointedly from Donna to Marc.

"No," and Marc looked down at the now dingy floor.

Philip glanced around. This used to be a nice house with clean, lavish furniture and now it was dirty and the furniture probably-pawned, totally obvious they had fallen on hard times. It was still his property and if he wanted he could sell it. But he didn't want to, and he didn't want the house period. Too many memories lingered here.

"Whose baby is it?" asked Philip, not really caring, except somehow he felt sorry for Donna. Maybe she had known what Marc was really like for sometime and it was Marc she was frightened of, not him.

"Mine, *Sir...*" and the Sir was said with such sarcasm and a very Italian-looking young man with tattoos everywhere, appeared from the back room and slung his arm round Donna. "And before you ask, Don Andrea, my brother was Tony!"

"Really... isn't that interesting," and Philip nodded his head towards him and the next thing the Vegas punk knew he was face-onto the wall with his arm behind his back.

Pauli had him locked there, nice and tight to the wall. Pauli was an expert at this.

"And your name would be, Tony's brother?" Pauli took over with his deep accent.

No reply.

"Wrong answer... one more time. Don Andrea wants to know your name, Tony's brother... better be the right answer this time. This isn't my finger in your back, boy."

"Vinnie, name's Vinnie," and Vinnie appeared to need the bathroom, or rather had needed the bathroom.

"Better answer. Vinnie what... might be an even better answer," reminded Pauli.

"Vinnie Carbina. Tony was my baby brother. You killed him, Don Andrea... you fuckin' killed him. Blew his head off..." and Vinnie yelled at Philip.

Philip leaned towards Vinnie. "Do you know why I killed your brother? Do you? Turn him round, Pauli. He shot and killed my friend in front of his wife. You don't kill a Don and get away with it. So I ended him... and perhaps now it's your turn!" Philip nodded his head at Pauli.

Vinnie closed his eyes. No bullet. Nothing.

"Did Donna come to you willingly? Answer me... did she?" Philip demanded, almost accusing Vinnie of rape.

"Yeah..." and he looked straight at Philip. "She came to you, didn't she?"

That caught Philip off guard. "She did and that was in the past, an accident." He glanced at Marc, who looked a little nervous now his that ally was held at gunpoint. "Donna, do you want to stay here with this punk?" asked Philip glancing at the girl.

"No, Sir, nor with Marc. They forced me to have sex..." and she stopped, worried that if she said more and Philip and his men left her there...

"Get your things together. Anything you need to take. You can fly back with us and we will make arrangements for you to have the baby... hurry, though, and we will wait for you down here."

"You can't just take her away, Philip. She's Marc's girlfriend... and since when are you so charitable anyway?" intervened Sally.

"Since today, as you seem to be holding her here by force. I can do exactly what I want to do, and as for you, you don't look very sick to me. Let me tell you right now, you will never see the twins again… ever. My wife takes care of them and Philipa, and so she will do with my baby she is now carrying. And if you ever try to see them, you will wish you hadn't. Ex-wife or not." He turned to face his man. "Pauli, teach this young punk a lesson that he won't forget and remind him not to follow Donna or anyone of us ever again… and we will let him live." He looked back at a man who was once his son. "You, Marc, are a disgrace to the Vega name…" and Philip stopped while Pauli and another man escorted Vinnie out of the hallway.

"I am not a Vega! You made sure of that… both of you…" Marc looked from one to another. He also heard the part about Emma being pregnant… again.

"I wish to god you were not, but unfortunately you are, Marc." Sally looked him in the face. "I think Philip has discovered the truth, and if he hasn't, he will now. Damien Vega was not your uncle. He was your father! I slept with your brother, Philip, just one weekend right before we were engaged and you were out philandering with one of your *mistresses*. Did it out of spite, just to pay you back! Oh, I knew everyone did it then… back in those days sleeping round meant nothing. The more mistresses you had the more revered you were… and you certainly had a lot!" She laughed. "Damien wasn't even as good as you are in bed, Philip… not by half, but he produced our first born, and now you know why I wanted to get married so fast. Marc wasn't your son!" and she laughed again, coughing up blood. She was indeed sick.

Chapter 47

Philip had found out the truth, but airing dirty laundry didn't seem quite right. Letting Sally die in Florida did. Plainly obvious to them all she was telling the truth, both about Marc and about Philip's constant philandering... until Emma. Philip could hear Vinnie in the other room pleading for his life, and he could see his ex-wife decidedly sick in front of him.

Marc looked shocked. "Damien was my father? Dear god... he was rotten to the core..." and he stopped speaking. That was one hell of an admission. "Did he know?" and he looked at his mother.

"He knew the day before your uncle, here, almost beat him to death... oh, that's right, Philip. You executed him instead..." added Sally. "Things get out, Andrea."

Rossi and Mikey looked at each other. Why was their boss taking this? He couldn't possibly feel anything for her.

It was then that the real Philip emerged and the dark side of him appeared. "Enough, Sally! You may have given me three sons, but that does not give you any rights! I came here to warn you and Marc to stay away from the family. I had heard you were sick and wanted to see your sons and now you never will." He moved right into her space. "You ever leave Florida, or pose any threat to my family and especially my wife; I won't just have you ended... I will do it. And as for you, Marc, it doesn't change anything. You had your chance at the Vega line and you blew it. Patrick has already been *made*. And you ever come near my wife again and you are dead! You get the picture? If you don't, Rossi will be only too happy to enforce it. He's never liked you, much as most of the household didn't." Now Philip

243

was being cruel and he was enjoying it. This was the other side of Philip Vega, the one Emma had seen in the Ferrari. He would only be pushed so far.

"I get the picture loud and clear. It's all for your new family. How does Patrick feel now? Still in love with your wife? That's gotta be hard to take, a twenty-five-year-old look- alike in love with her. But by all accounts, you are far better in bed than anyone else… explains all the women at the house… and, I wonder how many more kids you have you don't even know about…"

Philip brought his arm back and his hand hit Marc so hard across the face that he went sprawling across the hall and into the kitchen, blood spurting from his nose and mouth. It took him a few seconds to collect himself together, and then he jumped up from the floor grabbing a large bread knife from the kitchen table. Immediately there were two .22's pointed at him, ready and very willing to fire confirming Philip's speech about them not liking him. Rossi and Mikey would have terminated Marc right there and Rossi looked at his boss for his instructions. Philip glared at Marc.

"You ever let me see your face again and I will let them shoot you… dead!" Philip was furious and when that happened… someone paid.

Even Sally was frightened by Philip. She had never seen him this volatile and she backed into the doorway out of his way.

"Where's Donna?" and he yelled for her. "Get in here, Donna… neither one of these so called men is ever going to hurt you again…"

She came from the stairs where she had stopped dead in her tracks at the violent display in front of her.

"You ready? Then let's go. All my business here is concluded. You have been warned, all of you! No more warnings, only .22's." He turned and walked out of the house for the very last time in his life, never looking back.

Donna didn't even look at Marc or Vinnie as she hustled by them trying to catch up to Philip, carrying her few possessions with her. Pauli and Rossi followed with Mikey reiterating the facts to them all in the house. They watched from the window as Philip and his men left in the limo, a life they all once had. Vinnie leaned back on the nearest chair.

"I'm out, Marc! Not going up against the Vega's again. Let him take Donna; let him take what he wants. Don Andrea is one mean son-of-a-bitch… and I do believe him when he says next time it's a .22. He didn't have any problem killing my brother…" and Vinnie grabbed his jacket and was gone out of the backdoor looking more like he had run into a ten-ton truck than Rossi's fist.

The mood in the limo was very tense. No one said a word, not even Donna. She clutched her belongings to her and she seriously reminded him of Emma coming back from England. He hoped that Emma would understand why he brought her out of the household. He thought she would, but maybe he should call and warn her first. They arrived at the airport and Philip climbed out, moving to one side of the car. It was now dusk, shades of pink filled the sky and all Philip wanted was his wife and child. He speed dialed her cell.

"Baby…" and there was a pause. "Can you hear me?" Bad connection. He guessed the jet's engine wasn't helping things too much, and he stuck his finger in his other ear. "Getting back on board the jet. Back home way before midnight. Wait for me, baby… wait up for me. I love you…" A bad line was not the time to tell her about Donna. Maybe put her in Marc's old room till tomorrow and then sort it out. Maybe that wasn't a good idea. She could sleep in the spare room over the garage.

Philip was totally disgusted with Marc and Sally. If he hadn't have been a gentleman he would more than likely have told her what he really thought of her and why he divorced her. His thoughts were interrupted by Pauli telling him the jet was ready when he was.

"Yeah, right…" and Philip boarded his plane from a private airfield where money still talked.

Once more he sat at the back of the plane reflecting on today's events. Pauli brought him a scotch and Philip took the bottle from him. It was a turbulent flight reflecting the day's events.

It was a bad landing and Donna threw up. Again it reminded Philip of Emma. As soon as they had taxied, Philip called her. This time she could hear him.

"Baby… we've landed in L.A. Be home in less than an hour. I need you, baby. Need to talk to you and need to make love to you. I just need you…" and he closed the phone.

When she saw the car, she ran outside in the falling rain and the half-light. Philip didn't wait for anyone to open his door. He went straight into her welcoming arms and held her close to him, wetting the front of her negligee with the damp of his leather. Neither of them cared, all she knew he was home and all he wanted was her. Philip ushered her inside shedding his leather as he did.

"Mac… I have to talk to Emma first and it's late." He looked at his Rolex. Wasn't too late but he was tired. "Give me an hour or so, and I'll be back down. Go help Pauli." He didn't even see Patrick, just made haste up the stairs and the first stop was the baby's room. "Need to see her, Emma…" and they both stood in the doorway watching her sleep and Philip realized just how much his new family did mean to him.

Downstairs Mac went to the car and Pauli and he escorted Donna to the spare room over the garage. She was crying bitterly and Pauli felt certain sympathy for her. Ripped from her home and from everything she knew, but safe. They settled her in, made her as comfortable as they could, talked to her for a while and then walked back outside along the front of the house.

Pauli stopped for a cigarette, sheltering under the eaves from the rain. "She's just here for a while. It was a mess, Mac. Mr. Vega will tell you all, but I don't think it's over. Oh, Vinnie, the punk from Vegas, is over. If I see him again, orders or not, I will kill him. But Marc and Sally, not over… very much not over. I think Marc, at some point, will seek revenge on Mr. Vega, especially now that he knows he is Damien's son. If I had been the boss instead of whipping him, I would have ended him! He would now be dead!" and Pauli thought tonight his boss had made a mistake.

Chapter 48

Before the meeting, Philip explained the day's events to Emma, and then they made warm understanding love.

She leaned on him, naked at the day she was born. "Philip, I don't think she should just be bundled off to have her child. Let me talk to her. See what we can arrange. That's almost an apartment over the garage. Oh, I know what happened before, but I can't imagine being raped and carrying an unwanted child…"

Emma never ceased to amaze Philip. Then again, he should have known she would react like this. She was a mother and pregnant herself, and he pulled the warm blanket round her. He told her they would discuss it more downstairs with Patrick and Mikey. He left her then and she could hear them talking as she passed by the library door on her way to Donna's room with food.

When the girl opened the door to Emma, she burst into tears and cried till she could cry no more. Donna told Emma what happened the night of the party and how it was totally her fault. She had come to realize that Marc was nothing like Philip in any way. With nowhere else to go she had stayed with him, almost threatened by him and Vinnie and, truth was she really didn't know who the father was. She doubted the child was a Vega… but they hadn't let her leave, either taking or pawning her possessions, giving her no way out till Philip arrived.

Emma couldn't help but feel sorry for her. That was her nature. She would ask Philip if Donna could stay at least till the baby was born. And Philip and Patrick had decided pretty much the same.

It was almost time for Donna's baby. Things had quieted down for the family. No more problems from Vegas and now Christmas loomed in front of them, and this one was to be spent in L.A. There would be many more times for Christmas in Colorado, much as Philip wanted to go there for this one.

Patrick flew back down from the Vineyard the week before Christmas and he had taken Emma to Rodeo Drive to shop for Philip's Christmas gift. Emma was eagerly looking at gold bracelets, had just picked one out and paid for it, when Patrick's cell rang.

"Sir," and Patrick knew before Philip told him that his mother had passed away. It wasn't a shock and he wasn't distressed for himself... for the twins, maybe. "Mac, stay with Emma a moment," and Patrick stepped outside into the street. "I hear you, Sir... and Marc... when did he leave there? Do you think he will come for you? And Emma? I won't scare her. We'll finish her shopping and then come home." He paused reflecting. "Sir... my loyalty is still to you and always will be." And he hung up the call and went back to the group.

"Patrick... was that Philip?" She knew, too, and she knew, now that Marc was on his own... literally.

"Yes, Emma, it was. My mother passed away today." In his eyes was a sorrow for someone he used to know, someone who gave birth to him.

"I'm so sorry, Patrick. We should go straight home. The twins will need you. Philip will need you. Shopping can wait!"

And that's just what he loved about Emma. It was never about herself. Always Philip or the children... when really this was about her. Tomorrow was her wedding anniversary and Philip had planned on taking her to a hotel for the night, and now that was probably gone. Patrick knew about it. Emma didn't. It was a surprise for her from her husband, Santa Barbara for a couple of days, without any children. The two of them and security. Patrick wondered if Emma's life would ever be normal.

As they arrived home, security at the gate had been doubled. Obviously Philip had received more than just a phone call, and sat waiting for his son in the library, with Mikey and Pauli at his side.

"Firstly... I am sorry about your mother. That being said, since I called you, Patrick, Marc called me. He blames both Emma and me for your mother's death. Said I took Donna too, and no, he doesn't know she is still here, nor will he. I think I will still take Emma to

Santa Barbara… take her away from this for a couple of days. You guys can deal with things here. Marc won't get in the grounds and he certainly won't know where Emma and I are. We'll take the Ferrari and Mac and Alex can follow in the SUV. Don't tell anyone else what's going on, not even Donna. Less people that know the better. Emma's pregnancy isn't going as well as the last one and she needs a break. Maybe the baby was too fast after Pip. Pity we hadn't gone to Colorado." Philip stopped, seriously considering changing plans and going, but all his men were here and here was their home and he wasn't about to run. He stood up and moved to the window, looking out over the grounds. "Okay… so we'll leave around mid-morning, take the coast road, and head to the hotel. It's The Biltmore, by the way, in case you do need me, and I'll have the cell, so will Mac and Alex. May stay an extra day or two. See how it goes. Back on Christmas Eve. Pip will be fine between the nanny, the twins and Donna. While I am gone, Patrick, you and Pauli will be in charge here. And while I am gone you take every precaution, and I mean every one, to keep this family safe. If anything happens to my children… any of them… someone will pay!" and with that he left the room.

Emma didn't get a choice about the trip, nor about taking Philipa with them. Philip had the maid pack their bags and at eleven the next day they left for the Biltmore. In the car he handed her a brochure for the hotel.

"This is where we are going? Really? No wonder you had me dress like this," and she looked down at her black pant-suit and black high heels. At four months gone her baby bump was once again like someone who had eaten too much dinner. "It looks fantastic, Philip… It says there is a spa, pool and TV…"

"Emma… Emmy… you won't be using those things… all you have to think about is resting, eating and me…" and he focused very hard on getting there. "Take a nap, baby. You'll need it," and he picked up a little speed as they hit the coast road.

The SUV was right behind them never losing site of the Ferrari's seventy miles per hour, slowed only for Emma. Philip decided to drive straight through so that she could see the wonderful view of the ocean highlighted to perfection by sunlight dancing on the waves. Philip pulled over at one point to let her see it more clearly. As she stood at the oceans edge, he pulled a camera from the glove compartment and snapped his wife standing, looking to far off lands. She stood there, perfection in his eyes, mother of his child and the children yet to come.

"Hey, come on, baby… let's go. Getting chilly," and they climbed back into the car. "Would like to be there for dinner. Nice candlelit dinner on the balcony of our room looking out at the sunset. How does that sound… don't know about you, but I am hungry."

"You're just a growing guy, Philip. I thought that was me that was growing," and she laughed at him. "But, yes, I am a little hungry," and she hopped into the car beside Philip.

They checked into the Biltmore by early afternoon. It was just as the brochure said it was… glorious, overlooking the ocean, with a lobby of people bustling to welcome them to the hotel. Philip let the attendant park his car but with a warning there would not be a scratch on it… would there! One didn't show up in an expensive Ferrari like this one unless you were loaded, or someone important… and both applied. Philip Vega was very obviously wealthy and that caused power service for them. As they walked through the lobby and to their room, Emma was a little in awe. Her high heels clicked on the marble floor and it made Philip look at her body, one he planned on looking at a lot more closely in the next half hour.

Ushered into the number one suite, Philip tipped the porter handsomely. Emma wandered around like she had never seen anything like this suite before and walked out onto a magnificent balcony directly across from the ocean, with a view to die for.

Philip came up behind her and encircled her with his arms, and she leaned back on him so happy to have him to herself even for just a day or so. She shivered.

"Cold, baby? Let's go inside and have champagne in the Jacuzzi. Looks pretty nice in there," and Philip whisked her inside pulling the patio door tightly closed behind him.

She knew where that was leading and she wanted that as much as he did. They could get room service; in fact they could live on room service. After they had made love, long, lengthy love, in warm waters with bubbles, they drank champagne and ate those tasty chocolates from the bedroom accompanied with fruit from the lavish welcome basket in the suite.

Emma was blissfully happy and relaxing against Philip when the there was a knock on the suite door.

"Room service…"

"Be right with you… Mac…" and Philip realized that Mac was in the next room with Alex, and he hurried from the Jacuzzi, grabbing a bath towel round him and disappeared to get the door, sliding into the terry robe as he did.

It was then that someone entered the bathroom from the outside patio door. There hadn't seemed to be any danger.

"How did you get round that way, Philip…" and Emma lounged in the water, glanced up and stopped speaking. It wasn't Philip that she saw standing there watching her. It was a man dressed all in black, and then, as he pulled the balaclava from his head, Marc's face came into view and in his hand was a .357.

Chapter 49

"Hey, Emma, baby… you want the food in there or out here by the warm fire? Emma? You okay, baby?" and Philip left the food and came back into the lavish bathroom. The look on his face told it all. In front of him stood Emma, her wet body dressed in her T shirt and panties and behind her, holding a gun in her back, stood Marc his arm wrapped around her waist. "How the hell did you get here and what the fuck are you doing, Marc? Let her go. It's me you want. She's not part of this!"

"Really? If you hadn't been so obsessed with Emma when you met her, you wouldn't have brought her into the family and we would still all be just the same. But no, you had to let your emotions get in your way with this one instead of just your dick…"

Philip wanted to reach out and kill him where he stood, but he knew any slight movement and Marc would shoot Emma. "What do you want, Marc? I didn't kill your mother… Damien, yes, I did… and yes, he did have it coming." Philip's eyes narrowed. "You touch one hair on her head and I will kill you with my bare hands. Now, let her go and you and I will go outside and settle this."

"Right, with two bodyguards next door? Speaking of which, where are they?" Marc looked around in mock gesture. "I don't see them in here… maybe because they are asleep, possibly because I took them coffee with a nice sedative in there, left over from my mother's bathroom cabinet. They thought I was room service," and Marc had a slightly insane look on his face.

"Are you losing it, *boy*. They would know you. What did you do?" and Philip moved just slightly.

"Just like I said… but I left it by the door for them… Now what are you gonna do, *Mr. Vega*… take me on man to man? I know you could do it. I know you could take me, too, just like you took my father. Does Emma know what you did? Probably. You tell her everything and you never told my mother anything. That hurt her, you know. You shut her out, and you never really liked me. I could tell… and if you move another step towards me I will drop her before you even get close." His voice was a little agitated now, and he shifted his body from one foot to the other.

Philip knew he was telling the truth by his steady hand, and for someone who professed not to like guns, he was doing very well. He had to try and talk him down. His own gun was on the chair about three feet from him and the other one was by the Jacuzzi. Somehow Philip had to get to one of them. He looked at Emma's face. She was paralyzed with fear and tears rolled down her cheeks like she knew she was going to die.

"It's okay, baby. He's not going to hurt you, Emma. Even if he had the guts to shoot, it would bring too much attention. They would catch him before he gets out of the building." Then he focused back to Marc. "Let her go. Point the gun at me and we will go onto the beach. You want to kill a pregnant woman?" and it hit Philip like a ton of bricks he did want that, just as Damien had. "That's the idea isn't it…"

"At last, you get the picture… you took Donna away from me and now I am taking Emma…"

"One big difference. Donna wanted …" Philip didn't get to finish.

"Yeah, she wanted you, just like all the women do… Emma know that, too?"

"That's not true, Marc and you know it!" Philip was buying time, hoping to god that Mac or Alex would burst through one of the doors and take him out. "Donna stayed with you. She loved you," now he was lying for his own ends. "She still loves you. You can get her back; look after her and the baby… we can help you." Philip's voice was on an even keel.

Now Marc's hand wasn't as steady. "It's not my baby…" and the gun waved. "It's Vinnie's… I can't have children…" and Marc kept on talking, "and you, you will have five children, and I'm not one of them," and his voice was raised, but Philip was having the affect on him he wanted, distracting him from Emma. "I am not your son…"

So that was it… he wasn't the son of the father he wanted.

Philip looked at the door behind Marc. Mac stood there gun in his hand, a little woozy but he was there. Silent and deadly.

"No… you are not, but that isn't either mine or her fault. That was your mother's fault. No matter where I was, I always came home to her after we were married. After the twins were born, I admit maybe not so much… but you, you want my wife and that isn't going to happen…" and Philip glanced at Mac.

"Marc!" Mac made his move. "Let her go, or I will shoot you."

Philip reached for his gun and enough distraction was caused to make Marc turn slightly away from Emma and Mac aimed his .22… and pulled the trigger. He hit Marc in the side dropping him to the floor, just as Philip reached his .357 and turned to fire.

"Emma, drop down!" he yelled at her. "Hit the floor, baby!"

Marc lay there gun still in his hand and Mac went to kick it away from him to safety. Instead, the gun emptied its chamber… straight into Emma's back. She didn't cry out, she had expected to die. She lay there, her eyes open staring at Philip, tears running down her face.

"No, Emma… not you, not you! You bastard, Marc!" Philip screamed, and both he and Mac emptied every shot they had into Marc until it was a lifeless bloody mess on the Persian rugs, turning the white to red. Philip dropped the empty gun and fell on the floor beside her, cradling her in his arms.

Mac stared at the horror in front of him, hardly believing it.

"Get help… do something! Get a doctor! For god's sake help her…" but inside Philip knew it was too late. His robe was covered in blood, his hands and her, mainly her. "Emma, dear god, forgive me, please forgive me! I love you so much," and he kissed her lips one more time trying to breathe life into her. He felt the warmth of her kiss back and then she was gone, both her and his baby she carried.

When the police arrived Philip still sat on the floor holding her to him. He could not believe she was dead. Mac and Alex tried to persuade him to let the paramedics take her. He would not. Mac called the house and Patrick sounded distraught as he gave orders for Pauli and Mikey to leave with him instantly for Santa Barbara.

It was after midnight when they arrived and the police were still at the hotel. They had laid her on the bed and Philip had donned jeans. He was a broken man and they all knew it. The police knew him as Philip Vega, nothing more. Didn't matter how many guns were in the room and the shooter was a stalker, even though he was blown to pieces, with hardly any body to bury.

Mac let the family into the suite, Mac and two policemen. Patrick broke down in tears as they showed him Emma. She was wrapped in sheets waiting for the body to be taken away, an empty shell of a woman who had not given up till the last. Never screaming out to Philip to save herself, knowing she was going to die in his place. Patrick sat down next to his father on the couch and rested his arm on his shoulders.

"You couldn't have done anything, Sir. We think he followed you here from the house… oh, god, dad, I am so sorry," and the look on Philip's face disturbed him, like he would never be happy again. Patrick saw him look up at Mac, and he knew for Mac it was over… he had let something happen to her and he had been warned.

Conclusion

There was no Christmas that year and possibly for that family, ever again. They flew to Colorado taking her body there, closing the house in L.A. for now, and, possibly, for ever for Philip. The funeral was private, family and friends only. She was buried in the family plot where one day Philip would join her, dressed in the black dress that he first saw her wearing. Roses filled the church, white ones, and the kind that Emma liked. Everyone was dressed in black and wearing shades. The twins cried uncontrollably for Emma. They had lost both mothers in such a short space of time.

Patrick stood next to his father, a father who was totally broken inside, but to the outside world as tough as nails. He wore a heavy black coat and underneath he still carried a gun or two. He listened as the priest read words over the grave. He watched as they lowered her coffin into the ground and he heard strains of the music 'wish you were here' in his head. In his hand he held a white rose still in bud, and he kissed the petals as if in full bloom and laid it on her coffin. He glanced up to see his baby in the nanny's arms and he saw Donna standing ready to give birth any day. A life for a life. And he knew now what he must do. He couldn't live without Emma, but there were still some things to do first, before he turned his empire over to Patrick. He knew it would be in good hands... Mikey and Pauli at his son's side. And then there was Philipa... apple of his eye, Emma's and his child. Patrick was her godfather and he would raise Emma's daughter knowing how much that Patrick loved her and knowing his son would never marry. At least he had his father's child to comfort him... and an empire.

When Philip wasn't strengthening his dynasty from Colorado, he was drinking, and drinking heavily. He didn't care, not anymore, hoping the bottle would kill him. It failed! His hair grew longer and he never shaved. His only mistress was the bottle, and now Philip turned another year older, sitting alone in his rooms at night. Most mornings Mac would find him there reeking of wine and scotch, with bloodshot eyes and slumped over his desk where he had slept in the same clothes as yesterday.

But Philip had one more thing left to do in his lifetime, something he should have taken care of a year back. He turned away from the limo that they took each day to her grave, and strode out into the snow, his handmade Italian leather boots once more crushing the soft snow beneath them. Slowly he put his hand under his coat and slid his arm round the back of his jeans. Retrieving the gun from its hiding place was an easy task. He kept the weapon by his side and turned to face his bodyguard. Philip raised the gun high and saw the look in Mac's haunted blue eyes.

Mac Hunter fell to his knees. He did not beg for forgiveness. He knew his boss would kill him at some point and amazed himself that death had not come knocking on his door sooner. Snow seeped water up his black jeans and touched his long grey coat.

"You may just as well of killed her yourself. I told you you would never know where or when and now is the time… But before you die, there is something you should know." Philip paused. Revenge was often sweet. "Marc was not Damien's son. He was your son, Mac… your son! I knew you slept with Sally, both you and Damien that weekend, and I know it was the only time you both did. I always suspected he was yours. Why do you think you rose so fast in the ranks, you were the father of my god damn son. Pity you didn't know and I know you didn't. Sally wasn't even sure. She thought Damien was and so I let her think that, even though Marc was blonde. He looked more like her than anyone else. I couldn't really blame her for that one weekend when she was hitting back at me. I could have forgiven you that and did… until your son killed my wife." Vega's voice rang out in the crisp air, and his eyes were cold and calculating. "But… Mac, you killed your own son and he killed the woman I loved more than life… Time to die, Mac. Time to die!"

Philip aimed the gun at Mac's head, pulled the trigger and with one clean shot ended the life of his longtime bodyguard. He slumped down in a pool of crimson-red snow, twitching in death and then he was still, dead eyes staring into cold air.

Philip turned away without showing any remorse. He stood there and looked across to the grave that sported an icing of snow on the flowers of yesterday… her grave, and he waited for the second car to collect him. He could hear the engine and could see the headlights of EV1, and just for a moment he hesitated as he looked once more at her grave…

"Not even in death, Emma, will I leave you… I promised you that… I miss you so much, baby… too much to live without you," and Philip Andrea Vega put the gun under his chin and pulled the trigger. Then his weapon of choice dropped from his hand and he fell, as if in slow motion to join her, his body resting on the snows of her grave, crushing the white roses, to hold her in his arms once again.

THE END.

www.ingramcontent.com/pod-product-compliance
Lightning Source LLC
Chambersburg PA
CBHW070221030726
47505CB00006B/1751